What's Done in the Dark

Other books by Gloria Mallette

Distant Lover

The Honey Well

Promises to Keep

Weeping Willows Dance

Shades of Jade

When We Practice to Deceive

What's Done in the Dark

GLORIA MALLETTE

KENSINGTON PUBLISHING CORP.
http://www.kensingtonbooks.com

DAFINA BOOKS are published by

Kensington Publishing Corp.
850 Third Avenue
New York, NY 10022

ISBN 0-7582-1157-0

First Trade Paperback Printing: January 2006
10 9 8 7 6 5 4 3 2 1

Printed in the United States of America

Acknowledgment

I thank God Almighty for each breath I take, for each step I make, for each night I sleep, for each day I awake, for each meal I eat, for each drop I drink, for each sight I see, for each sound I hear, for each hand I feel, for each kiss I get, for each word I write, and for each dream I realize.

What's Done in the Dark

What we do, no one has to know.
What we know, we never have to tell.
Behind closed doors, we do what we will,
out in the open, our faces never reveal
what we hide behind the darkness of the veil.
Time and error are often unkind.
A slip of a tongue, a careless mind,
an eye unexpected, a happened upon find.
What's done in the dark will find its way
into the vast bright light of the fated day.
                                    —Gloria Mallette

PROLOGUE

Celeste was miserable. The muscles in her behind were burning, her legs were stiff and achy, and her back hurt. Listening to eight-and-a-half hours of taped hits from the sixties and seventies, and sitting in the backseat of her father's car was torture. Yawning, she arched her back, stiffened her body, tightened her buttocks, and stretched her arms high and wide, pressing the palms of her hands into the cushiony tan roof of the old green sedan, and while she stretched her left leg out across the seat, her right leg was only partially extended; her foot had gone under the front passenger seat only so far. In that front seat, her mother, Stella Reese, was asleep. She'd been sleeping since they left Warren, Ohio, and crossed the border into Pennsylvania, heading back across Interstate 80 to New York City. Even when her father, Richard, pulled into a rest stop to use the rest room and to get something to eat, Stella had not awakened, she was that tired. They'd spent three days in Warren at Cousin Edith's wedding, her third, where Stella had been her favorite cousin's matron of honor—more like her gofer. Cousin Edith's three grown children were of little help because they didn't like it that she was getting married again, and Stella, with her take-charge self, was in her element. The only thing Stella didn't do was make the white wedding gown that she'd whispered to Celeste was inappropriate.

All in all, it was a nice wedding, but it was for old folks and Celeste hated that her mother had made her go when she wanted to stay home and hang out with her boyfriend, Sean. He was the first real boyfriend her parents allowed her to have, and they had been going together for only two months. And now that school was over for the summer, they could be together a whole lot more, but oh, no, her mother wouldn't let her stay home.

"I'm not leaving you and Katrina home alone together. The house might not be standing when your father and I get back."

"So why don't you make Katrina go. I'm always the one you make go somewhere."

"Because Katrina's older and more responsible. You're seventeen and with all those friends you have, and not to mention that little boyfriend of yours, Sean, no telling what kind of trouble you could end up in. Go pack. And I don't wanna hear any more lip."

As much lip as Celeste wanted to give her mother, she didn't; it wasn't worth the energy or her mother's customary, "as long as you're under this roof" speech. She'd only end up going on the trip anyway, mad as hell, not speaking to either one of her parents, and miserable to boot because she had to spend hours cooped up with them in the car and with family members she had seen maybe twice before in her life. At least on this trip both her parents were her allies—and not Katrina's. The worst part of the whole trip had been the drive. Didn't her parents know that airplanes had been invented to make traveling a lot less stressful and a whole lot shorter in duration? Her father liked to drive everywhere. He was even talking about buying a Winnebago of all things and driving across country to California. If there was a God, Celeste prayed that she would be out on her own by that time so her parents couldn't force her to go along with them.

Katrina was lucky. Although she was twenty and still lived at home, she was never forced to go anywhere with their parents. Of course, no one would ever say it out loud, but Stella and Richard both knew that Katrina would bitch every single mile going and coming like she did when they drove down to Atlanta back in 1983, five years ago, for a family reunion on Richard's side of the family. Celeste could tell by the way her father had gripped the steering wheel and squeezed his eyes shut that he was fighting against driving off and leaving Katrina behind at the rest stop. That was a miserable trip. Katrina never stopped whining and complaining, and seemed to take great pleasure in picking on her the whole way. Katrina was that much of a witch, which is also why Celeste couldn't stay home like she wanted to. No matter how minor their disagreement, she and Katrina would inevitably end up screaming at each other, which within minutes would escalate into them going for each other's throats. Their last fight, two weeks ago, was over who would get the last banana. Katrina felt she should have the banana because she'd called for it first: "That banana is mine." Celeste felt she should have the banana because she hadn't had one in two days whereas Katrina had eaten a banana every day for the past week. After fighting and pulling on the banana, the banana was squeezed into mush by their grabbing hands so neither got to eat it. Boy, were Stella and Richard angry when they saw the scratches on their necks and arms, the broken coffee table, and the smashed banana and the mushy black banana skin smushed into the green carpet in the family room.

Stella and Richard blamed both her and Katrina, but if they really thought about it, they would have realized that it was Katrina who was at fault. Katrina couldn't stand the sight of her. For a long time, Celeste had tried to be friends with her one and only sibling, but Katrina wasn't having it. Katrina just didn't like her and never tried to hide it. Celeste could remember when she was three being pinched all the time by Katrina—always when her parents weren't in sight. When she was ten, Katrina cut the strings on her violin. "I'm tired of you giving me a damn headache every night. You sound like you're trying to kill a cat."

Celeste didn't think her playing was all that bad and cried pitifully.

Katrina got punished more for saying the word "damn" than for cutting the violin strings. The violin belonged to Celeste's school and her parents had to pay for replacing the strings but that was about all, which led Celeste to think her parents hated her playing as well. That was when she gave up trying to learn how to play the violin, and when she also gave up trying to be Katrina's friend. Since then, she'd told her parents often enough that she didn't like Katrina. "She's mean," she said every time Katrina did something vicious to her, which was quite frequent. They were older now, but nothing had changed. Other than Katrina constantly calling her a spoiled brat, Celeste still couldn't understand why Katrina didn't like her and didn't look forward to seeing her after being away for three days. Originally, they had planned on staying four days in Ohio, but they were coming home a day early because Richard couldn't stand sleeping another hot night on the old, wobbly army cot set up at the foot of the full-size bed that Celeste slept in with her mother. She got to sleep in the bed because she had horrible menstrual cramps and sleeping on the cot didn't help.

Richard didn't have a bit of fun and quite literally exhaled when he pulled up in the driveway of his own two-story, roomy Cape Cod house in Laurelton, Queens. "No place like home," he said, cutting the engine and turning on the dome light so that he could see all they had to gather up.

"The house is dark," Stella said, looking at all the windows on the front of the house, upstairs and down. "Katrina must be out, unless she's back in her bedroom."

Pulling on her leather thongs, Celeste was hopeful. *If she's out, I won't have to see her stupid face tonight. Thank God for small favors.*

"Where would she go on a Sunday night?" Richard asked.

"Somewhere with Damon," Celeste replied. "You know how tight they are."

"It's after ten. Doesn't she have to go to work tomorrow?"

Stella answered, "No, she took off."

"Again? That's not a good way to start out."

"Richard, it's only a summer job at Burger King," Stella said, picking up her pocketbook from the floor between her feet. "Katrina'll be fine once she finishes college and gets a regular job."

"Yeah, right, Ma. You know Katrina doesn't like to work. She said she's gonna marry somebody rich so she won't have to."

"Well, she better do it soon," Richard said. "She's not gonna make a living staying in bed all day or partying every night."

"Yes she can, Dad. She could become—"

"Celeste!" Stella said. "Don't you start. You, too, Richard. Both of you leave Katrina alone. She'll be fine."

Celeste snickered behind her hand. Her mother knew what she was about to say, and that's because Katrina thought she was the bomb and used her body to get any guy she wanted. What did that say about her?

Stella pushed open her door and again looked at the house. "I left a message for Katrina telling her that we would be coming in tonight. You'd think she'd be home."

"Where did you leave the message, Ma? On the house machine or the one in Katrina's room?"

"The house machine, I think."

"Ma, you know Katrina never checks that answering machine."

"Yeah, that's true, I forgot."

Again Richard yawned. "Man, I'm tired. The next time we go anywhere, I'm staying in a hotel."

"Me, too," Celeste agreed, as she collected the empty potato chip bag, candy wrappers, empty soda cans and plastic slushie cups tossed on the floor. "Ma, I don't like sleeping with you."

"I don't like sleeping with you either; you toss and turn too much, but you and your daddy are just spoiled."

Richard pushed a button under the dash and popped the car's trunk. "If you consider me spoiled because I like sleeping in a king-size bed and having my own damn bathroom to use when I need to, then so be it, I'm spoiled." Then opening the door he slowly pushed himself out of the car. "And another thing, I don't like being cornered by family with their hands out."

"Who asked you for money? You didn't tell me anything about that."

"Your nephew Joe, and your cousin Ralph."

"Did you give them anything?"

"Sure did—a handshake and an 'I'm broke' speech. What do they think, we're rich?" Stretching out fully, Richard walked stiffly to the trunk and grunting, started unloading the suitcases.

"I didn't know they'd asked you for money," Stella said, deciding to keep her mouth shut about giving Edith fifty dollars, Joe thirty dollars, and Ralph fifty dollars.

"I'm with Dad, Ma. I'm for staying in a hotel, and for flying the next time we have to go anywhere." Taking her bag of garbage and her small carry-on bag, Celeste got out of the car, glad to be able to fully stretch out her legs. "Dad, planes fly to Ohio, you know."

"Good, save your money. Next time we'll meet you there."

"I'm not going back to Ohio," Celeste said, meaning it, and she wasn't ever driving anywhere that took more than an hour to get to.

"That's your family, Celeste," Stella said.

"Your family first, Ma, and they're boring."

"Celeste—"

"Let her be, Stella. She's a teenager, everyone's boring to her."

"That's right. I'm going inside to call Sean."

"Before you do, miss, come get these bags," Richard said, indicating two large plastic shopping bags full of clothes that Stella and Celeste had shopped for in Ohio that were still in the trunk. "And hurry up and open up the door and get the lights on." Richard's hands were full and he didn't feel like digging into his pocket for his house keys. "I have to go to the bathroom."

Stella stayed behind. "And, Celeste, come back and help me get the rest of this stuff out of the back."

"I have to go to the bathroom, too," Celeste said, using her key to unlock the door.

"I bet you do," Stella said, knowing that Celeste was anxious to get her hands on the telephone.

"Dad, I'll use the upstairs bathroom." Dropping the bags in the front hall, Celeste quickly turned on the lights in the hallway and in the living room, and then taking the stairs two at a time, rushed up to the bathroom on the second floor. As soon as she took care of her business, she headed for her bedroom to cool out and call Sean, but just as she was passing Katrina's bedroom, she heard a noise coming from behind the closed door. She looked down at the bottom of the door and saw a thin line of light. Katrina was home. Celeste pressed her right ear to the door. She heard the sound of someone shushing someone. Normally, she would not go into Katrina's room uninvited, which was never, but she was intrigued. Celeste pushed open the door. Out of the corner of her eye, she saw the closet door as it was closing.

"Who told you to open my damn door?" Katrina was on the far side of her bed hurriedly trying to pull on her panties. Her hair was all over her head.

"I saw that," Celeste said, her eyes glued to the closet as she boldly stepped inside Katrina's room. "Who's in there?"

"Celeste, U'ma kick your ass." Katrina searched frantically for her bra. "Get outta my room!"

Teasingly, Celeste said in a hushed voice with her hand to her mouth, "Ma, Dad, Katrina's home. And she got company."

"U'm gonna kill you, Celeste. There's no one in my room. Get out and close the door."

"Is it Damon? Ooh, Ma and Dad are gonna kill you. You're not supposed to have him up in your room."

Katrina fumbled with her bra but couldn't get it untwisted to get it on right. She yanked it off her arm and threw it at Celeste. "Get out!" She took a step toward Celeste, but she glanced at the closet door and stopped. "Please, Celeste," she said in a softer voice, "just leave. I'll owe you."

"That's all right. This is payment enough. Damon, you better come out before my dad gets up here. The window's open."

"Celeste, stop talking crazy. There's no one in my closet."

"Then why do you look so scared." Celeste started for the closet.

Katrina rushed over and blocked Celeste, pushing her back toward the door. "Get out before I kick your ass."

Celeste was no longer seeing the humor of the situation. Katrina was caught and what better way to get back at her. "You better get dressed before Ma and Dad get up here."

"I hate you."

"What else is new? Ma! Dad! Y'all better get up here!"

Again, Katrina pushed Celeste. "I'm gonna beat your ass!"

"Let's see if you get yours beat first." She pushed Katrina back.

Richard and Stella rushed into the room. "What're you girls fighting about now?" Stella asked, out of breath. "Katrina, if you're home, why are all the lights out?"

Katrina stood bug-eyed, mouth open, staring at her parents.

"Girl, put your clothes on!" Richard said, standing behind Stella.

Katrina scurried back to her bed to search for her white tee-shirt in the rumpled bedsheet and spread. Quickly finding her oversized tee-shirt, she hurriedly tried to put it on but her head and arms got caught up in the shirt. She yanked irritably on it until she was able to pull it on right.

"Now, what's going on up here?" Richard asked.

"Celeste barged into my room without knocking."

"That's because I heard something."

"You heard me, stupid! I am in my own room, you know."

"Yes, and you're butt-naked. Dad, I heard another voice in here."

"That's a lie! Ain't nobody in my room but me."

Richard and Stella both glanced around the room. Seeing nothing but Katrina upset about Celeste barging into her room, they both looked at Celeste.

"Celeste, you know you girls are supposed to stay out of each other's rooms," Stella said. "It's ridiculous that you two can't get along."

"I'm sick of it myself," Richard said. "I want it to stop."

"I didn't do anything wrong," Celeste defended.

"You came into my room—uninvited!"

"Is that true, Celeste?" Stella asked.

"Yeah, but—"

"Celeste, we've only been home five minutes. I'm tired. Must you start up with Katrina the minute we step foot in the house?"

"I didn't—"

"Get out of my room!"

"Celeste, go to your room, " Richard said. "Tomorrow—"

"Y'all always taking Katrina's side. Y'all never listen to me." Celeste charged at the closet door, getting there before Katrina could stop her. She yanked open the door exposing the half-naked man hiding there. But it wasn't Damon as Celeste had suspected, it was Sean—her own boyfriend. A boyfriend she had only kissed.

All hell broke loose. While her father was snatching Sean out of the closet and hauling him toward the door, Celeste, when she recovered from the shock, which was quite swiftly, charged—claws out, teeth bared—at Katrina. Before her mother could come between them, Celeste pulled a handful of Katrina's hair out of the top of her head. In that moment, she hated her sister.

CHAPTER
1

Seven hours to flight time—twelve-fifteen P.M.

Celeste couldn't sleep—she was too excited. She had been up and moving about since four-thirty, just minutes before Willie turned over and covered his head to block the harsh overhead light, and long before the morning sun peeked into the bedroom window. For two weeks now, Celeste had been ticking off her list of things to pack. Her large suitcase was open on her side of the bed with everything neatly folded inside. The only things not packed were her toothbrush, her deodorant, and her comb. Oops. Scratch that. This trip, she didn't need a comb. Her hair was braided. This trip, she was being smart—her braided hairstyle was going to save her a lot of time and energy—no rollers, no blow-drying, no combing. She was going to swim, air-dry her braids in the hot Caribbean sun in the Bahamas and Bermuda, and dance the night away with nothing on her mind but a Sin on the Beach high and making love to her man.

For a year and a half Celeste had been looking forward to her first vacation in nine years. The last vacation had been on the occasion of her marriage to Willie. Then they had gone to Virginia Beach—the poor man's version of the Caribbean. Celeste glanced over at Willie on his back on the bed with nothing but a pair of black briefs to cover his fabulous nakedness. Yep, the boy still looked good. For sure, she was definitely going to revisit her honeymoon on this trip—she was going to wear Willie out. Since their honeymoon, they had not had the money or the time to go on an extended vacation of any kind. All of their money had gone into buying and fixing up their brownstone—Celeste's pride—and now paying a baby-sitter five afternoons a week when Justine's second grade class let out. Justine was her joy; Justine was the reason Celeste's heart sang. Her brownstone, on the other hand, was her just reward for working hard all her life. While she had no regrets about all the money spent on the brownstone, she couldn't say the same about her family. From the start, her mother had been against her buying a house in Bedford Stuyvesant, which was once upon a time one of the poorer sections of Brooklyn, but, shoot, she and Willie had needed a place to live that wasn't going to gag them every time they had to cough up the monthly rent. Her father used to say, "A home is what goes on inside the walls, not what goes on outside the walls," but her mother would always retort, "Then let's see you make a home in a landfill." That pretty much summed up how Stella Reese felt about much of Brooklyn. She and Katrina both seemed to have forgotten that they had once lived in Bedford Stuyvesant, for two years, in the seventies after Dad lost his job and they were forced to go onto welfare. Katrina swore to this day that she was never on welfare, but at the time she had no memory lapses when it came to eating the food that those monopoly-looking food stamp dollars bought. That's because her ass was hungry and a hungry gut doesn't turn its nose up and question where the food came from.

Unlike Katrina, Celeste remembered the hard times and learned from them—nothing came easy—which was why she and Willie were able to move into a brownstone that had been all but abandoned. Right away, they fixed up the master bedroom, the second-floor bathroom, the kitchen, and slowly, over seven years, renovated one square foot at a time around them. They had no problem with moving into a community that had nowhere to go but up.

Just weeks after they returned from their honeymoon, she and Willie had driven up and down the brownstone-lined streets of

Bed-Stuy, as the natives of the community called Bedford Stuy-vesant, admiring and dreaming about one day owning one of the grand, ornately adorned turn-of-the-century row houses of brown slate. Between the two of them working—Willie as a communications specialist and she as a debt collection agent—they couldn't afford a house of any size, but they were looking anyway. Hey, one never knew. They had just gotten married and felt that the one-bedroom apartment they lived in in Flatbush, which had been Willie's, was too small and, as far as Celeste was concerned, too full of lustful memories of lascivious romps for Willie. She wanted her own place where neither had memories of past lovers, and just when it seemed like they would not luck upon a brownstone for, literally, a dream and a fistful of dollars, they did.

A brownstone on Macon Street was advertised in the *New York Times* Classified Section, an unlikely place for a house in Bedford Stuyvesant, so it really stood out. The asking price was fifty thousand dollars. She and Willie were both skeptical. Anyone in the know knew that shells—brownstones with nothing inside them but the dust from wood eaten away by termites—in Prospect Heights, Fort Greene, and Clinton Hill were going for one and two hundred thousand dollars. The ad had to be wrong.

"Bedford Stuyvesant or not," Willie said, "what kind of house goes for fifty thousand dollars in New York City?"

Celeste was disheartened, yet curious anyway. She and Willie drove from Flatbush to take a curious gander at this fifty-thousand-dollar brownstone. Surprise, surprise, it was as advertised. It was a brownstone. The brown exterior slate was flawless—it wasn't flaking or cracked—it needed only to be steam cleaned. The house inside, however, needed a lot of tender loving care—hell, it needed a bulldozer, a sledgehammer and a barrelful of cash. Although, miraculously, the three-story building had sturdy wooden floors, working plumbing, and electricity flowing through its wires, every dismal, opaque-colored wall of dark brown, deep avocado green, or brazen hot pink in the twelve-room house was peeling or cracked, and the floors had to be stripped of the yards of corroded linoleum that was stacked five layers deep on every floor throughout the house, including the bathroom and kitchen floors. The three bathrooms and two kitchens still had huge, rusty cast-iron, claw-foot sinks and tubs, and the light fixtures were all original two- and three-socket metal hubcap-looking fixtures that looked as if they came off of an old Cadillac. But Willie wasn't fazed. He saw the potential of the house, and so did Celeste. Willie claimed for an additional fifty thousand dollars and doing the work himself, he could, over time, make the house into a showpiece. That was if they could come up with the purchase price, which they immediately had problems raising since the banks weren't willing to loan money for a house that realistically, needed about a hundred thousand dollars' worth of work.

The twenty thousand dollars they were able to come up with on their own wasn't enough when the deceased owner's son, Joseph Ross, living in Virginia, wanted the entire fifty thousand in cash, up front. Thinking that they were defeated, Willie said, "This isn't the only house in the world. We could save up for a few years and get a better house." But Celeste wanted this house. She refused to accept defeat. She had already researched the house, so she knew that Joseph Ross's sister, Barbara Walkins, was the person listed as the contact for the house. Using her skill as a collection agent for Akron Financial Collections, Celeste was able to do a skip trace and get the unlisted telephone number for Barbara Walkins down in Atlanta, Georgia. From the word "hello," Celeste poured on enough charm to make a horse drink from a Dixie cup. After a two-and-a-half-hour conversation about the house, her family's life in the house, and the neighborhood before the blackouts and destruction of 1967 and 1977, Barbara said, "I like you. I'm going to tell my brother to give you the house."

And, literally, Joseph Ross did. He dropped the asking price down to thirty thousand dollars and then turned around and asked for fifteen thousand in cash and took back a fifteen-thousand-dollar mortgage. Celeste and Willie paid off the house in two years, and finally, after nine years, the house was just about where Celeste wanted it to be. She and Willie had done much of the work themselves. Willie said once, "Who knew what these hands could do?" Boy, was he proud, and he had every right to be. Their house was beautiful. They had one more bathroom to renovate on the top floor. Then they were done. They were taking time out now to go on a much deserved vacation, and Willie, with his sleepyhead self, was going to get all the loving his beautiful body could handle.

Standing over Willie, Celeste smiled down on her man, her sweetie pie. Willie looked so good, she could eat him up—she glanced at the clock radio on the night stand: five-twenty—no time, but she kissed Willie full on the mouth anyway, savoring the softness of his lips without the sourness of his morning breath. Willie didn't stir. Celeste pinched his left nipple.

Frowning, his eyes squeezed shut, Willie groaned.

"Wake up, sleepyhead."

Grunting, Willie turned over on his side away from Celeste.

She tapped him once on the behind. "Willie, get up. I don't wanna get to the airport late and have to wait forever and a day on those long-ass lines. You know security is tight since nine eleven."

Willie muttered, "What time is it?"

"Five-twenty."

Willie still didn't bother to open his eyes. "Baby, we don't have to leave until nine o'clock, and even that's too early. Will you let me sleep?"

"Willie, you didn't finish packing, and I'm telling you right now, I am not packing for you." Celeste glanced over at Willie's suitcase on the floor in the corner. The only things inside were two pairs of swimming trunks and a pair of leather sandals. "Geez, Willie, do you think you'll be wearing a pair of swimming trunks everywhere we go?"

"If I feel like it."

"Willie!"

"Damn, baby, relax. I can finish packing in five minutes. So would you, please, let me get my sleep out." Willie grabbed Celeste's pillow and covered his head with it.

"Okay. Fine." It annoyed her that Willie's one major flaw was that unless he was going to work, he didn't think anything else in the world was worth being on time for. Back when they were fixing up the house, many a day he had gotten lazy and deemed the house "liveable," which meant that he was tired of spending his money and all of his spare time working on the house. He'd go back to working on the house only when he got tired of hearing her bitch at him, like she was doing now.

"Willie, if you wait till the very last minute to pack your bag and you can't find everything you need, you better not scream for me to help you find a damn thing, because I won't! I'm done."

"Damn, woman! It's too damn early for you to be bitching at me."

"Then get up and do what you need to do! Did you put gas in that gas-guzzling SUV last night? You know we won't have time to stop and get gas if you're running late."

Willie held the pillow tighter to his head and ears. He was so tired of hearing Celeste bitch, just to spite her, he wasn't getting out of bed until eight-thirty—he could do that because he had filled the tank last night after he'd gotten his fill of some good loving.

"Okay, Willie, don't answer me, but if that SUV doesn't have a full tank, I am going to pack all of my luggage on top of your hard-ass head and use a crop on your hard behind and ride you all the way out to LaGuardia."

When Willie didn't respond, Celeste went back to checking her list of things she needed for the trip. If she brushed her teeth, she could pack her toothbrush, too. She went off into the bathroom to do just that. It was early yet, but she may as well get her shower over and done with as well.

With the water running in the shower while she brushed her teeth, Celeste didn't hear the telephone ringing back in the bedroom.

Willie answered crabbily, "Who is it?"

"We need to talk," was the hasty reply.

Willie knew immediately who the caller was—Andrew Coleman, his supervisor at Dialacom. "Not right now, we don't. Do you know what time it is?"

"Sorry, Willie, but I had to try and catch you before you left."

"Well, I'm not up yet, and I'm not on company time. I'll see you in two weeks."

"I can't wait two weeks, Willie. I need to know what you're going to do."

"Coleman, I haven't decided as yet what my course of action will be, but I can tell you this much, Tyrel Johnson's name will be cleared."

The other end of the line was silent in Willie's ear. "I'm hanging up."

"Wait, Willie. I need to explain some things to you. Let me come by and talk to you."

"No."

"Come on, man," Coleman said. "I can meet you at your house or anywhere you want. I'm already on the road. I can be at your place in ten minutes. You're still over on Macon, right?"

"Coleman, don't come to my house." Willie sat halfway up in bed. "I'm not dealing with this shit before I leave town. If you wanna do anything, you need to right some wrongs before I get back. Then I won't have to show my hand."

Again, there was an uncertain silence on the other end. "You hear what I'm saying, Coleman? Do the right thing, man."

"Man, don't you think I wanna do that?" Coleman was shouting. "It's not as cut and dry as you think. If I recant my story, reinstate Johnson, I'm the one—"

"Yeah, you're the one that'll be brought up on charges." Willie could feel his stomach muscles tighten into knots. "Coleman, you got Tyrel Johnson fired and brought up on charges for something you did. The man is in jail because you stole fifteen laptops. If I hadn't secretly set up that video recorder in the supply room yesterday morning, I wouldn't be the wiser, would I? It's too damn bad I didn't get to see the damn tape until last night, after I left work, or you'd be sitting in jail instead of Tyrel."

"Listen to me, Willie. I can straighten everything out for Johnson. I can get back most of the laptops. I put a computer back yesterday. I know you saw that."

"You got that right."

"Look, Willie, I'll say that the computers were misplaced, that there was a mistake. I'll get Johnson reinstated, and the charges will be dropped."

"You do that—first thing Monday morning." Willie wasn't fooled by the lie. Coleman was a thief and, by default, a liar.

"I will, Willie, I swear. Just don't turn the tape in. And you know what I'll do for you, Willie?"

"Let me guess—get me fired?"

"No, no, Willie, I swear, I'd never do that. I'll get you a raise, a promotion. That's right, you'll be Senior Communications Specialist. You'll get a five-thousand-dollar raise. What do you say, Willie? You keep quiet, I'll take care of you, I promise. We got a deal?"

"No deal."

"Shit, Willie! I can't afford to lose my job. I can't go to jail! I got a family."

"You should've thought about that when you were sneaking laptops out of the office in that big-ass briefcase of yours."

"Goddamnit, Willie, I made a mistake. I—"

"Man, I ain't got time for this crap." Willie slammed the telephone down and quickly turned over in the bed with his arms folded tight. He was going to get his nap out no matter how pissed off he was. He flopped over onto his back and laid his arm across his eyes to shield them from the overhead light.

Damnit! If only he had viewed the tape before he left work. Then he could have turned it in, but oh, no. He didn't see the tape until ten-thirty last night. Clearly, Coleman could be seen taking a laptop from his briefcase and putting it back on the shelf in the supply room. Earlier in the morning, Tyrel had been arrested for stealing the fifteen laptops. Coleman, obviously, thought it best he return the laptop he had already taken earlier that morning before anyone discovered it was missing. The man was low to steal from Dialacom, but even dirtier to put the blame on Tyrel, who worked as the supply room clerk. A few days ago when Willie first heard about the stolen computers, he knew immediately that Tyrel was blameless. Weeks before, he had been out to lunch with Tyrel when Tyrel found twenty dollars in the restaurant. Willie was speechless when Tyrel turned the money over to the manager. Hell, if it had been him, he would have wasted no time shoving that twenty deep into his pocket, but Tyrel had said, "My gain is someone's loss. I wouldn't feel right." Tyrel taking that stance had particularly amazed Willie because Tyrel was only twenty-four years old, and it wasn't like he was making a whole lot of money. He had come from the mean streets of the South Bronx and had run the streets as a gang banger in his teen years. It was while he was locked up in jail that Tyrel had found religion—the Muslim religion. Willie had to ask himself, would a man who turned in found money steal from a company that took a chance and gave him a paycheck? He didn't think so. When he returned from vacation, he would turn in the tape if Coleman hadn't cleared Tyrel's name. For now, the tape was stuck down in the living room sofa between the arm and the cushion where he'd slipped it after watching it. It was just as safe there as anywhere else in the house. Willie turned onto his stomach. He was determined to sleep at least another hour.

Riiiiing!

The telephone ring screamed in Willie's ear. He snatched up the receiver. "Look, man! I told you—"

"Willie?" a young girl's hushed voice asked.

Willie immediately sat up. He glanced at the door. He could hear the shower water running halfway down the hall, but he covered the mouthpiece with his hand anyway. "What are you doing calling me here?"

"Baby, I miss you."

CHAPTER
2

Willie's heart was racing. "Renee, what if—"

"I know, but I had to talk to you."

"Why? What's up?"

"Baby, I just wanted to talk to you."

"Suppose my wife had answered the phone?"

"If she had, I wouldn't've said anything."

"At this hour, that would have made her suspicious as hell. And, you shouldn't be calling me on this line—just my cell phone. And what about you? Are you calling me on your cell phone or—"

"Dang, Willie, I ain't stupid . . .

Willie thought otherwise.

". . . I know better than to call you on my house phone when my parents—"

"Okay, okay, so what do you want?"

"I miss you," she whined.

"Listen to me. You could mess me up big-time calling here."

"I wouldn't have to call you there if you'd left her two months ago like you promised. You're not gonna leave her, are you?"

Willie kept his eyes fixed on the open door and his left ear listening to the sounds outside his bedroom door. "I'm not gonna talk about this on the telephone. I'm hanging up. I'll—"

"I'm sorry! Don't hang up. I just called to tell you, baby, that I'm missing you already."

"I told you I'd call you when I get back in two weeks."

"But, Willie, I won't be here when you get back. I'm going down south on Monday for three weeks, remember? I'm supposed to register for college."

That Willie did forget.

"Baby, I won't be back till the end of the month, and even then, unless you tell me that you're leaving your wife, I'll be back just to pack up the rest of my things. That's why I wanna see you before you leave."

"But I just saw you last night."

"I know, but this'll be the first time we'll be apart so long. I'm gonna miss you."

"C'mon, baby, the weeks will pass before you know it." Willie rushed to the bedroom door. The shower was still running, so Celeste would be at least another two minutes. He closed the bedroom door for good measure, but his voice was still hushed. "I'll miss you, too, baby. I'll bring you back something special, okay?"

"Yeah, but I want something really special right now. I got my thighs wide open, waiting for you, big daddy."

Willie thought about those sweet, tight young thighs wrapped around his body. "Aw, man."

"Wanna know what I'm doing, Willie?"

"Damn, baby, don't be messing with me." Willie began rubbing himself. He had a pretty good idea what his sexy young lover of the past year was doing. He began to lick his dry lips.

"I'm real horny, Willie. Don't you want some more of this good stuff?"

Willie felt himself harden in his own hand. Again, he glanced at the closed door. He sat on the side of the bed. "You're a bad, bad girl."

"You wanna come spank me, big daddy?"

Sucking in his breath and closing his eyes briefly, Willie massaged himself. He could almost feel himself inside Renee's warm, tight hole. He had taken a chance sneaking out of the house last night, but that sweet young stuff was hard to ignore.

"Willie, you said you weren't leaving for the airport until nine o'clock, right?"

Willie started shaking his head. "Don't even ask."

"Please, Willie. Make up an excuse. She'll believe you."

"Yeah, but at five-thirty in the morning, there isn't anything I forgot to do."

"You could say that you need to get some gas. That's how you got out last night."

"Yeah, and I already had a full tank then." He had filled up after work.

"So, do she know that?"

Thinking hard about the danger of running out so early, Willie weighed the sweet rewards against the risks. "Are your parents home?"

"Yeah, but it's Saturday and they always sleep late on Saturday. They won't hear me leave."

"You don't know that. At this hour, sounds are magnified. They might hear you coming down the stairs or locking the door."

"I doubt it. My mother sleeps like she's drugged. You could put a bullhorn to her ear and scream her name, and she won't hear it . . ."

"No."

". . . and my father got in late last night. He was tired when he went to bed, so he won't—"

"No!"

"But, Willie—"

"I said no, Renee. I want your sweet ass, but I'll be damned if I want it bad enough for both of us to get caught. If your parents heard you going out this early, they'd want to know why. I don't want you getting in trouble; you've been in enough this past year."

"Okay, okay, but, Willie, I got to see you, baby."

"It's not doable. Let's forget it."

"Please, baby. I want you so bad I was dreaming about you."

Willie's chest swelled. "Yeah? Was I good?"

"Damn good. You had me throbbing in my sleep. That's what woke me up. I can still feel your tongue from last night."

And Willie could still feel what his tongue had been touching.

"Don't you wanna do that again before you leave, Willie? Don't you wanna wash your face with my—"

"Damn! Okay, okay. I'll pick you up in ten minutes. We can do it in my SUV."

"That's no fun. I hurt my neck last night, and I don't wanna do it on the street again. What about that motel out on Atlantic Avenue?"

"You mean that seedy little joint over in East New York where the door locks can be picked with a feather?"

"Yeah. We went there before, remember?"

"And that was because we were driving past it and you were stripping in my car."

"Well, I was hot."

"No doubt, but I can't—"

"Shh! Hold on a minute . . . Yeah! . . . Hey, Dad."

Willie pressed his ear to the phone. He could kill Renee for calling him this early.

"Who're you talking to this hour of the morning?"

"My friend, Will—Willamina. Her name's Willamina. All the kids call her Willie."

"It's kinda early for phone conversations, cut it short."

"I'll be off in a minute."

Willie listened to the silence on the other end.

"I'm back. He went to the bathroom, but he's back in his room."

"We'd better forget about it," Willie said. "He might've overheard what you were saying."

"Oh, he didn't hear anything. He went back to bed. Willie, let's go to that motel. Please, it wasn't so bad there. Besides, it's not like you can take me to the Plaza."

The pressure from his persistent young lover, and the pulsating tightness in his groin, was killing Willie. Again he glanced at the clock and listened for Celeste. "If I go out to Atlantic, she'll wonder what's taking me so long."

"Tell her you got a flat."

"That's too cliche."

"Yeah, but it happens, right?"

Thinking . . . thinking . . . Willie glanced at the clock

"Ooo, Willie, I'm juicing. Don't you want some of this?"

"Damn, girl, what you trying to do to me?" Willie glanced at the door. He might just be able to—

"Please, Willie, I'm about to come all by myself."

"Damn." Willie's mind was full of Renee's beautiful brown, naked body lying under his own body. "You better make this worth my while."

"I tell you what. As a going away present, I'll let you do what you been wanting to do for a long time."

"Don't play with me."

"I promise, I won't stop you this time."

Willie felt the heavy weight of the pulsating in his hand. He was in pain. He rushed back to the door. He opened it a few inches and looked down the hall toward the bathroom. The water was still running in the shower. If he was going, he had better go before Celeste got out. At that moment, the water was shut off.

"Are you dressed?"

"In one minute I will be."

"Meet me at the corner in six minutes, no, five." Willie quickly hung up. He jumped into his jeans. He didn't tie his shoes, nor did he button up his shirt as he rushed past the bathroom and yelled out, "I forgot to gas up last night. I'll be right back."

Celeste stuck her head outside of the bathroom. "What did you say?"

Willie kept walking. "I forgot to gas up."

"Willie! Why do you always wait till the last minute? Wait a minute. I thought you got gas last night. Willie! Why do you always wait till the last minute to do anything?"

The sound of Willie trotting down the stairs and the slamming front door were the only answers to Celeste's rhetorical question. For years she had been trying to make Willie put gas in his car whenever the gauge dropped to one-quarter, but Willie never would. He said every car had a reserve of two gallons in the tank even if the gauge was on empty. Yeah, right. Celeste wouldn't bet her life on it if she had to drive Route 66 out in California. That's why she started fussing with Willie the minute she saw the gauge dropping to the quarter mark. And today of all days, she'd kill him if they ran out of gas on the way to the garage out near the airport where they were leaving his SUV for the two weeks they were away. Well, this time, Willie at least remembered and was getting out early enough to return and finish packing. The gas station was only a few minutes away. He'd be back in time to finish packing, eat breakfast, and drop by her parents' house to say good-bye to Justine.

Next stop, the blue skies and the aqua blue waters of the Bahamas and Bermuda.

CHAPTER
3

Willie didn't notice the headlights of the car that followed him to the motel. What he did notice upon entering the dinky room was that the air conditioner was working—just barely. It loudly cranked out its tepid air, filling the room with a stale, musty smell, but that smell was a distant memory with the fragrant scent of a pair of black lace panties around his neck and the heady, redolent scent of lovemaking filling his nostrils. And now, dripping with sweat and out of breath, he rolled off the top of his own personal nymphomaniac. Renee was practically insatiable. He lay flat on his back, his right arm resting on a perfectly flat, tight stomach. He was whipped, but he was happy. He smiled to himself. *Boy, this young stuff is hellified.*

"That's what I'm talking about." Renee smiled as she turned over on top of Willie.

Sleepily, Willie asked, "What?" He shifted slightly so that he could breathe easier with her body atop his chest.

Renee grabbed a handful of Willie's hot, sticky manhood, cuffing him possessively. "This! It's the joint and it's all mine."

Willie grinned lazily. "You got that right."

"I'm the only one that makes it happy, right, Willie?"

"Yeah, baby."

"You gonna leave that bitch like you promised, right? We're gonna be together, right?"

"Baby, don't spoil it. Let's talk about this when I get back." He kissed the top of Renee's head to quiet her. He didn't like her cursing Celeste; it grated on his nerves. As good as the sex was with Renee, he regretted cheating on Celeste. In all the years that he and Celeste had been together, he had never before cheated on her. But eleven months ago, the one time he let himself be talked into going out for drinks with the guys after work, he ended up in a club where there were girls half his age, wearing less clothes than the law allows over bodies that their own mamas wished they had, and he bumped into this fine young thing. Damn! In the dim lighting of the club, they got to dancing, they got to grinding, kissing, drinking, and before Willie knew it, he was humping the sweetest piece of young ass, in the back of his SUV, like a championship stallion riding a wild mare. He hadn't had sex like that in years and wasn't willing to give it up for hours. Damn good stuff—young stuff! When he got home, his guilt kicked in, and he hurriedly showered, telling Celeste that he had to wash away the pungent smell of cigarette smoke that clung to him and his clothes from the club.

It blew his mind still that he'd let the affair go on this long when he had no intention of leaving Celeste, but she would definitely leave him, if not kill him, if she ever found out. When the affair started, for days he couldn't bring himself to touch Celeste, and when the calls started coming, enticing him to sneak out, like a dog, he gobbled up as much sex as he could. He felt bad afterward, but while he was getting it, he was loving it—like now. It was as if Renee's ass was made to be palmed by his big hands.

"Baby, don't let any of those young country boys touch what's mine, you hear?"

"Willie, you know I don't want nobody but you."

"You say that now, but you're a hot, sexy woman that needs to be made love to—often."

"Yeah, but only by you." Renee stretched felinely atop Willie, rubbing herself along his newly budding erection. She pushed herself up higher until her nipple was on his lips.

Willie opened his mouth and began sucking as if he were hungry for the milk of life.

"When you leave that witch you're married to, you can have it like this all the time."

"C'mon, baby. You're gonna spoil our last few minutes together."

"Okay, okay. Whatcha bringing me back?"

Willie was enjoying the silky feel of Renee's body rubbing atop his hard-on. He closed his eyes. "I'm bringing you something from the ocean." He began thrusting upward with his body.

"I don't want no sea shell, Willie. I want something nice. Something expensive."

"Baby, you deserve the crown jewels."

"Willie, I'm serious."

"So am I." He was ready to hit that sweet ass. "I'll get you something really special, but what about me, baby? Do I get that special something you promised?"

Renee dropped her head and laid her face alongside Willie's. "You won't hurt me?"

"Not a bit."

"Are you sure, Willie? It kinda hurt that time you tried before."

"I'll go real easy, I promise. Hey, you know what?"

"What?"

"I'll bring you a gold bracelet."

That excited Renee. "You promise?"

"Yeah, baby." Willie started sitting up, nudging Renee's body over to the side as he did. Renee was hesitant as she rolled onto her stomach.

"Don't make me bleed, Willie."

"I won't, baby. Trust me." Willie was drooling with anticipation. He helped Renee up onto her knees with her warm ass backed up against his groin. He pulled the black lace panties from around his neck and slipped them under the pillow. He then lowered his face and ran his wet tongue along Renee's spine down to her behind. He kissed each of her cheeks as though he were kissing the tender bottom of a newborn baby.

Renee giggled with each kiss.

"See. I love this sweet ass. I wouldn't hurt this sweet ass."

"You better not."

Willie went about fulfilling his fantasy. He began slowly trying to ease himself inside Renee's sweet virginal rectum. Tensing up, she moaned and tried to pull away. He held her tight against his body.

"Relax, baby." Willie was beginning to breathe hard. "I won't hurt you." With his left hand, he gripped Renee's hipbone and held her firm. With his right hand, he slowly worked himself inside a place where no man had ever gone. He didn't hear her moaning or see her raising and lowering her head, grimacing with her discomfort. He was only aware that he was where he wanted to be.

Beads of sweat popped from Willie's forehead, his chest, and his shoulders as he began to grunt his pleasure. The loud, warm-air-blowing air conditioner did nothing to cool the room down. *Oh, yes, this ass was certainly worth sneaking out of the house for.* He could feel Renee beginning to move with him. He pushed himself farther up inside her.

"Ow!" Renee exclaimed, but she didn't pull away. Instead, she pushed back into Willie. She took his left hand and placed it underneath her body, right on the spot where she was throbbing.

"Oh, baby, yes!" Willie was in heaven.

Together they gyrated in a rhythmic dance of thrusts and grinds. Willie forced himself to hold back—he didn't want this dance to end too soon; he was finally fulfilling a longtime fantasy. Celeste would never let him do this to her, she was such a prude. He and Celeste had even had a falling out a time or two when he tried and wouldn't stop when she asked him to. The last time, five years ago, she reared back and butted him in the face and kicked wildly until he had to let her go. She didn't care that he was so hard that he ached or that she almost kicked him in that most sensitive area. He concluded then and since that Celeste was selfish, but that was all right. He had her love, yet he was still getting all the ass he wanted—firm, young ass at that.

"Oh, baby . . . that's . . . right." Willie strained for each breath. "Take . . . care . . . of . . . your . . . man. Damn, this is good!"

"Do it to me, big daddy. Harder!"

And Willie did. He screwed harder, he sweated harder, he panted harder. He didn't hear the motel door ease open. He couldn't hear; he was near to exploding. He raised his head higher. He grit his teeth as a powerful surge coursed through his groin. "Oh, yes, ba—"

The sledgehammerlike, skull-crushing pain that slammed Willie in the back of the head stole the intense pleasure of the explosion in his groin. A loud grunt whooshed from his open mouth as he collapsed heavily atop his lover's back. Renee flopped onto her stomach and face under the weight of Willie's sweaty body. He was still full and emptying inside her.

"Willie!"

From the room rushed the intruder on shoes that made not a sound, but the slammed door startled Renee.

"Who's there? Oh, my God, is someone in here? Willie . . . Willie!"

No one answered, not even Willie.

"Willie!" Renee tried to push herself up off of her face. "Get offa my back!"

Willie didn't move.

"Willie, stop playing." Renee could feel the sweat from Willie's body run down the sides of her own body and her right cheek. "Willie, you're too heavy. You're wetting me up! Get offa me!"

Willie not responding unnerved Renee. "Willie, stop playing." She tried pushing Willie off top of her while attempting to crawl from under his weight. She felt him plop from inside her.

"Willie? Willie, are you all right?" With one final backward push of her hip and her right arm, Renee shoved Willie off top of her and onto his back. She glanced at the door. It was closed. "Willie, I think someone was in here. Willie—"

The wide-eyed fixed gaze in Willie's stare and his wet tongue hanging from his open mouth stilled Renee's question. Then she saw the blood on Willie's neck and pooling under his head on the bed. Inhaling one mighty gasp, she clamped her mouth shut with both hands to stifle the scream that strained to burst from her throat, yet a horrific, muffled scream rushed from her anyway. Jumping off of the king-size bed, she stumbled back into the wall.

"Oh, God . . . oh, God."

With her hands covering her mouth, Renee slid down the wall to the floor with her knees drawn tight to her chest. She couldn't understand how Willie could be bleeding.

"Damn you, Willie!"

Celeste snatched Willie's brand-new, micro mini, silver cell phone and, with all of her might, threw it at the wall across the room. It exploded on contact and landed on the floor in shattered pieces, just as Celeste hoped it would. She didn't care one bit that Willie had paid three hundred dollars for his state-of-the-art camera phone; she wished only that it had been Willie's head that she was throwing. For the last four hours, besides running back and forth to the front stoop, she had called Bryson, Willie's brother, who hadn't heard from him, the police precinct, and St. Mary's Hospital and Kings County Hospital, all to no avail. There was no William Alexander in the emergency room at either hospital, so Willie hadn't been in an accident or locked up for any reason. Celeste was beside herself with worry on one hand and mad as hell on the other. Willie was supposed to have gotten gas last night. Where in the hell was he?

For what felt like the fiftieth time, Celeste stood high up on her front stoop, hands on hips, frowning every time the traffic light at the corner of Macon and Throop changed and Willie's black SUV didn't turn into the block. Each time she wanted to scream, "Damn you, Willie!"

"Celeste, I thought you were leaving out early this morning," a woman's voice said.

Huffing loudly, Celeste crossed her arms and stomped her foot. She was so mad she couldn't even speak to Gertrude Price, her next door neighbor. She and Gertrude were pretty good friends, although Gertrude had her by fifteen years. Gertrude had three sons and one daughter, ranging in age from eighteen to twenty-five, all still living at home, all still depending on Gertrude, none self-sufficient or of any help to their mother. Their father, Walter, wanted them all to move out, but Gertrude wouldn't hear of it. She was the type of mother who liked to be depended upon. Since Celeste had moved into her house, she and Gertrude had looked out for each other's houses when the other wasn't home and taken in each other's UPS and post office deliveries. In a way, she depended on Gertrude, too.

Gertrude stood in her front yard looking up at Celeste. "What's wrong?"

"Willie's not home, and I don't know where the hell he is."

"He's not home?"

"No! He went out around five-thirty this morning to get gas and hasn't come back yet."

"He hasn't called?"

"No!"

"Maybe he—"

"I've called the hospitals, I've called the precinct, nothing."

"Well, maybe he ran other errands and just forgot to tell you or ran into an old friend—"

"Gertrude, I swear to God. If Willie is somewhere doing something stupid like running his mouth with some 'old friend,' I am going to kill him."

"Like I am gonna kill that fast-behind daughter of mine. She hasn't gotten home yet either."

"From when? Last night?"

"She wasn't home when I went to bed at nine-thirty. Shawn said she came in around ten, but she snuck her butt out again. God knows what time she left."

"Gert, that child is probably at that Melvin's house. You know she can't stay away from him."

"If she's with that no-good bum, I'm gonna chain her stupid ass to the radiator. That fool don't mean her no good. He's hoping that she'll get a job and support him."

From her vantage point high up on the stoop, Celeste saw a young shapely girl come around the corner from Throop Avenue. "Isn't that your wayward daughter coming into the block now?"

Gertrude leaned over her front gate to get a better look down the block. "Yeah, that's Naynay. Wait till I get my hands on her. Look at the way she's dressed."

Riiiing!

"That's my phone," Celeste said. "It might be Willie." Celeste raced into the house, praying that it was Willie.

Hoping that Willie would sit up, Renee kept staring at him. Willie didn't move.

"Oh, God, Willie, what am I supposed to do?"

Looking around for a telephone and not seeing one anywhere in the room, Renee suddenly remembered that Willie always had his cell phone on his belt. Walking wide around the bed, she rushed to Willie's cast-off jeans on the lone wooden chair in the room. She fumbled with them as she turned them first legs up and then waist up. There was no belt.

"Willie, your phone. Where's your phone?" She patted down his pants pockets from which she pulled out his wallet and keys. No cell phone. "Oh, God, Willie. This can't be happening. Willie, please get up!" Putting the keys and wallet back, Renee began to anxiously twirl her hair around her fingers. *Oh, God. The police'll think I killed Willie. They'll put me in jail. I gotta get outta here!*

Renee rushed over to her own jeans and skimpy midriff top rolled up neatly on top of the low dresser covered with black burn marks from the many cigarettes that had rested there. She pulled her skin-tight jeans over her bare bottom and pulled her midriff top down over her naked breasts. Slipping her feet inside her high-heeled mules, she started for the door and realized that she had no way of getting home. She went back to Willie's pants and took the thick wad of money from his wallet that he must have had for his vacation, but then thinking better of it, she put all of the money back and took only a twenty-dollar bill. Before rushing out into bright, early morning light, Renee stuck her head outside the room and cautiously glanced around to see if anyone was in sight. No one was. Before bolting from the room, she looked back one last time to see if Willie would suddenly sit up and shout, "I got ya!" He didn't. As she quietly pulled the door closed, Renee didn't notice her black lace panties peeking out from under the edge of the pillow on the far side of the bed.

She ran across the parking lot on winged feet past Willie's SUV onto Atlantic Avenue. It was just past six-thirty in the morning, the traffic was sparse, just a few early risers out on a Saturday morning, but Renee didn't want to be noticed by anyone. Self-consciously she touched her right cheek and felt the stickiness there. She looked at her hand. Blood! Willie's blood was on her. She wiped frantically at her face until she thought all the blood was gone, but there was no mirror to tell her it was so. Lowering her head, Renee hurried down Atlantic Avenue toward Penn-sylvania Avenue, hoping all along the way, block after quiet block, that she'd see a livery cab. She saw none, and at the corner of Warwick and Atlantic, she stopped at the pay phone and with trembling fingers dialed 911. She had to tell someone that Willie was dead.

CHAPTER
4

Angry tears filled Celeste's eyes as she slammed the front door for what seemed like the hundredth time. She could not believe that Willie was doing this to her. She had begged him to get gas last night. But no! Willie did whatever the hell Willie wanted to do whenever Willie felt like doing it. Now he was running around, God knew where, obviously not caring that she had wanted to leave early for the airport. It was now ten forty-five, and she hadn't heard a word from him. He was going to make them miss their plane.

"Suppose he's been in an accident?" Bryson asked for the third time.

"Well, his ass had better either have amnesia or be in a coma because if he's not, I am going to kill him when he gets home!" Celeste cried as she hung up on Willie's brother. As heartless as it sounded, the only way Celeste would excuse Willie for being late would be if he had been in an accident, and he had better be at death's door. If not, by now he could have called home. He was only going out to get gas, but she had always told him to take his cell phone with him. After all, wasn't the cell phone for emergencies? But oh, no, Willie had gone out and left his cell phone on the dresser. Stupid! But even that was no excuse. There had to be a zillion pay phones on the streets of Brooklyn, including in the gas station, whichever one he went to.

Celeste struggled awkwardly down the stairs with the pullman-size suitcase she'd packed for herself. She set it alongside the matching carry-on and the suitcase she had hastily finished packing for Willie. She had balled up and tossed all of his clothes inside without a care as to how wrinkled they'd be. All she knew was that she was not going to be the one to iron out a single wrinkle once Willie unpacked in the hotel. Served him right. Damn, but right now, the way it looked, they wouldn't be unpacking this afternoon.

"Oh, hell no, Willie. You can go to hell! I'm going on this trip!" Celeste snatched the telephone and dialed 411.

"Welcome to Verizon local and national 411," James Earl Jones's rich baritone-laced voice said. "What listing please?" a woman's mechanical voice inquired.

"Black Pearl Car Service."

Buzzzz!

Celeste hung up the telephone and rushed to the door, opening it wide without first looking out through the peephole to see who was there. The two men—one African American, one White—standing before her, Celeste did not know and was certainly not in the mood to hear from.

"I'm not interested!" She slammed the door in their faces. Celeste hadn't stepped away from the door when the bell rang again.

She yanked the door open. "Look!" She put her hand on her hip and glared at the man right in front of her. "I said I was not interested in anything you're selling." She was about to close the door again when one of the men quickly put his hand out to stop her.

"Ma'am, do you know a William Alexander? Does he live here?"

Celeste's heart thumped. The anger that had been choking her all morning seemed to stop her from breathing altogether. She stared at the taller of the men, the black man, with the tiny neat locks clinging to his scalp. That's when she noticed what hung from the breast pocket of his dark blue suit jacket—a gold police shield on a flap of black leather.

"We're from the Seventy-fifth Precinct. Are you Mrs. William Alexander?" the detective asked.

Celeste didn't like the sound of that question. She cut her eyes from one detective to the other. She didn't like the sorrowful look in either of their eyes. While her anger at Willie had filled her chest with a tenseness that had left her breathless in her rage, this sudden, smothering sensation of fear that crept up her spine and spread over her chest numbed her.

"Ma'am, are you Mrs. William Alexander?"

A little voice somewhere in Celeste's head prompted her to answer, "Yes."

"Ma'am, may we come inside?"

Celeste began wringing her hands. They were calling her ma'am. Something had to be terribly wrong. "Willie went to get gas. He's not back yet, but he should've been back hours ago. Willie always does things at the last minute." Celeste knew that she was jabbering, but she couldn't stop herself.

"We're about to go on vacation, but if Willie doesn't get here soon, we're gonna miss our plane. We haven't had a vacation in nine years, and Willie knows that I've been planning and planning and planning this trip. And he has the nerve to . . . you just wait till he gets back here. I am going to—"

"Ma'am—"

"Do you know where Willie is? Do you know why he's late?"

"Yes, ma'am, but, ma'am, it's best if we come inside," the taller of the detectives said.

"Why?"

"Please, ma'am, the news isn't good."

A bolt of lightning pierced Celeste's heart. She felt as if every nerve was on fire. Her tongue was suddenly dry. She felt as if she was dragging a ball and chain as she lead the detectives into the living room. What were they about to tell her? Had she bad-mouthed Willie so much that her words had come true?

"Has Willie been in an accident?"

"Ma'am, would you like to sit down?" the taller of the detectives asked.

"Stop calling me ma'am!" Celeste's knees were buckling despite her struggle to square her shoulders and stand strong. She reached behind her for the overstuffed armchair she knew to be there. "Would you please just tell me where Willie is!"

"I'm sorry, ma'am, but your husband is dead."

CHAPTER
5

Until Celeste saw Willie laid out stone cold on a stainless steel slab in the city morgue, she did not believe that it was he whom the detectives spoke of, and that's when the plaintive wailing started sounding in her head, but not coming out through her mouth. Until she sat for hours staring at Willie laid out in his casket, his eyes sealed shut forever at the front of the church with arrangements of flowers from friends and family surrounding him, she didn't allow herself to believe that Willie had gotten his brain knocked out while making love to another woman. It seemed the latter pained her more than his death. She had not lain a single red rose on top of his casket. She had not leaned against her mother or father for support. She had stood transfixed in her anger at Willie, glaring at his casket, silently cursing him, damning his soul to hell. Until she saw him sealed up in that glossy box of walnut and brass and lowered into the bowels of the earth, it hadn't dawned on her, that she had not shed one tear for Willie from the moment the detectives told her where he had been found. She would have spit on his grave if it were not for Justine; she would not understand her display of contempt for the father she'd adored.

Three weeks ago Celeste turned her back on Willie's grave site and walked away, dry-eyed and bitter, knowing that all curious eyes were on her. All, except for her family and Willie's family, wondered about her squared shoulders, her raised head, her cold, tearless eyes, and her stilled tongue. She wanted to tell them all that the man they mourned was an adulterer, a liar, a fornicator, but again, she had Justine to think about. It was hard enough trying to explain to Justine why she had not taken her back to the cemetery to visit Willie's grave. "We'll go one day when I can handle it," she said, knowing that Justine didn't understand the full import of that explanation, but it was the best she could offer. Willie's brother, Bryson, finally volunteered to take Justine to the cemetery, and Celeste permitted it because it was the least she could do for her child. Other than that, she knew there would never come a day that she could handle standing at Willie's grave without wanting to dig him up and use his face as a punching bag.

Celeste asked no questions of Justine when Bryson brought her home. She tried her best to act interested in what Justine was saying.

"Mommy, I still can't believe that Daddy's in the ground," Justine said sadly. "I wish he was still alive."

"So do I, sweetheart." *Just so I can kill his ass all over again.*

Bryson lowered his eyes; he seemed to know exactly what Celeste was thinking.

"Mommy, Uncle Bryson said Daddy's gonna have a headstone on his grave like everybody else, but it's not ready yet."

"I guess it's not." Celeste really didn't care. She'd told Bryson and the rest of Willie's family if they wanted a headstone on his grave, they had better put one on themselves, because if it was up to her, the only thing that would ever mark Willie's grave would be a brick with the word "bastard" printed on it with a magic marker. As for her and Willie's plan to be buried in the same plot, that was never going to happen. She didn't even want to be buried in the same cemetery with Willie, much less the same plot of ground. Just in case their spirits decided to get up and walk the earth, she didn't want to stumble into Willie even by chance.

"It'll be another month," Bryson said. "The inscription has to be carved on."

Celeste peered at Bryson. "I hope the inscription is befitting the man that lies there."

"Celeste, come on. The inscription—" Bryson glanced uncomfortably at Justine. "It's the right inscription."

Celeste rolled her eyes away from Bryson. *It had better be.* She had told Bryson that he better not put "loving husband" on Willie's headstone. In fact, the word husband was not to be inscribed at all.

"What's an inscription?" Justine asked, looking to Celeste for the answer.

Celeste turned away from her child. She didn't want Justine to see in her face that this was one of those times she couldn't hide her contempt for her adulterous father.

"The inscription is what's written on the headstone," Bryson explained. "It'll have your father's name and his dates of birth and death. It's so that people will know that he once lived."

"Oh." Justine fell silent as she slumped down onto the floor and began to pick at the nap of the carpet.

Celeste felt Justine's sadness even before she saw it on her face. She hadn't been able to say the things Justine needed to hear about her father—he was a good man, he will always be with you, you're so much like him, you smile like him, you have his eyes— to make her feel better because Willie had stolen those words from her tongue. The things she wanted to say most were mean— he's not your father, he's a liar, he's a cheater—and would hurt Justine too much.

"Justine, why don't you go up to your room and finish getting your clothes together. Your grandfather will be here soon."

Justine continued plucking on the carpet. "I don't wanna go."

"Come on, baby. You know you wanna go. So, please," Celeste said a little too tensely, "don't give Mommy a hard time. Please."

Moving like a tired old woman, her head lowered, Justine slowly dragged herself up to her bedroom on the second floor.

Bryson waited until he thought Justine was well out of earshot. "Celeste, you can't be so cold around Justine; she doesn't understand."

"I know that."

"She misses Willie."

"I know that, too."

"So help her."

"I can't."

"Celeste, you have—"

"Bryson, leave me alone!" Celeste could hear that deafening wail in her head. "It's not my damn fault that Willie went and got himself killed while fucking some bitch in some cheap-ass motel when he was supposed to be home, here with me, packing his damn bags for a trip I waited years for."

Riiiing!

Tears threatened, but Celeste wouldn't give in to them. "It's not my damn fault that Willie's daughter misses him. I—"

Riiiing!

"You're right, Celeste. It's not your fault that any of this happened, but Justine doesn't understand about fault or blame." Bryson glanced at the telephone. "Aren't you gonna answer the phone?"

Riiiing!

Celeste huffed. "Do I look like I'm about to answer that damn phone?"

"Damn, Celeste. Suppose it's important?"

Riiiing!

"Nothing is important right now except my daughter, and I need to get my head together for her. And while she's gone, I will call her as often as need be."

"So you're not taking any calls?"

Again Celeste huffed. "Did I take yours?"

"So if I hadn't shown up here, I would never have gotten you on the telephone, and since you don't have your answering machine on, I wouldn't've been able to leave you a message?"

"You got it."

"You can't keep doing that, Celeste."

"I can if I want to."

"Damn, Celeste. Man. You can't keep hiding."

"I'm not hiding, Bryson. I talk to whomever I want."

"So Erica and I aren't part of the privileged?"

"Oh, please, Bryson."

"And what about your neighbor, Gertrude? On the way in, I saw her. She said to tell you that she's keeping you in her prayers, and anytime you wanna talk, she's home. I guess you've been ignoring her, too."

"Would you *please* leave me the hell alone and let me live my life the way I want. *Thank you* very much!"

Bryson threw up his hands. "I guess I need to just worry about Justine. I'll call her at your parents'."

"Do what you want, Bryson, but my parents and I will take good care of my daughter."

"And so will I and my family. Let's get an understanding here, Celeste. I'm not gonna let you shut us out of Justine's life or your life. You're angry with Willie. Don't take it out on the rest of us. You keep building up that wall of scorn against me, I'll knock it down. I mean it."

Celeste had to steel herself against outright weeping. She never knew that Bryson cared so much for her. Oh, they had always gotten along, and his wife, Erica, was one of her closest friends, but she hadn't counted on Bryson being the shoulder that she could lean on. It was good to know that he hadn't deserted her, but she wasn't about to let him run her life.

"The hell with you, Bryson. I won't let you bully me."

"That's real nice, Celeste. I'm not trying to bully you. But you go ahead. Say what you want. I'm not mad—I understand. Just like you need to understand that all Justine knows right now is that her father is dead."

Damn! Here we go again. Celeste could feel the vein pulse in her temple. Her head was killing her. "And that's exactly why Justine is going to stay with my parents out in Queens. They can help her more than I. I'm no good for Justine right now, I'm too messed up. I know you can understand that, Bryson."

"How long is she staying with your parents?"

"Till school starts."

"That's more than a month, Celeste. Is it a good idea for Justine to be away from you that long?"

"It is if I say so, and I do!" She stalked off into the kitchen with Bryson at her heels.

"Okay, so you get rid of Justine—"

Stopping abruptly, Celeste turned on Bryson. "I am not getting rid of my daughter!"

"Then what do you call it?"

"I call it doing what's best for her."

"And what is that, Celeste? Separating her from you? What are you gonna be doing?"

"Minding my own damn business."

"Damnit, Celeste! I'm not trying to hassle you. I'm trying to look out for you and Justine."

"That was your brother's job, Bryson, not yours."

Bryson knew not to respond to that remark; it was bait that he wasn't taking. "Okay, Celeste, when are you going back to work?"

"When I feel that I can handle inquiring eyes."

"Come on. You haven't told anyone on your job about how Willie died. If they ask, just say he had a heart attack."

"Did you forget that there was an article in the *New York Post* and the *Daily News* about Willie's body being found in that motel room? I guess everyone already knows he was killed while he was coming."

"You don't have to be cruel. Willie—"

"Bryson, I'm not the one that was cruel. Willie ran out on me to be with another woman."

"You gotta give Willie the benefit of—"

"Did you know Willie was cheating on me?"

"No, I . . . I—"

She cut her eye at him suspiciously.

"I didn't!"

"Hey, sometimes you act like you know something."

"Well, I don't!"

"Are you sure?"

"Celeste, if I had known something, I would have stopped him."

"Well, somebody should've. He died stuck up in some bitch like a dog with a hard-on."

"Damn, Celeste! Forget how Willie died. We should be talking about Justine anyway."

"Bryson, I will never forget how Willie died, and *we* shouldn't be talking about Justine. *I'm* doing what's best for *my* daughter."

"It's like that, huh? You're hell-bent on shutting me out, like you've done with all your friends. Well, you can't do that, Celeste. Willie might be gone, but you're still my sister-in-law, and Justine is still my niece. I'm gonna look out for both of you."

"Would you please leave me alone?" Celeste felt as if Bryson was smothering her. His concern for her and Justine, no matter how well intentioned, was annoying her.

"Justine can come to my house just as well as she can go to your parents'. She can be with her cousins."

"And she will be."

"Okay, but right now, Celeste, Justine needs to be with you. She just lost her father and—"

"Which is, again, Willie's fault." For a minute Celeste couldn't remember why she'd come into the kitchen. She opened the refrigerator door. "If Willie had been concerning himself about his daughter's well-being, he might have thought twice about sneaking out of the house like some dog in heat. "

"Willie made a mistake, Celeste. He—"

Celeste slammed the refrigerator door so hard, bottles on the shelves on the inside of the door rattled. "So that's what you call it? A mistake? Bryson, a mistake is taking a wrong turn into a one-way street, or thinking that you put a quarter in a parking meter when you put a nickel. So you're saying that Willie made a mistake? So he left here that morning to get gas and took a wrong turn, three miles away, and stumbled into a motel room and fell on top of some bitch, and screwed himself into getting his skull split open? I'm supposed to believe that, right?" Celeste stormed out of the kitchen back into the living room.

Again, Bryson followed. "Okay, so mistake is the wrong word. Willie—"

Celeste whirled around. "Bryson, stop trying to play me for stupid! Willie was cheating on me. On the very day we were supposed to go away, he *chose* to meet his whore in a motel for a last hump and lost his life. Willie was a low-life bastard. There is nothing that you or anyone else can say to me to make me see him or this god-awful nightmare any differently."

"I'm not trying to, Celeste. I'm trying to help you through this, like Willie would want me to. But you're not letting me. You're so angry. You—"

"I have every damn right to be angry!"

"Maybe you do, but you're confusing Justine."

"Well, excuse the hell out of me, but right now, that can't be helped. I'm just as confused as she is."

Bryson took Celeste's hand. "I under—"

Celeste snatched her hand free. "No! You don't understand." She fought to keep from crying. "Bryson, Willie put a knife through my heart and turned it until he ripped me to shreds. I feel like he's still turning that damn knife."

"Don't you think I understand that, Celeste? Willie was my brother, and I hate that he did this to you, but we don't know everything there is to know about how Willie died. I think if you concerned yourself with what happened to Willie, who killed him, maybe—"

"The hell with maybe, Bryson. I really don't care who killed Willie. Whoever it was did me a favor."

"Damn, Celeste. Sure, Willie was wrong, but he didn't deserve to go out like that."

"See, Bryson, that's where we have differing opinions, but then I'm not surprised. Willie was your brother, but the hell with that. Willie was my husband. I believe Willie went out exactly the way he deserved. What he was doing behind my back, I found out about upon his death. He was caught with his penis in a hole it should not have been in. My, wouldn't it be poetic justice if the whore he was with killed him?"

"That's just it, Celeste. Suppose Willie was forcibly taken there and set up to make it look like he was with a woman. That detective that's on the case thinks that's a possibility."

Celeste put her hands on her hips. "Bryson, are you forgetting that the manager said that Willie was the one that signed for the room, and that the DNA tests showed that it was Willie's semen on the sheets?"

"No, but damn. Try to give Willie the benefit of the doubt. Willie was a good husband and a good father, and you know it. None of us know what really happened that morning. Willie could have been forced to—"

"Bryson, I know you know better than that. Willie would have fought and died at the gas station if it was like that." Celeste began prowling around the living room. "I trusted Willie. I never thought he would cheat on me. Boy, was I wrong. Obviously, Willie had been cheating for some time to sneak out of the house like that."

"He went to get gas, Celeste," Bryson said defensively. "He did have a full tank when his SUV was checked."

"Yeah, but who knows when Willie got that gas or where. He must've paid cash. There was no receipt from the service station he should have gone to. Whoever Willie was with was no stranger, and I don't believe for a second that it was a prostitute that he just happened to run into in the gas station, whom, if he was so inclined, he could have fucked right in the back of his SUV. The bastard."

"Willie wouldn't—"

"Stop it, Bryson! Stop defending Willie. Willie was cheating on me, and you know it. So stop defending him to me."

"Willie loved you."

"Really? Then why did he do this to me?" Celeste hit her chest with her fist. "I can't sleep, Bryson. I can't sleep because in my mind, I keep seeing Willie with some faceless woman in that motel room, making love to her and laughing at me waiting at home for him to return."

Shaking his head, Bryson sat heavily on the sofa. "You have to stop thinking like that. Willie did love you."

Celeste shook her head no.

"Willie loved you for real, Celeste. I know that as a fact."

Celeste chuckled drily. "If Willie loved me, he would not have done this."

"He made a—"

"Bryson!" Celeste stopped prowling. "Don't you dare say *mistake!* What Willie did was a conscious choice, and I will never forgive him for it. He hurt me. He hurt Justine. I won't forgive him for that either. Willie betrayed both of us, and that betrayal is worse than his dying. God!" Celeste hugged herself tightly. "Bryson, I am in such intense pain that I can't even cry. I feel like there's yards of duct tape wrapped around my head, covering my mouth and my nose, suffocating me, like there's no air getting into my lungs."

"Celeste," Bryson said, going to Celeste and taking her into his arms. "I'm sorry. I—"

Celeste pulled out of Bryson's embrace. "Don't comfort me. I don't want to be made to feel better. I want to feel this pain so I can keep hating Willie."

"Oh, man, Celeste, that's not good."

"It is for me, Bryson. But you know what? In a little while, I'll be fine. I have to be. I have a daughter who is going to need me for a very long time to fill the void that her daddy has opened up in her life."

"I'm here for Justine, and for you, too, Celeste. Me and Erica both. All you need to do is—"

Celeste held up her hand to stop Bryson from talking. "Guess where I went last week. No, don't guess. I went to that motel, to the very room that Willie died in."

"I figured you would."

"Damn right. Bryson, I stood in the middle of that room and tried to see if I could feel Willie there. I couldn't. The room was empty of any kind of life force. It was like a house that had not been lived in for a long time."

"That's because no one lives there, Celeste. It's a transient motel."

"I know that, Bryson. Anyway, I tried to find out from the clerk at the front desk who the woman was that Willie was there with, but he said he didn't know. He said he had only seen Willie that morning."

"The police had already told us that, Celeste. You could have saved yourself that trouble. You don't need to be burdening yourself with trying to find the woman Willie was with. The police are doing all they can. If she can be found, they'll find her. They were able to lift her fingerprints from Willie's SUV."

"Well, I hope they find her real soon. I'd like to meet the woman who could get Willie to run to her for one last fuck before going away with me. She must be really special."

"Let it go. You're only prolonging your anguish. You need to—"

"Don't tell me what I need to do, Bryson! Your bastard of a brother hurt me. I have every right to know every little detail of this mess. Eventually, I will find out who Willie was with. And when I do, I am going to plaster her name across the front page of every newspaper in this city."

"I'm telling you, Celeste, you're too angry. You're gonna make yourself sick."

"Oh, didn't I tell you about this stabbing pain in my chest that jabs at my soul and pierces my heart every time I see Willie's face, which is every time I look at Justine, every time I look around this house that we sweated to get just right, which is every time I breathe."

Celeste could feel herself welling up. But it wasn't tears she wanted to shed. It was the cloak of betrayal that covered her mind and soul that she needed to rid herself of. She swiped angrily at the tears on her cheeks.

"Mommy!" Justine called from the top of the stairs. "Can I take my scooter with me?"

"Yes!"

Buzzzz!

"That's Granddad!" Justine bounded down the stairs.

"Are you finished packing?"

"Almost."

"Almost isn't finished. Girl, go back up those stairs and finish packing and please make sure there are more than one pair of socks and one pair of underwear in your bag. And take that makeup case out of your suitcase because it will never close."

Justine stopped at the top of the stairs. "How did you know my makeup case was in my suitcase?"

Buzzzz!

"Just take it out." Celeste opened the door. It was her father. She threw her arms around his neck and held on tightly. When Richard Reese set the shopping bag he carried on the floor and closed Celeste up in his strong embrace, she shut her eyes and just let his warmth and strength seep into her body. She inhaled his Brut cologne and felt safe with the familiar scent he'd worn since she was a little girl.

"How are you, Mr. Reese?" Bryson asked, coming to the door.

Richard continued to hold Celeste with one arm while he shook Bryson's hand with the other. "Good to see you again."

Finally feeling as though she had collected herself enough, Celeste let go of her father.

"Ahem," a woman's voice behind Richard said. "Am I supposed to stand here holding this all day?"

Richard stepped aside to reveal who had come up on the stoop behind him.

Oh, shit. Katrina. Celeste couldn't believe her eyes. Katrina hadn't been to her house in years.

Katrina came on into the house carrying a foil-covered, large aluminum baking pan. She said nothing to Celeste.

"Hello to you, too, Katrina." Celeste said snidely. She couldn't believe the audacity of her sister to be so ill-mannered that she'd enter her house without speaking.

"Hey," Katrina said, "thought I'd come along to see how you're doing."

Celeste didn't buy that for a moment. The truth was more likely that Katrina had come along to see for herself if she had fallen apart. "I'm just dandy."

"Mother sent this." Katrina held out the aluminum pan. "It's fried chicken. There's some potato salad, some macaroni salad, and a tossed salad in the bag. She said you probably weren't eating."

Celeste picked up the shopping bag her father had set down on the floor. She looked inside. "She didn't have to send all this. I'm going to be here alone, or did she forget?"

"Not hardly," Katrina said under her breath but loud enough for Celeste to hear her.

For an uncomfortably edgy second, Celeste glared hatefully at Katrina. She could almost see herself pushing Katrina out of her house.

"Celeste," Richard said, "where do you want this stuff?"

Celeste shot her father an accusatory glare. He looked away from her immediately.

"I'll take it," Bryson said, taking the pan of chicken from Katrina and the shopping bag from Celeste.

"Bryson, right?" Katrina asked.

"That's me."

"How have you been? The last time I saw you was—"

"At my brother's funeral." Bryson walked off into the kitchen. A hushed silence was left in his wake. Celeste leveled a hateful look at Katrina, but Katrina was on her way into the kitchen.

"I'll just help him with the food."

Celeste slipped her arm through Richard's, and together they went on into the living room. She lowered her voice. "Why did you bring her?"

"She said she wanted to see how you were doing. She followed me over in her car."

"You should have driven straight to the Bronx Zoo."

"Don't start, Celeste."

Celeste pulled away from Richard. "She already started, Dad, or didn't you notice?"

"Lower your voice."

The voice in Celeste's head was screaming, *Get that bitch outta my house!* but she was cool. "Katrina hates the ground I walk on, Dad, and you know it. She didn't come to my graduation, she didn't come to my wedding, she didn't come to my house warming, she didn't come to my baby shower, nor did she come to the hospital when Justine was born, but, interestingly, she did come to the hospital when I had that ectopic pregnancy a few years ago, and she was the first to arrive at Willie's funeral."

"Celeste, you and your sister haven't always been there for each other."

"That's not true!" Celeste glanced at the kitchen door and quickly lowered her voice. "I have always been there for Katrina.

Just two years ago, I was the one who picked her up from the hospital when she broke her leg on that skiing trip and took her to your house when her stupid husband wouldn't take time off from his job in Washington to be with her. I was the one that drove all the way up to the Poconos to get Gordy when he damn near drowned in camp four summers ago because Katrina was out of town. I'm the one that always dropped everything and ran to Katrina when she needed me, but she has never done that for me. She didn't lift a finger to help me get through Willie's funeral. All she did was stand around with a stupid smirk on her face. Oh, and I'm sure you noticed that neither her husband nor her eldest daughter were at Willie's funeral."

"Well, Gordon—"

"It's obvious to me, Dad, that Katrina didn't think enough of me to have her whole family there to support me. Is that too much to ask of my only sister?"

"Celeste, Gordon wasn't in town and Patrice—"

"Stop making excuses for them. The truth is, Katrina only shows up when there are bad things going on in my life. She shows up just to see if I'm humiliated or defeated."

Richard sighed heavily. "You and your sister have got to learn to get along, Celeste. You—"

"Dad!" Celeste felt as if she was talking to herself. "How could you say that after everything Katrina's done to me? After what she said to me, remember? You were there when she said she hated me, that she hated that she was even related to me, much less my sister."

Richard began to nervously rub his nape. He was never comfortable being in the middle of Celeste and Katrina's accusations against the other. "Celeste, you and Katrina are sisters. You girls have got to learn to get along. Now, I believe this time Katrina is genuinely concerned for you. She—"

"Dad, I lost my husband, not my damn mind. Katrina is here to gloat. I'd bet my life on it."

"This is not the time, honey, for—"

"Forget it." Celeste moved away from her father. "Dad, you never understood the dynamics between me and Katrina. Mom does, but, like you, she takes Katrina's side."

"I'm not taking sides, Celeste. I never have."

"Maybe you should; then perhaps you'd see what I see."

"Celeste, you're both my girls. I love both of you equally. I—"

"Dad, you're off the hook. I don't expect for you to ever understand what I'm trying to tell you about my and Katrina's relationship. But that's all right. I don't care anymore. But, I'm telling you, take Katrina out of here when you leave, because I'm not in the mood for her foolishness. So be forewarned, if she fu—messes with me, I am going to kick her behind."

"Celeste, all your sister did was walk in the door and you've gotten yourself all worked up for nothing."

Celeste never understood how her father could be so deaf, dumb, and blind to what he surely had borne witness to over the years—the many petty but vicious fights between her and Katrina over a simple act like walking in the door.

"Dad, do you remember the time Katrina walked in the door at your house three years ago and ruined Thanksgiving dinner for you when she said, 'Dad, I hope you didn't cook the turkey. That one you cooked last year tasted like shredded cardboard.' "

Richard frowned. He hadn't enjoyed any of the dinner while Katrina was there.

"And do you remember what she said to Mom? I know you do."

"Celeste, let's not open old wounds."

"Dad, Katrina told Mom that after all these years, you and she could afford to hire a caterer so that all of the dishes could be edible."

This time, Richard rolled his eyes up to the ceiling. "Your mother wanted to kill her."

"Yeah, but she did what she always does—chalk it up to, 'That's just how Katrina is. She speaks her mind,' " Celeste said, mimicking her mother's soft speaking voice. "Dad, Katrina has never just walked in anywhere and not left everyone's emotions in shambles."

Richard threw up his hands. "Okay, okay. I'll take her out of here when I leave."

"Thank you," Celeste said, relieved. She felt as though she needed to lie down just to calm down.

"Where's my granddaughter?" Richard asked.

"Upstairs packing everything but her toothbrush and under-wear."

Richard started for the stairs. "I'll make sure she has everything."

"Dad." Celeste stopped Richard from leaving. "I'll take care of Justine's things in a minute. I need to talk to you."

"Sure, honey."

Celeste glanced back toward the kitchen door. She didn't want Katrina to overhear her.

"What is it?"

"I haven't told Justine anything about the circumstances surrounding Willie's death."

"That's best."

"Yes, but she's been asking questions. I told her that Willie had a heart attack. So, please don't—"

"Don't worry, honey. Your mother and I have already discussed this. We'll make sure Justine doesn't learn the truth."

CHAPTER
6

Celeste was furious. Her father was going to hear her mouth. Long after he'd left with Justine—without Katrina—Katrina was still sitting around talking to Bryson. Celeste had continually drummed her fingers on the kitchen table and then on the arm of the chair in the living room until her tips were numb. What the hell was Katrina trying to prove hanging around her house? In all the years Celeste had lived in her house, Katrina had crossed her threshold two times, one of those times being today, and the other on the occasion of the dinner she'd had a year after moving into her brownstone. Katrina had hated the unfinished house and the dinner. The dinner had been a disaster. So this visit marked two visits too many. And the fact that Katrina was talking to Bryson was even stranger. On the rare occasion that Bryson and his family had joined Celeste and Willie at Celeste's parents' house for Thanksgiving dinner, Katrina had always gone out of her way to ignore Bryson and Erica. Katrina was much practiced in that rude behavior because, growing up, she had systematically done that with all of Celeste's friends, except Sean, but Celeste refused to let herself dredge up thoughts of what Katrina had done with Sean. It was still too painful to think about. But, actually, most of the time, Katrina had ignored Willie, and that was because Willie was Celeste's husband. The truth was, Katrina liked no one who was connected to Celeste. This was just another fact of life that Celeste, over the years, had worked hard to make herself accept, that was after she'd accepted that just because they were sisters it didn't mean they had to like each other.

Laughing flirtatiously, Katrina playfully tapped Bryson on the arm. "Oh, that's just too funny, Bryson. So did you ever learn to do the electric slide?"

Disgusted, Celeste groaned under her breath at Katrina's annoyingly phoney laughter and glib chatter.

"Not a step," Bryson said flatly.

"I'm surprised. You have a great body. You probably move like a jaguar."

Bryson didn't crack a smile. "Lead feet, remember?"

"Oh, you can't be that bad. I could teach you—"

"Katrina." Celeste couldn't take it. "Would you like for me to call you a cab? It's getting late."

"I have my car, thank you." Katrina's eyes never left Bryson. "Really, Bryson, I can only imagine what your body was like in your late teens and early twenties. You had to be awesome because you're fabulous now."

"Yeah, that's what my wife tells me."

Good for you, Bryson! Celeste could not believe Katrina was openly flirting with Bryson. She had to be trying to get under her skin.

Again Katrina put her hand on Bryson, but this time on his thigh. "I love a man who works out. I—"

"Katrina!" Celeste said quickly. "Where's Gordon this evening? He must be off work by now; it's pretty late. Don't you have to fix dinner for him and the kids?"

"If you must know, Gordy's spending the weekend at Mom and Dad's, Lorna's old enough to get her own dinner—she is fifteen, you know—Patrice is away, and Gordon's in Washington. He splits his time between his New York office and his Washington office."

"That must be hard on you with him away so much."

It's hard as hell, but you'll never know it. "Not really. Gordon comes home often enough to not be missed. And actually, being apart only makes the coming together that much sweeter, if you know what I mean?" *But the truth is, we haven't had sex in over five years. I know Gordon leapt at the chance to work in Washington just to get away from me.* "So, I'm as free as a bird tonight."

Celeste could barely contain her cynicism. "A vulture," she said under her breath.

"What about you, Bryson?" Katrina asked, cutting her eye at Celeste. "What's your weekend like?"

Celeste almost leapt from her chair. "What the hell do you mean, what's his weekend like? Bryson has a family, a wife to go home to, or did you forget that? Until tonight, you never spoke more than ten words to him. What's up, Katrina? You lonely with Gordon out of town?"

"Wow," Bryson said, looking at his wristwatch. "Look how late it is."

Katrina smirked. "Gordon being out of town isn't a permanent condition." Although at times Katrina felt as though it was. Gordon was coming home less often and staying fewer days, with the excuse that he was working on a major project and weekends were workdays. Often he left in a huff after an argument, which he always blamed her for starting, but it was really him starting the fights.

"Maybe not," Celeste said, feeling her stomach quiver, "but it's a hell of a way to get away from you. How is your marriage, Katrina? Has Gordon asked for a divorce yet? If he hasn't, then he's just as insane as you."

"Oh, you should know about insanity, Celeste. Aren't you insane with grief over your hubby's sudden demise?"

"Okay," Bryson said, standing suddenly. "This is getting out of hand." He took a giant step over the coffee table to get out of the way of the ugly words being thrown across him.

"I'm not in the mood for your shit, Katrina. Why don't you go home?"

Katrina clicked her teeth. "That's why I don't come around you. You're always in a nasty mood."

"Damn," Bryson said. "This is too deep for me."

"Believe me, you've been doing me a favor by not coming

around." Celeste couldn't believe what she was about to do. "So why don't you keep that favor going—get the hell outta my house."

"Katrina," Bryson said, "it might be a good idea if you went home."

Katrina glanced disdainfully around the living room. "Your house could use a professional decorator."

"Fuck you."

Again Katrina smirked. "No, you're the one that's gonna need someone to fuck you."

CLAP! Bryson loudly clasped his hands together, startling both Celeste and Katrina. "It's getting pretty late, Katrina. Maybe you should go."

"No problem. I'm done slumming."

All the memories of all the terrible things that Katrina had done to her rushed into Celeste's mind. "You have always been such a bitch."

"It takes one to know one." Katrina began moseying toward the door.

"Just get the hell out of my house, Katrina."

Katrina turned. "Oh. By the way, Bryson, have the police gotten any closer to finding Willie's killer?"

Celeste shrieked, "What the hell do you care?"

"I don't."

"Katrina," Bryson said, "you need to go—now."

"Don't keep telling her, Bryson. Let her keep messing with me."

"Geez, Celeste, I don't know why you're so mad at me. I'm not the one that Willie was humping when he got himself killed."

"That's it!" Celeste started for her. "I'm gonna kick your ass."

Bryson grabbed Celeste, holding her back. "Go home, Katrina!"

Celeste wanted desperately to get to Katrina. "You nasty witch!"

"My, you're a mite sensitive, aren't you, Celeste?"

Celeste struggled to pull free of Bryson's hold. "You're evil, Katrina. I'm tired of your shit. I'm not like Mom and Dad—I'm through tolerating your evil ass. As far back as I can remember, you've always been a hellion of a bitch."

"So have you. Personally, I can't stand the ground you walk on."

"Aw, come on, Katrina," Bryson said. "Just leave. We know how you feel."

"Here's a news flash for you, Katrina. I can't stand you either. You've always been the worst kind of sister. How dare you come—"

"Sister! Hell, I think I've already told you that I hate that you're even related to me, much less my sister."

"Come on, ladies. Don't say anything that you'll both regret."

As angry as she was, Celeste couldn't believe that she could still be hurt by Katrina's words. Yet as it was with the first time Katrina told her that she hated that she was her sister, it still felt as if a cold blade of steel had sliced through her chest.

Katrina smirked. "Believe me, I won't regret a word." She tucked her pocketbook under her arm.

"Ditto! As far as I'm concerned, I've never had a sister."

Bryson tapped Celeste's cheek, trying to get her attention. "Celeste, she's leaving. Don't say anything else."

"No, Bryson, let me and my sister air our shit. It's long overdue."

"Hey, I'm down," Katrina said. "Yeah, let's get it all out in the open." Katrina inhaled and exhaled as if to clear her lungs. "You know, Celeste, from the time you were born, you were nothing but trouble. And I don't mean just to me; you were trouble for Mom and Dad. "

Celeste couldn't ignore the stinging in her nose. "That's it, isn't it? You hate me because I was born and stole all the attention you were getting."

Again Katrina smirked. "You'd like to think that, but, no, I hate you because you were selfish, demanding, and loud. If you didn't get your way, you'd bitch louder than a fog horn."

"Well, excuse the hell out of me for being a baby."

"Oh, it's not as simple as that. You've always been a pain in the ass."

"Katrina, you've always been jealous of me."

"You're nothing to be jealous of."

"Oh, no? You're three years older than me. Until I came along, you had Mom and Dad all to yourself. The minute I was born, you probably wanted to kill me. Hey, I can understand that, but we're now both grown-ass women, not little girls sucking our thumbs and wetting in our diapers. For the life of me, I can't understand, when we don't even see each other, how and why your hatred for me grows with each passing year."

"Then let me explain," Katrina said. "You're a know-it-all, Celeste. You're always trying to be somebody's mother. I'm older than you; I don't need you to tell me what to do about anything. You got that? Keep your advice for those simpletons on your job that need you bossing them. I don't need you. I never have."

"I've never tried to tell you what to do."

"Oh, no? What about the time you called my house and told me about that carpet sale downtown?"

"What?" Celeste gawked at Katrina. She looked to Bryson to see if he understood. He shrugged his confusion. "Was that a sin? Did I overstep my bounds?"

"I don't need you to tell me about any sales. I have money to buy whatever I want, on sale or not. What you were telling me to do was go buy what you thought I should buy, like I couldn't afford to buy anything not on sale."

"How stupid are you? I wasn't trying to tell you any such thing. I was telling you about a great carpet sale. You had just moved into your house, and I thought—"

"Well, you thought wrong. I don't need you to tell me anything. In fact, I—"

"This is fucking ridiculous." Celeste choked back tears. "You know what, Katrina? I refuse to spend another minute talking to you. Get the fuck outta my house!"

"Gladly." Katrina glanced around the room with her upper lip scrunched up to her nose as if an awful smell assailed her senses. "I have to go play my lottery numbers anyway."

"Still trying to win that illusive pot of gold? If you added up all the money you've spent over the years playing the lottery, you might find that you've spent about a million."

"Hey, it's mine to spend. At least I have money to play with. Can you say the same?"

The wailing in Celeste's head was near blinding her. "I thought you were leaving."

Smirking, Katrina opened the front door. "By the way, Celeste. I always know where my husband is."

"Go to hell."

Katrina lifted her chin and walked out of the house, leaving the door wide open.

Bryson stood in the doorway and watched Katrina get into her car before he closed the door and locked it. Looking back at Celeste, he saw her trembling in her rage. Her eyes smoldered black in her anger, while her chest heaved as she gasped in her struggle to breathe normally.

"Celeste, you can't let your sister get to you like that."

Celeste went to the front window and snatched the sheer white curtains back so she could look out at Katrina, but Katrina was already out of sight. It didn't matter. Celeste didn't need to see the woman who was by birth her sister to wish her dead.

CHAPTER
7

If he had witnessed a terrible car crash, Bryson would not have felt any more traumatized than he did in witnessing the clash between Katrina and Celeste. He had been morbidly mesmerized by their acerbic bickering and really wanted to know, "I know what Willie told me about you and Katrina, but have y'all ever liked each other?"

Celeste released the curtain with a contemptuous thrust. "I am going to kill my father!"

"Celeste, you and Katrina—"

"Don't mention that bitch's name to me!" Celeste balled her shaking hands into tight fists. She pressed her lips together to keep from screaming. The effort only made her head ache worse.

Bryson could see that Celeste was shaking. "Celeste, why don't you come to the house for dinner? I put all that food your mother sent in the fridge. Erica asked me to bring you anyway. She'd love to see you."

"I hate her."

"Who? Erica?"

"No, Katrina. I hate Katrina." It dawned on Celeste that this was the first time in a long time that she had given voice to those words. It seemed forever that she hadn't liked Katrina, but until today, she hadn't felt the intensity of that dislike since the day she found her boyfriend in Katrina's bedroom closet. Supposedly, it had only been that weekend while Celeste was away that they had gotten together, but it didn't matter. It could have been five minutes or five years. They had had sex. They both had betrayed her. Tears that Celeste could not shed for Willie poured from her now.

Bryson put his arms comfortingly around Celeste's shoulders. "Go ahead. A good cry will make you feel better."

Celeste's tears suddenly dried up. She threw Bryson's arms from around her and angrily dried her face. "Then I don't need to cry." She went to the china cabinet where she kept the alcohol locked away in the bottom.

"Getting drunk won't solve anything."

"I'm not so ambitious. I'm only trying to get numb."

"Maybe you and Katrina need to just stay out of each other's way. She—"

"I know you saw Katrina come across my damn threshold. I didn't cross hers."

"No, but she—"

"Bryson, I have stayed out of Katrina's life for years, and having no contact with her has made little difference. Actually, no difference at all. Katrina hates me. That's all there is to it."

Celeste poured herself a double shot of Bacardi dark. "Is it a sin to say I hate my sister?"

"Probably."

"Then I'm a sinner—big-time. I hate her!" She closed her eyes and let the bitter brew wash down her throat like bad medicine.

Being that he had never seen Celeste drink liquor beyond a celebratory glass of champagne, Bryson watched silently as she made a sour face. He sat.

Celeste opened her eyes and exhaled a whoosh of hot air. She could feel the strong, hot liquid coating her empty stomach. She could feel every nerve in her fingers tingle. Taking her glass, she sat across from Bryson.

"Were you and Katrina ever close?"

"No!" She'd spoken too fast. "Well, that's not altogether true. If I go back far enough, I guess I can remember playing with Katrina as a very young child. In fact, we used to share a bedroom, but that would have been before we moved out to Laurelton."

"So what happened?"

"If I knew for sure, other than jealousy and sibling rivalry, I might be able to tell you. Katrina was thirteen when I was ten, which is when I sat up and took notice that she didn't like me."

"What had she done?"

"I don't know, cruel things. She just did cruel things to me—hitting me, breaking my toys, my dolls. She just got meaner. Maybe it was puberty. I don't know."

"There has to be more to it," Bryson said. "What I witnessed was straight-up, unadulterated hate."

Celeste took a sip of her rum. "Bryson, all I know is that one day I woke up and my sister hated me. It was like she was mad, pissed, real angry with me. I could do nothing right by her, and she hated me for it. When my parents weren't looking, Katrina would grab a chunk of my arm and pinch the hell out of me." Celeste rubbed her upper arm. "Damn, she pinched me so much back then, I can still feel the sting."

"Why?"

"For meanness, for nothing. Who the hell knows."

"What did you do? Did you just let her pinch on you?"

"There wasn't much I could do. Katrina was bigger than me. She'd beat my behind, I'd go crying to my father, he'd whip her behind and make her stop, but then Katrina would turn around and get back at me in other ways. She'd take my things, break them, throw them away, anything to mess with me, and I could not, for the life of me, fathom why she was hell-bent on hurting me."

"How long did that go on?"

"Until I was about thirteen and got big enough to fight back. When our parents weren't home, Katrina and I used to have some snatch-your-hair-out, roll-on-the-floor brawls. We'd be hurting and still cursing each other out when my parents got home, so we'd get punished for fighting and cursing and for messing up the house. We broke quite a few things during our fights, including several of my mother's collectible porcelain birds. Boy, was she angry with us."

"Damn. I thank the man upstairs that me and Willie got along. In fact, we only had each other. We only had one serious fight, and that was over a basketball game."

Celeste smiled. "I heard about that fight. You cheated."

"Yeah, well, I can admit that now, but back then, I denied it. Willie wasn't hearing it, and we fought hard. Willie kicked my ass. Celeste you should have seen Willie when he was on the court, he—"

"Please. No Willie stories tonight."

Bryson understood. "Yeah, okay. So when did you and Katrina stop fighting?"

"Need you ask that question? What did you just witness?"

"I mean physically."

"Oh. After Katrina moved out."

"Damn, y'all must have been about grown."

"She was twenty-three." Celeste shook her head at the absurdity of their behavior back then. "Up until Katrina moved out, the older we got, the smarter we got about not leaving any evidence of our fighting. After a while, one or the other of us would stay out of the house when my parents weren't home. Usually it was me; I had more friends to hang out with."

"I don't know, Celeste. It just doesn't make sense she harbors so much hate for you. There has to be a reason."

"Well, if there is, you let me know. I've tried all of my life to figure Katrina out. Like she said, she just hates me."

"Then, maybe it is jealousy."

"Bryson, Katrina's never had cause to be jealous of me. Not when we were kids, and not now as adults. She has everything I have and more."

"Then maybe it's not materialistic. Maybe Katrina liked some boy that you were seeing."

"Not when I was ten, but certainly when I was seventeen. Katrina stole my first boyfriend right from under my nose."

"Damn, Celeste. For real? How?"

"How do you think? Giving him sex when I wouldn't."

"Damn, that was low. I know you had to hate her for that."

"I did, and still do."

"Did your parents know what she did?"

"They were with me when I found out about it. We caught Sean in Katrina's bedroom. My mother beat the hell out of her, but that didn't stop Katrina. She made it her business to flirt with any guy who looked my way. But I was a quick study. I stopped bringing guys home. I didn't bring Willie to my parents' house until we were engaged, and Katrina wasn't even living there, but, hell, little good that did. Look what Willie went and did on his own."

"Be fair, Celeste. You can't possibly put Willie in the same category as Katrina. You said yourself that Katrina always hated you. That's not the case with Willie. He always loved you. He made one bad-ass mistake. He—"

"Bryson, don't you get it? Willie's betrayal is greater than Katrina's. I trusted Willie. Katrina, I never trusted. As far as I'm concerned, they're both vile. I don't think I'll ever completely trust anyone again."

"But, Celeste, you can't let what other people do to you jaundice your perception of everyone. Look, come back to the house with me. You should talk to Erica; she misses you. Celeste, you can't keep shutting out your friends."

"I can if my friends can't understand that I can't stand to hear them tell me I deserved better, or that I'll get over what Willie did. Bryson, I won't get over what Willie did. That's something I know as a fact."

"But everyone means well, Celeste."

"They think they do, but damnit, Bryson, they really don't. Their words of pity, their words of concern, are actually hurting me. The truth is, I deserved Willie." She laid her hand on her chest. "Willie used to be the best man for me. That's why I'll never get over what he did, and—"

"But that's why your friends are trying to be there for you. They wanna help you."

"Bryson, I am in no way deficient, mentally or physically, because of what Willie did. Therefore, I don't want anyone to feel sorry for me, and that includes you and Erica. See, I'm gonna get beyond this, you just wait and see, but I will never forget what happened." Celeste was again on the brink. The loud wailing in her head was getting louder, her headache was making her eyes hurt, and a queasy feeling was creeping up from her stomach to her throat. The rum was tearing up her empty stomach. She began kneading her stomach with her fingers.

"Bryson, be a good brother-in-law. Go home so that I can throw up all by my lonesome."

"It's the rum."

Celeste kneaded her stomach harder.

"I'll get you some bread." Bryson rushed off to the kitchen while Celeste sprinted for the upstairs bathroom to heave up the bile of her stomach and her mind. If she didn't want to end up old and bitter, she was going to have to rid herself of the toxicity with which Willie's betrayal and Katrina's hatred had poisoned her, or she was not going to be any good for Justine or herself.

CHAPTER
8

The short drive home across Atlantic Avenue into Crown Heights—a more upscale enclave of Brooklyn—did absolutely nothing to calm Katrina's anger. Admittedly, she had tried to bite her tongue to stop herself from saying what she really thought about Celeste's nasty attitude, or what she really thought about how Willie had died, but damnit, just being in the same room with Celeste was enough to set her off. If Bryson hadn't been there, she probably would have said a whole lot more, but she didn't want Bryson to think that she was picking on Celeste—which was what Gordon always accused her of. Her own husband never sided with her against Celeste, and that always irritated the hell out of her. Yet, Gordon swore that he didn't have a thing for Celeste, but she didn't believe him. Gordon seemed to always find something to talk to Celeste and Willie about at the few family get-togethers they attended, which she could never understand. What the hell did he have to talk to Celeste about anyway? Celeste was such a boring person. There was nothing remotely interesting about anything she had to say. Why was it that Gordon didn't see that?

Yuk! There was a sour taste in Katrina's mouth. Thinking about Celeste always put a sour taste in her mouth. She really did hate Celeste. There was just no two ways about it. Hearing Celeste's name always set her nerves on edge, but seeing Celeste, hearing

Celeste's whiny voice, talking to Celeste, or even thinking about Celeste just made Katrina's skin crawl. How they could be sisters was beyond her. One or the other of them had to have been switched at birth, and more than likely, it was Celeste.

"Ma!" Lorna screamed.

"What?"

"Look what you did! You cut your finger."

Katrina looked down at her right hand—her finger was bleeding. She had been finely chopping an onion to add to a can of salmon to make salmon patties.

"Damn." Turning on the faucet, Katrina began running cold water over her middle finger, making it sting.

"It's not so bad," Lorna said, watching the water now run clear down the drain. "You didn't even know you were cut, did you?"

Katrina wrapped a clean paper towel tightly around her finger. "Go get me a Band-Aid." While Lorna went off to the bathroom, Katrina pressed her finger to make sure it had stopped bleeding. She was lucky she hadn't cut herself worse; the serrated knife she was using was sharp as hell. "That damn Celeste!"

"What about Aunt Celeste?" Lorna asked, coming back into the kitchen. "What did she do?"

"She pissed me off—as usual." Katrina wrapped the Band-Aid around her finger.

Lorna sighed. "Ma, you get upset every time you deal with Aunt Celeste. So why did you even go to her house?"

"How do you know where I was?"

"Granddad called. He was pretty upset."

"About what?"

"He was upset because you hadn't gotten home yet. He said he wants to talk to you. You better call him."

"What am I, a kid?" Katrina put her hand on her hip. "Am I supposed to feel intimidated because my father called? I don't think so. I'm a grown woman."

"Chill out, Ma. Granddad only wanted to know if you were still at Aunt Celeste's. He said to call him when you got in."

Katrina went back to chopping the remainder of the small

onion. It wasn't difficult to figure out that her father wanted to chide her for staying behind at Celeste's when he'd tried to make her leave with him.

He had taken her aside. "Celeste might not be up to having much company tonight."

"She doesn't seem to mind Bryson's company. I'm sure she won't mind if I hang around."

"Bryson's helping her with his brother's things."

"So. I'll help her, too."

The look her father had given her was cynical. "What're you up to?"

"Just trying to be a sister to my sister, Dad."

"Katrina, you're up to no good. You're leaving with me." He'd taken hold of her arm, but she wasn't going anywhere. She'd quickly pulled away from him.

"See you later, Dad," she'd said aloud and sat down before he could do anything about it without causing a scene.

"Ma, you should call Granddad so he'll know you're home."

Katrina slammed the knife on the counter. "Lorna, I couldn't care less if your grandfather knows I'm home or not. I don't answer to him or anyone else about my comings and goings. And you stop telling me what to do, too."

Lorna sucked her teeth. "Dang! Don't be biting off my head. I didn't do nothing. I was just giving you Granddad's message."

Katrina exhaled loudly. She quickly scooped up the finely chopped onion and tossed it into the bowl of drained salmon. She added an egg. All afternoon she'd had a taste for deep-fried salmon patties—one of her favorite things to eat. She could eat salmon patties with grits, with rice, with macaroni and cheese, or with plain old ruby red catsup. The truth was, there were times when she ate a whole batch of salmon patties with nothing but her fingers and a glass of ginger ale. Good eating! Katrina's stomach growled. She had been hungry while at Celeste's, but she would have to be starving and near death to eat anything out of Celeste's kitchen, although there was the food her mother had prepared, but hell, that was like eating Celeste's food. It was in her house. Celeste probably couldn't cook worth a lick anyway.

Katrina began stirring the onion into the salmon. "Did your father call?"

"No."

"Great." Katrina stirred harder. "This is the second night he hasn't called home. I've been trying to reach him since yesterday."

"Maybe he had to go away, Ma."

"In case you hadn't noticed, Lorna, his ass is already away. He practically lives in Washington. I don't think Gordon even cares about what's going on here."

"What is going on here?"

Katrina cut her eyes at Lorna. "Don't you have something you should or could be doing elsewhere in this big-ass house?"

"Dang, Ma, you don't have to—"

"Hey! Don't use that tone with me. I'm not one of your little girlfriends."

"Man!" Lorna started out of the kitchen. She said under her breath, "I can't wait till I'm eighteen. I'm gettin' the hell outta here."

"What did you say?"

Lorna turned back. "I said, I can't wait till I'm eighteen. I hate being around here when you're all worked up over Aunt Celeste. Every time you get mad at her, you beat down on me, like it's my fault y'all don't get along."

"I do not *beat down* on you when I'm mad at Celeste. You just ask too many questions that don't concern you."

"But I live here, Ma. I'm supposed to be concerned about what goes on here. At least that's what you told me last year, when you wanted me to tell that sanitation inspector that someone put all those bags of plaster and wood in front of our house during the night and that they didn't come out of our house."

Smart-ass! "Yeah, well, I wasn't about to pay a fine when no one told me that we weren't supposed to put that stuff out for the city to pick up. Besides, this is different. How I feel about Celeste is my business."

"But, Ma, you should hear how you sound when you buggin' about Aunt Celeste. You always sound like you wanna kill her, and when it's like that, you always take it out on us. If Daddy was here, you'd be beating down on him, too."

Katrina wanted to defend herself but couldn't. Gordon had said the same thing just before he left for Washington three weeks ago. "Sometimes I hate coming home. If you're not bitching about your job, you're bitching about your sister. Even if you don't see Celeste, Katrina, you're talking about her."

"That's because she gets on my nerves."

"But you're never around her! How can she be getting on your nerves?"

"You just don't understand, Gordon. You and your siblings always got along. Me and Celeste, we were born to be enemies. That's just the way it is."

"No, I understand. You're a miserable person, Katrina. That's all there is to it, and you make life miserable for the rest of us."

It was almost a full week before Gordon called home. He spoke to the kids, but he always hurried off the line if she asked to speak to him. It wasn't that he was so busy in Washington; he was avoiding her.

"Ma," Lorna said, "if you can't stand Aunt Celeste, you shouldn't've gone to her house. I know that's why Granddad called."

Katrina angrily folded her arms and glared at Lorna. "So it's my fault for even going over to her house? If Celeste wasn't such a bitch, there wouldn't have been a problem. She's the one that always starts with me."

"So if it's like that, leave her alone."

"I'm not bothering her! And why do you care? Celeste isn't your problem."

"Dang, Ma! I'm just trying to understand what the deal is between you and Aunt Celeste. The few times I ever get to see her, she never says anything bad about you, and she's always nice to me and Gordy and Patrice, even though you got Patrice hatin' on her like you do."

"Patrice hates Celeste on her own and with good reason. She hates conceited, stuck-up, opinionated, self-righteous people."

"Aunt Celeste is all that, Ma? She don't seem that way to me."

"Are you blind?"

"I guess so, 'cause I like Aunt Celeste."

"How the hell can you like her when I don't?"

"'Cause I'm doing what you told me to do."

"And what the hell is that?"

" 'Do as I say and not as I do.' "

Katrina glared at her stupid child. "Don't be a smart-ass, Lorna. I've told you time and again, Celeste is a bitch. She made my childhood miserable."

"But how, Ma? You never say what she did to you."

"You wanna know what she did to me? Celeste was a snitch, Lorna. Celeste always told on me. She always got my ass in trouble. And on top of that, everything I wanted Celeste had to have, and most times she got it. When I was thirteen, I finally got for Christmas my own television. That same Christmas, Celeste got a television, too. She was ten. What does that tell you?"

"Ah, well, maybe Grandma and Granddad could afford two TVs."

"Lorna, that wasn't it. I'd been begging for a television for two years. My mother told me that kids younger than thirteen shouldn't have televisions in their bedrooms. Celeste was ten. Her spoiled ass got a television when she was younger than me."

"But y'all were kids then, Ma. All that stuff's old. Can't y'all get along now?"

"I don't like Celeste, Lorna. What can't you understand about that? She was spoiled rotten, and I couldn't stand her. I don't see how you can like her when I don't."

"Because you told me to develop my own opinion about people and to not judge them by what others say about them."

Katrina's hand was itching to slap Lorna for throwing her own teaching back in her face. She was a smart-ass just like Celeste, but it was true that she had taught all of her children to be independent thinkers. Yet when it came to Celeste, they were supposed to be on her side.

"You want me to stop liking Aunt Celeste, Ma? Will that make you happy?"

Katrina glared at Lorna. "I tell you what. Since you like Celeste so damn much, despite what I've told you, why don't you go live with her ass!"

"You buggin', Ma."

"Go ahead, get out! Go live with that bitch!"

"Ma, will you chill. That's what I'm talking about. You're losing it."

Maybe she was losing it. She couldn't stand that Lorna liked Celeste; it really annoyed her. At her grandparents' house, Lorna was always the first to find her way into Celeste's arms for a hug. The sight always nauseated Katrina. She didn't want Celeste touching any one of her kids.

"Ma, I'm not taking Aunt Celeste's side against you. I'm just saying she's always nice to me."

"Are you saying I'm not as nice to you as Celeste is?"

"No, Ma!"

"Then what are you saying, Lorna? It sounds to me like you're saying that you like Celeste more than you like me, and I'm your damn mother."

"I didn't say that!"

"Don't you raise your voice at me!"

"Ma, you're not hearing me." Lorna stepped closer to Katrina. "You never hear any of us when you're mad at Aunt Celeste. You get off into this freaky mile-high zone every time you see Aunt Celeste. And if you argued with her, you're even worse. You always say you can't stand her, which is why I don't understand why you went over to her house."

"I went because I felt like it." Katrina went back to stirring her onions and salmon. She added a pinch of salt and three hearty dashes of black pepper.

"But, Ma, that's not fair to us, especially to me right now because I'm here with you by myself. You're in a bad mood, and you're taking it out on me."

Katrina busied herself with pouring oil into the frying pan sitting on the stove. "This discussion is over." She turned a medium fire on under it. "Did you eat?"

Lorna pouted.

"Well, did you?"

"I had a bag of potato chips. I was gonna eat later over at Shannon's house. I'm waiting for her to get home."

"I'm still the mother in this house. Did you ask me if you could go over Shannon's?"

"Ma, why you trippin'? I asked you this morning if I could spend the night over Shannon's, and you said yes!"

"Well, I don't remember." Which she didn't, but she was glad Lorna wasn't going to be around for the weekend. With Gordon, Gordy, and Patrice away, she and Lorna would be bitching at each other nonstop. Lorna was truly nothing like her. Lorna had her father's face, but Celeste's snooty ways. Now that Lorna was fifteen, she had a fresh mouth and a self-righteous attitude about anything Katrina had to say. They never agreed on anything, and their moods were never in sync. It was as if their asses were glued to a lopsided seesaw that never balanced. If Katrina was in a good mood, Lorna wasn't. If Katrina said peas were round, Lorna would argue that the term was spherical just to be contrary.

"Ma?" Lorna looked anxiously at Katrina. "Are you still gonna give me the two hundred dollars you promised? We're going shopping tomorrow, remember?"

"I promised, didn't I?" *Damn!* She didn't remember that either and didn't know if she had two hundred dollars on her. She'd never made it to the bank. She had stopped off at her parents' to drop off Gordy and got caught up in what her parents were saying about how bad Celeste was taking Willie's death.

"Lorna, get that container of rice out of the refrigerator." Katrina took from the cabinet a can of cream-style corn. Again her stomach growled. She had to eat soon. When Lorna handed the container of cold white rice to her, she didn't take it. "Girl, your hands aren't broken. You can help out. Use a small pot with a little water to heat up that rice."

Lorna's tongue was still as she went about spooning cold clumps of rice into the small saucepan. Afterward, both Lorna and Katrina placed their pots on the stove.

"You will eat before you leave," Katrina said. She began placing egg-size spoonfuls of salmon into the hot frying pan. By now everyone in the family knew that Willie had gotten killed in a sleazy motel room. The police weren't getting anywhere because no one knew who the woman was that he was with. Willie was a lowlife. Just the kind of man that Celeste deserved—a lowlife who deserved to die just the way he had—with his head bashed in.

Hot grease popped out of the frying pan, forcing Lorna back. She stretched her neck to peer at the sizzling salmon patties, but quickly drew back to keep from getting tagged by a spot of hot grease.

"Ma, can I ask you a question without you getting upset?"

"No, but ask anyway."

"How come you hate Aunt Celeste so much?"

"Didn't you hear anything I said?"

"I mean for real."

With a spatula, Katrina carefully turned her patties in the bubbly hot grease, while she searched for words that would make Lorna see, once and for all, that Celeste was a bitch and not as sickeningly nice as she pretended to be.

CHAPTER
9

Katrina was annoyed that Lorna insisted on talking about Celeste while she was trying to eat. She hated for anything to spoil the tasty onion flavor of her crunchy salmon patties.

"I told you Celeste was spoiled rotten. My parents gave her everything she wanted, even things that belonged to me."

"How they do something like that? That wasn't right."

"So, finally, you understand."

"So what did Aunt Celeste get that was yours?"

"My dolls. When I was eleven, my mother decided I was too old to be playing with dolls, so she collected all of my dolls and gave them to Celeste."

"Whoa, that was cold. How many dolls did you have?"

"About fifteen." Katrina picked up another salmon patty. She bit off more than half of it, but continued to talk. "I'm still angry with my mother for that. I tried to tell her I wanted to save my dolls for my daughters, but she didn't care. She gave them to Celeste anyway, and every time I saw Celeste playing with my dolls, I wanted to beat her up. Every chance I got, I'd break something off one of the dolls and then point out to my mother that Celeste was destroying *my* dolls."

Lorna didn't know what to make out of that. "Did you break all of them?"

"Every last one of them."

"Wow. I bet Aunt Celeste was mad at you."

"Like I cared." Katrina chewed hungrily on a mouthful of cream corn and rice.

"But, Ma, it really wasn't Aunt Celeste's fault that Grandma gave her your dolls. She didn't ask for them, did she?"

"Are you trying to defend her again?"

"No, Ma—"

"Celeste was a sneaky, manipulative little witch. I wouldn't doubt for a minute that she asked for my dolls behind my back."

"But you don't know that for sure. Grandma coulda—"

"Lorna, it was more than the goddamn dolls! Celeste tried to take my boyfriend from me when we were in high school, but she didn't get him."

Lorna's eyes widened. "For real?"

"Well, she tried anyway."

"How? What did she do?"

"By playing charades," Katrina said. "One afternoon some of my friends were over, and we were playing charades. I was liking this guy, Fred. We weren't *really* going together, *yet*, but he came over to be with me, but Celeste, with her nasty ass, got up on him and started grinding him . . ."

"No."

"I forget what we were supposed to be guessing, but Celeste got Fred all horny and hard, and he couldn't stop looking at her after that. So when my turn came, I got up on him myself and didn't stop until he was ready to . . . you know."

"Oh, man. Ma, you nasty."

"Hey, I used what I had and it worked. I got Fred. Celeste didn't."

"So that's how you started going with him?"

"Damn right. I showed Celeste that day that she couldn't take anything from me that I didn't want her to have."

Lorna was musingly quiet.

"What now?" Katrina asked. "You don't believe me?"

"Well, Ma, you said you weren't even going with that guy before then. So Aunt Celeste couldn't've taken him from you if you weren't going with him."

Katrina sighed heavily. "Look, Lorna. I saw Fred first. I was talking to him first. Celeste tried to put the move on him when he was my date. Therefore, she was trying to take him from me. Do I need to explain it on a second-grade level for you to understand? How would you feel if one of your girlfriends or even your sister went after a boy you liked?"

Lorna sucked her teeth. "I'd have to kick her as . . . behind."

"All right then." Katrina picked at the crunchy edge of a salmon patty. "I've never forgiven Celeste for that, but she's done so many other things to me over the years, even if I had forgotten that incident, there are so many more to choose from. Celeste is low. She's always been a very selfish person. I can't stand her."

Lorna jabbed at her half-eaten salmon patty. She hated crusty, greasy fish patties. "I guess Aunt Celeste got some stuff with her."

"That's what I've been trying to tell you."

"But she seem so nice. She—"

"Fooled you, like I said." Katrina picked up another salmon patty.

The telephone suddenly rang, pulling Katrina's attention away from the patty she was about to eat. She put it back on the plate. "Pass me the phone. It had better be your father."

"It might be for me." Lorna rushed to answer the telephone on the kitchen counter. She caught it on the second ring. "Hello?"

"Mrs. Gordon Dawson, please."

Lorna sucked her teeth and handed the telephone to Katrina. "Who is it?"

"It's not Daddy," Lorna said offhandedly.

Katrina sighed her annoyance that Lorna was still not asking who was calling before handing her the telephone.

Lorna headed straight for the cookie jar filled with chocolate chip cookies.

"Hello?"

"Mrs. Gordon Dawson?" the caller asked.

"Yes. Who's calling?"

"Mrs. Dawson, my name is Albert Waterman. I work with your husband, Gordon, in Washington, D.C."

Although immediately concerned, Katrina was struck by the effeminate tone of the man's voice.

"Why are you calling me, Mr. Waterman. Where's Gordon?"

"Mrs. Dawson, forgive me for calling with such terrible news, but Gordon is in the hospital. He's in a coma. He—"

Katrina stood. "What are you talking about?"

Lorna stopped chewing her favorite cookie. She stared at Katrina.

"Gordon is in a diabetic coma."

"Gordon doesn't have diabetes. Is this some kind of joke?"

Lorna gripped Katrina's arm, shaking her. "Ma, does Daddy have diabetes?"

"Shh!" Katrina swatted Lorna off her arm. That swat didn't deter Lorna; she didn't move away.

"Mrs. Dawson, I spoke with Gordon's doctor at Howard University Hospital. He wasn't joking."

"My God. How long has he been in a coma?"

"Since late yesterday afternoon."

"What!" Katrina shrieked. She began to pace with Lorna on her heels. "Since yesterday and I don't know a damn thing about it?"

"Mrs. Dawson—"

"Why the hell wasn't I called?"

"Mrs. Dawson, I just found out today myself. I'm calling just minutes after visiting Gordon at the hospital. What I can tell you is that Gordon blacked out—"

"This makes no damn sense." Katrina turned and bumped into Lorna. She pushed Lorna out of her way. "I'm Gordon's wife. My name is in Gordon's wallet."

"U'm . . . well, ah, Mrs. Dawson, I—"

"What hospital is my husband in?"

"Howard University Hospital."

"Well, Howard University Hospital will hear from me," Katrina threatened. "Gordon has been in a coma since yesterday and not one administrator saw fit to call me, his wife, to tell me what the hell was going on? I'm the first person they should have called."

"This is why I took it upon myself to call you personally. Part of the problem is that Gordon was out jogging. He didn't have his wallet on him."

"So how did you find him?"

"Ah . . . Gordon, Gordon was with a . . . an associate."

"This just doesn't make sense," Katrina said. "You said Gordon was out jogging?"

"Ah . . . yes."

"Gordon doesn't jog! He barely walks. He drives everywhere except to the damn toilet. And he'd drive there if the damn car would fit into the bathroom. Something's not right."

"Ma, you're stroking," Lorna said. "Chill."

Katrina had to sit down. She was having a hard time digesting what she was hearing.

"I can tell you first hand, Mrs. Dawson," Albert Waterman said, "Gordon does jog. I've gone jogging with him myself. So it was no surprise to me that he was out jogging, but it's been very hot here. In fact, it is because Gordon was out jogging in the hot sun that it was first believed that he had had a heat stroke or perhaps heat exhaustion. When Gordon was first brought into the hospital, he was given a saline solution to rehydrate him, but when that didn't work and he didn't respond, further tests were given, and that's when it was discovered that his blood sugar was dangerously elevated. Hence the diabetes diagnosis."

"I just don't believe that." Katrina shook her head. "The doctors are wrong."

"Mrs. Dawson, Gordon's situation is dire. I suggest you come to Washington as soon as possible."

"Oh, God." Katrina covered her mouth. Her eyes filled with tears just as Lorna squatted in front of her.

"Is Daddy all right?"

Katrina could hear the man telling her he would meet her at DCA, just let him know the flight. He was also giving her his telephone number, but the number wasn't sticking in her head. She didn't write anything down because she couldn't move.

"What's your name again?" she asked.

"Albert. Albert Waterman, but please, call me Albert."

"Well, Albert, would you do me a favor?"

"Sure."

"Would you call me again in an hour? I didn't get your number. I need to—"

"I understand. I'll call back in one hour."

"Thank you." Katrina was pulling the telephone from her ear when she heard her name being called. "Yes?"

"Mrs. Dawson, I'm really sorry."

Even while her tears were falling, while she was hanging up the telephone, Katrina was thinking about all she had to do. She sent Lorna, crying, off to pack a bag for herself—she was taking her with her. Albert had said Gordon could die. God, she wasn't ready for Gordon to die. There was still so much yet to be said between them. After twenty years, she and Gordon no longer had the best of marriages, but they had weathered storms that would have destroyed a lot of people. In the last year, there was a bit more strain in their marriage, but being apart was partly to blame for that. Gordon's job as chief engineer with the Department of Environmental Protection kept him in the Washington office more than it did in the New York office. He'd had a one-bedroom apartment in Silver Springs for the past three years, and although when he first took the job he had asked her to relocate the family, she had refused. She didn't want to leave New York City. She was a New Yorker born and raised and had no desire to live anywhere else. There wasn't a thing in the world she wanted to do or see that she couldn't do or see right here in New York. When Gordon had asked her to relocate, she'd told him, "I didn't lose a damn thing beyond the span of the Verrazano Bridge." Besides, heading south of New Jersey always reminded Katrina of the awful summers she and Celeste had spent with their grandparents in Charleston.

Grandma Mildred thought Katrina had a fresh mouth and wasted no time pulling a limb off that ugly, bent-over old tree in her backyard and whipping her skinny little legs till painful red blisters and welts covered them. The worst beating she got was when she convinced Celeste to let her cut her hair with a pair of rusty garden shears. Her legs were raw and blistered for a week.

She hated Grandma Mildred after that. As soon as she was old enough, twelve, she refused to go south for the summer again.

Shaking her head to erase the memory of that god-awful beating, Katrina thought it weird that she should be remembering cutting off Celeste's hair and getting beat for it. Well, perhaps it was apropos—the evening had started out on a sour note because of Celeste, and it was ending on an even worse note perhaps because Celeste had jinxed her. If Gordon died, Celeste would have caused it. The bitch.

CHAPTER
10

Celeste felt like a third wheel. Until Bryson and Erica's ten-year-old twins, Kevin and Kevon, went off to bed, Celeste had been feeling like a fifth wheel. She could kick herself for letting Bryson talk her into going home with him for dinner all the way out in Bayside, Queens, especially when she ate very little of Erica's vinegary three-bean salad and dry, stringy ham. The macaroni salad Celeste didn't bother to try—it was darn near swimming in mayonnaise that looked regurgitated. None of which surprised Celeste—everyone in the family knew that Erica couldn't cook her way out of a house made of rice paper.

Erica was as nice a person as anyone could ever meet, but damn, she could spoil the appetite of a starving man, and no one had ever gotten up the nerve to tell her that she was possibly committing a felony every time she served people her cooking. Celeste could never understand for the life of her how Bryson could eat Erica's cooking. Maybe for Bryson it was love, maybe even dead tastebuds, but either way, Celeste got out of eating by saying she'd had no appetite since Willie died, and that was no lie. Erica and Bryson both understood and left her alone, but then they begged her to stay and watch a movie Bryson had rented. Another mistake. Celeste couldn't concentrate on the movie of dazzling special effects for feeling like that third wheel.

Bryson had his arm around Erica, which was as it should be, but seeing them all cozy like that only reminded her that Willie's arms would never again be around her, nor would he ever be pressed up against her side, his nose in her hair, his lips on her ear. No matter how Willie had died, this would have been true, but it was Willie dying in the arms of another woman that made his thievery of the promise of his love in her old age so painful, so unforgivable. She and Willie were supposed to grow old and wrinkled together, so they could draw on the memories of their early years when she was gorgeous and sexy, and he, fine and virile.

It was thoughts of what Willie stole from her that made Celeste want to cry. "It's late. I'm going home."

"I thought you were spending the night," Erica said.

"Nope. I'm going home."

Bryson stopped the movie. "No wonder you insisted on driving your own car."

"Because I didn't want you to have to drive me back to Brooklyn. Besides, I'd probably never sleep a wink out here—Bayside is too darn quiet."

"Yeah, it's nothing like noisy-ass Bed-Stuy," Bryson said, "but, Celeste, I was supposed to help you sort through Willie's things in the morning."

"I know, but I think I might get started tonight—especially if I can't sleep."

Bryson and Erica exchanged worrisome glances as they followed Celeste to the door. "But I said I'd help you," Bryson persisted.

"I know, but I need to do this myself. I've been procrastinating." Celeste opened the door herself. "Besides, if I can touch Willie's things without anger, maybe I'll start to feel better. Maybe. I don't know, but I need to find out. I'll call you if I can't go it alone."

Unseen by Celeste, Erica tapped Bryson on the leg—prompting him. "Okay, but if you find a box, a gray strongbox, it's mine. I asked Willie to hold it for me."

"Why? What's in it?"

"Receipts for my business."

Suspicious, Celeste arched her brow. "Bryson, you own a computer service and repair shop. Are you saying you're doing something illegal in that shop?"

"He better not be," Erica said, playfully tagging Bryson on the upper arm. "But seriously, Celeste, it's nothing illegal."

"Well, if it's all good, then why did Willie have to hold the box in our house? You don't have enough storage space in this nine-room house to keep it here?"

"Come on, Celeste," Bryson said. "You're making it more than it was. It was no big deal. It was just something I wanted Willie to hold for me."

"Then how is it that I don't know about this box in my house?"

"Because it's nothing. Willie probably forgot to tell you about it. Anyway, it's probably locked, so don't go getting nosey."

"What's in it? Illegal receipts?"

"Now you got her curious," Erica said.

"I sure am. Where did Willie hide it?"

Erica and Bryson looked uneasily at each other.

"You don't know where the box is, do you?"

"I just don't remember where Willie said he put it."

Celeste couldn't put her finger on it, but something wasn't right. The fact that Bryson and Erica both were looking at her like two children waiting to see if their mother would believe their lie confirmed that there was something about that box that was unsaid.

"That's your story. I'm going home."

"Celeste—"

"Good night, Bryson." She shot Bryson a reproachful glare but hugged Erica before heading out into the quiet, sultry night.

"No hug for me, huh, Celeste?"

Celeste back flipped her hand at Bryson and got into her car.

"Cold, Celeste. You're cold."

Like guardians, Bryson and Erica stood at their open door watching over Celeste until she drove off.

"Babe, if she goes through Willie's things alone and finds those pictures, it'll kill her."

Bryson's eyes were locked on Celeste's rear lights off in the distance. "It's gonna kill her anyway."

"Then shouldn't we tell her?"

Bryson neither agreed nor disagreed. He just hated that Willie had left him to deal with the fallout of his affair.

Minutes after exiting the Belt Parkway back into Brooklyn, Celeste took her time driving along Atlantic Avenue past dark shuttered storefronts and brightly lit fast food restaurants and gas stations. Brilliant reds, ambers, and greens of the changing traffic lights transfixed her at times, prompting the occasional motorist to honk his horn to move her along. The only time she sped up was when she saw that she was coming up on the motel where Willie died. She never saw it as she passed, and once she passed it, she slowed down again. After all, she wasn't in a hurry to go home to an empty house. She'd only been in a hurry to get away from Bryson and Erica—they reminded her of what she no longer had. While thoughts of Willie stayed with her the rest of the way home, she didn't let how he'd died take hold. She was tired of being bitter. It was the fun Willie, the playful Willie, she wanted to think about. And although she smiled at the memory of him sneaking up behind her and tickling her, she also teared. Those times were gone forever, and it saddened her as well as scared her.

By the time she pulled in front of her brownstone, it was two-fifteen in the morning. She dried her eyes and told herself she was done crying. She had work to do, and tears were time consuming.

At her front door, Celeste froze. She'd inserted her key in the keyhole, but the door was already unlocked. Her heart pulsed. Her first instinct was to run next door, but she had to know if in fact someone had been inside her house. She slowly pushed the first door open. Even in the faint light from the street lamp, she could see that the inside second door was swung wide. The hairs stood on her arms. *Oh, God.* Someone had been in her house. Celeste held her breath as she tiptoed, wide-eyed in the darkness, to the light switch on the wall on the other side of the second door. The sudden brightness confirmed her worst fears—she had been burglarized. Her living room was ransacked.

"What the—" Who would do such an awful thing to her?

CHAPTER
11

Bryson and Richard Reese both made it into Brooklyn just minutes apart. Celeste had called 911 immediately, but Bryson reminded her to call Detective Vaughan and Detective Wilder, the lead detectives on Willie's murder case.

"Mrs. Alexander, you're the only one who can tell if anything's missing," Detective Wilder said, coming back into the living room.

"Everything is a mess," Richard said. "Celeste might not be able to tell right away."

Celeste agreed with just a look at her father. She had gone through the house with him and Bryson, and from what she could see, everything was there; but something had to be missing or else why would someone break into the house?

"The intruder came in through the front door, but the door wasn't forced. Mrs. Alexander, does anyone else have a key to your house, besides you?"

Celeste started to say, "my husband," but caught herself. Willie's keys she had given to her parents to hold in case she was ever locked out.

"I have a set back at the house," Richard volunteered.

"Oh," Celeste said, "and there's the extra set that Willie used to keep at his job in case he ever lost his first set."

"Where is that set now?" Detective Wilder asked.

"Back in the kitchen in the drawer where I keep extra keys," Celeste said. "I got them when Bryson and I collected Willie's things from his office a week ago."

Detective Wilder jotted a note to himself. "So for two weeks those keys were still in your husband's office?"

"Yes."

"Are you sure the keys are back in the kitchen?" Detective Vaughan asked from the doorway.

"Yes. I checked before you got here."

"That's interesting, since the burglar got in with a key," Detective Vaughan said. "We'll get the crime scene unit in here to dust for prints."

"You know what's strange?" Bryson asked, looking around the living room.

"Everything," Celeste replied. "We've been in this house almost ten years, and never once have we been burglarized. Why now?"

Detective Vaughan unbuttoned his snug-fitting jacket. "Until recently, Mrs. Alexander, your husband has been here. You're alone now. Perhaps someone in the neighborhood is looking to take advantage of that."

"Could be," Bryson said, "but, Celeste, you and Willie have come and gone from here for years. You both worked. Most days the house was empty for at least ten hours, and you've never been burglarized, right?"

"Never," Celeste confirmed. "Look, Detective. I have really good neighbors. Mrs. Price, next door, always watches out whether I'm home or not, and before Willie died, we were preparing to go away on vacation. We weren't worried about being burgled."

"Then is it possible that this break-in has something to do with your husband's murder?" Detective Vaughan held Celeste's fearful gaze. "Mrs. Alexander, we've checked every possible lead surrounding the murder of your husband at the motel, and we've come up empty. The longer we go without witnesses, without clues, without motive, the longer it'll take to solve this case. We have DNA, but we have no body to attach it to. This is the time to try and recall any and everything about your husband, including whether he had any illegal dealings."

Celeste almost laughed out loud. "There was a time when I would have said definitely not, but considering how and where Willie died, I can't say anything for sure."

"I can," Bryson said. "My brother never did anything illegal in his life."

"Just that affair," Celeste said.

"Okay," Detective Vaughan said. "Mrs. Alexander, I told you before that we'd investigate your husband's murder to the best of our ability. We'll continue to do so. Now, regarding this burglary, your brother-in-law said it's strange? Talk to me about it."

"Well, it's just that we had iron gates put on all the windows on the two lower floors, front and back, and all door locks were double bolted. All of that, along with the eyes and ears of my neighbors, especially Gertrude next door, it is strange. However, I don't feel it's anyone from the block."

Detective Vaughan flipped his small notepad closed. "Okay. Then the question is, where did the intruder's key come from? Could that key be a duplicate of the key left unattended in your husband's office for two weeks?"

"Also," Detective Wilder began, "there was a set of house keys and a set of car keys found with the victim at the motel. You had a break-in, Mrs. Alexander, but there are four color televisions, four DVD/VCRs, numerous other valuables, including jewelry out on the dresser in the front bedroom, yet none of those things were taken. Whoever broke in was looking for something very specific. The question is what?"

The same feeling of molestation that she'd felt when she first walked through her house knowing that someone had touched her personal possessions without her being there went through Celeste now. For an overly long, awkward moment, Celeste, Bryson, Richard, and the detectives all exchanged questioning glances.

"Well, I've noticed something," Bryson said to Detective Wilder.

"What?" Celeste asked, looking around.

Bryson turned back to the television. "Look at the cabinet where the video tapes are kept."

Every videotape had been pulled from the shelves, removed from its jacket and strewn all over the room—obviously flung. Celeste hadn't noticed until now. She stared at the valuable movie collection that she and Willie had started purchasing once the bulk of their money was no longer going into renovating the house. So far, they had about two hundred and fifty movies. Willie had switched over to DVDs only a few months ago. He said they took up less space. Also in their collection were home movies of any occasion they celebrated, as well as plenty of fun tapes capturing Justine and Willie horseplaying around the house. There were very few tapes that captured Celeste because she was the one always behind the camcorder.

"I took note of that," Detective Vaughan said.

"What were they looking for?" Richard asked. "A movie to watch?"

"It's the same thing upstairs in Celeste's bedroom," Bryson said. "And if you think about it, nothing else is as messed up as the areas around the tapes. The drawers were all pulled out, but again, what were they looking for when there was jewelry right on top of the dresser?"

Celeste started over to the cabinet.

"Don't touch anything," Detective Vaughan said. "Not until the crime scene unit has gone over everything."

"And when will that be?" Celeste asked.

"In a few hours. We'll get someone over here."

"I hope so." Looking from one tape to the next, Celeste suddenly remembered something. "Wait a minute. The night before Willie died, he brought a tape home."

"A tape of what?" Detective Wilder asked.

Celeste couldn't remember. "That, I'm not sure."

"Did your husband say anything about the tape?" Detective Vaughan asked.

Again Celeste shook her head. "I don't remember."

"Do you know if the tape was a rental or—"

"I don't remember." She raised her hand to her forehead. "I think . . . no, I just don't remember."

"If a tape is what they were looking for," Richard said, "could what was on that tape be the reason Willie was killed?"

Celeste sat. "Dad, you're scaring me."

"Well, you oughta be scared. It seems to me someone broke in here, possibly looking for a tape you don't know anything about. If they got it, fine, but if they didn't—"

"Hold up," Bryson said. "We can't assume Willie's death and this break-in have anything to do with each other."

"This is correct," Detective Vaughan said. "We also can't assume the intruder did or didn't get what he came for. The question is, will he come back?"

"Look," Celeste said, "you people are really scaring me."

"Then you need to think hard, Celeste," Bryson said. "What was there about the tape Willie had?"

Celeste closed her eyes. She was thinking as hard as she could, trying to remember what Willie had said, if he'd said anything, about the tape he'd brought home. "I know that Willie was watching the tape down here in the living room. It was late. I was upstairs in the bedroom. He came upstairs after eleven, and he said . . . ah." Celeste opened her eyes. "Willie said he had the proof."

"Proof of what?" Detective Vaughan asked.

Again Celeste tried to pull on the memory of that last night with Willie. Again she shook her head. "I don't remember. I don't think we talked about it. I was running all over the place doing last-minute packing for a trip I ended up not taking."

Bryson quietly looked away.

"Mrs. Alexander, do you think what your husband was referring to had anything to do with his job?" Detective Wilder asked.

"I don't know."

"What kind of work did your husband do again?"

"He was a communications specialist with Dialacom in Manhattan."

"The cell phone company?" Detective Vaughan asked.

She nodded.

"Was he having problems with anyone on his job that you know of?"

"Willie was a people person," Bryson said. "He got along with everyone."

"Job relationships are different, sir. We'll check it out, although we did do a cursory investigation of his workplace, but because of the nature and location of the crime scene, there wasn't much gathered there."

That feeling of shame that had shrouded Celeste like a black veil since she was told where Willie was found smothered her now. She lowered her eyes.

"Mrs. Alexander," Detective Wilder said, "it would be a good idea if you could stay somewhere else tonight."

"Is there going to be a policeman on duty here, all night?"

"I'm sorry, but not likely. This isn't really a crime scene."

"I'm staying right here."

Detective Wilder persisted. "Just to be safe, you—"

"I wish that bastard would come back here."

"Celeste, I know how you feel," Richard said, "but maybe you should think about staying with me and your mother for a few days."

Celeste stood. "And leave my house unguarded? I don't think so."

"But, Celeste," Bryson said, "you just said Gertrude, next door, watches the house when you're not here."

"Little good that did this time, but then Gert was probably trying to keep her eyes on her fresh-behind daughter. Whoever got in here didn't break any glass—he used a key. I'm staying. I'm calling one of those all-night locksmiths to get over here and change the locks. Then I'm gonna get Willie's old baseball bat from down in the basement. I will bust the hell out of somebody's skull if they dare step foot in here again."

"Celeste, you're coming home with me," Richard said, "before you get yourself killed."

"Dad, I'm staying in my house."

"This is no time to be as stubborn as your mother. You're—"

"Mr. Reese," Bryson said, "I'll stay with Celeste until morning. I'll—"

"No, Bryson," Celeste said, "you *will not* be staying with me."

"Celeste—"

"Bryson, you have a family that you need to get home to. I'm staying in my house, by myself, where I belong. Thank you all very much."

Both Richard and Bryson said, "Celeste!"

"Okay!" Detective Vaughan shouted to get everyone's attention. "I have a solution. I'm off duty in an hour. I'll stay here with Mrs. Alexander until the locksmith changes the locks."

All eyes were on Detective Vaughan. His partner, Detective Wilder, scratched his nose. Celeste was intrigued. Detective Vaughan was a tall, muscular, nubby-dreadlock-wearing, chestnut-complexioned, good-looking man who reminded Celeste of Denzel Washington, without the bowlegs. Perhaps if she had not been so upset the day he came to tell her about Willie, she might have appreciated his good looks back then, although it was a bit disconcerting that she was noticing Detective Vaughan and his bulging biceps at all.

"Would that be okay with you?" Detective Vaughan asked, looking at Celeste.

Richard answered, "If you could do that, Detective, I'd appreciate it."

Celeste planted her hands firmly on her hips. "What do you people think, that I can't take care of myself?"

"What we think, Celeste," Bryson said, "is that you don't realize the danger you're possibly in."

"I know that someone out there has the key to my house, which is why it's imperative that I get the locks changed, and I can not do that if I'm not here. Therefore, I will be staying in *my* house, and I have *no* intention of disrupting the life of anyone else. Now, if Detective Vaughan doesn't have a family"—Celeste gave Detective Vaughan a questioning look to which he shook his head—"and he wants to baby-sit me, then it's on him."

"Then we're set," Detective Vaughan said.

"Do you play spades?" Celeste asked.

"I prefer poker."

"How about five-card stud, deuces wild? A dollar a hand."

"No problem," Detective Vaughan said.

Detective Wilder cleared his throat and beckoned with a slight

sideways nod of his head for Detective Vaughan to join him. They
went off into the outer hallway. On her way to find her telephone
directory, Celeste pretended not to overhear Detective Wilder
say, "You can't stay here. We're already out of our jurisdiction on
this burglary," and Detective Vaughan reply, "I'll be on my own
time. And, we're here because we're on the murder case," as she
passed them. Whether Detective Vaughan stayed or not, Celeste
was going to stay in her house, scared or not. Of course, she'd
feel a whole lot better if Detective Vaughan could stay—with his
gun in hand to scare the hell out of whoever broke into her
house.

"This is some night," Richard said, coming up behind Celeste
in Willie's den where she flipped through the yellow pages. "If
you're okay, I'm gonna head on over to Katrina's."

Celeste looked up from the telephone directory. "Daddy, you
can stay the rest of the night here if you don't feel like driving
back to Queens."

"I'm tired, but I'm going over to Katrina's because I'm taking
her and Lorna out to LaGuardia in a few hours. They're flying
out first thing in the morning for Washington. Gordon's in the
hospital."

"Oh, how bad off is he?"

"He's in a coma."

"My God. What happened?"

"From what your mother and I could get from Katrina, it seems
Gordon's got diabetes and didn't know it. He's in some sort of
coma."

"God. Katrina must be really upset."

"She's pretty tore up."

"I bet. Is there anything I can do?" Celeste asked, although she
was keenly aware that Katrina wouldn't want a thing from her.

"Not that I know of. Me and your mother are gonna take care
of Gordy and—"

"Maybe I should bring Justine home. After a few days, the two
kids together might be too much for you and Mother."

"The kids were going to be with us whether Katrina was home
or not. We'll just keep Gordy longer than we planned."

"But, Dad, I don't want you and Mother to—"

"Don't you worry about me and your mother. We can handle two kids. We survived you and Katrina, didn't we?"

Celeste chuckled wearily. "I guess you did."

"However, this time around, Gordy and Justine like each other. They get along just fine."

"Thank God for that." Celeste hugged her father. "Dad, thank you for being so good to me." And he really had been. Her father was probably the only one who would let her damn Willie's soul to hell for betraying her, yet listen to her say, "I miss him," without condemnation. It was too bad Willie hadn't lived to become a wise old man, but hell, he hadn't been a wise young man, had he?

CHAPTER
12

True to his word, Albert Waterman was waiting at the airport when Katrina and Lorna's plane landed. The minute Albert said, "I'm Albert," and daintily extended his hand for a handshake, Katrina knew that what she'd heard in his voice over the telephone was correct—Albert, as handsome as he was, was quite prim, quite proper, and quite gay. He wasn't flaming, but there was definitely a certain sweetness in his manner and in the casual chicness of his powder blue open-banded collar and neatly tucked shirttail. The very comfortable and very shiny blood red Toyota Avalon suited him perfectly, but Katrina wondered how good a friend could Albert be? Gordon had never mentioned Albert's name to her.

"Gordon's condition has worsened," Albert said. "The doctor says his body is shutting down."

In the backseat, Lorna gasped.

Katrina quietly touched Albert on the arm, hinting that he should watch what he was saying in front of Lorna. Albert understood and drove on in silence.

Entering Howard University Hospital, there wasn't a falter in Katrina's stride, but there was a skip in her heartbeat. She was scared. She was scared of seeing her husband, the man she'd danced the electric slide with more than twenty years ago, hooked up to life-support machines that were failing to restore his life's breath.

At the ICU nurse's station, Katrina declared, "I'm Mrs. Gordon Dawson. I'd like to see my husband."

The buxom nurse's cheeks drained of their pink rosy blush. "His wife?"

"Yes," Albert said, "this *is* his wife."

The startled way the nurse was looking at her renewed Katrina's fear. They had gotten there too late. She didn't get a chance to say good-bye.

"But, the patient has—"

Lorna clutched Katrina's arm.

Tears sprang to Katrina's eyes.

"Daddy's dead?" Lorna asked, herself tearing. "Ma—"

"No! No!" the nurse said, suddenly standing. "Mr. Dawson is not dead. I'm sorry if . . . if I . . . I—"

"I what?" Katrina asked angrily. "Why the hell did you look at me like that? You scared me and my daughter to death. Is my husband alive or not?"

"Mrs. Dawson, I'm sorry if I gave you the wrong impression. Mr. Dawson is alive, but he is in very critical condition. He—"

"That's foul." Lorna wiped her eyes. "You scared us!"

"You certainly did give us the wrong impression," Katrina said, relieved. "Where is my husband? I'd like to see him."

The nurse started to point in the direction of the many beds farther into the room, but changed her mind. "I'll take you to him, but I need to see a piece of ID."

This woman was working Katrina's last nerve. "What for?"

"This is ICU, Mrs. Dawson. Only family members or close associates are allowed in. We're required to ask for identification."

"It's routine," Albert said. "I had to show mine."

"Fine!" Katrina said, annoyed.

"I don't have any identification with me," Lorna said.

"She's his daughter," Katrina said. "Do you need me to vouch for that?"

"That won't be necessary." The nurse looked hard at the New

York State driver's license Katrina was showing her. "You *are* his wife."

"And I have been for twenty years. Do I need to produce my marriage license to prove it? I don't usually walk around with it in my pocketbook."

"Maybe you should," the nurse mumbled.

"Excuse me? What did you say?"

Lorna had heard the nurse clearly. "She said—"

"Mrs. Dawson," Albert said, "you should go right away to see Gordon."

The nurse walked off.

"I'll wait here," Albert said.

With her arm through Katrina's, Lorna followed the broad-bottomed nurse into the morbidly quiet ICU ward past sleeping, heavily medicated patients, all hooked up to one type of machine or other maintaining their fragile hold on life. Lorna held her hand to her nose, trying to keep out the nauseating stench of medication and sickness that permeated the air. In the far corner of the room, the nurse stopped at the foot of Gordon's bed.

Katrina and Lorna both gasped. Gordon's mouth was taped shut to hold a clear tube that snaked from between his lips to a machine at the side of his bed. Another tube was pushed up into Gordon's nose and was likewise taped. Even with the tape and the tubes, Katrina could see that Gordon's face was contorted. His head was propped back at an odd angle high atop two pillows that made him look awkward and uncomfortable.

"My husband hates sleeping on his back, and he never uses a pillow."

"Why does he look like that?" Lorna asked. The stuffy, stale smell of sickness was no longer bothering her as much as seeing her father look so old and helpless. Lorna dissolved into sobs against Katrina's shoulder as Katrina stared in disbelief at Gordon.

The nurse slipped away, leaving Katrina and Lorna alone.

While Katrina stared at Gordon through her own tears, she did nothing to console Lorna. She let Lorna cry on her shoulder and cling to her merely to have Lorna to lean back on to keep her own weak knees from giving way under her. When she'd seen Gordon three weeks ago, he was virile and strong with no hint of diabetes undermining his vitality. In retrospect, he had complained of urinating a lot, but he'd thought it was because it was a hot summer and he'd been drinking a lot of water. If Gordon had suffered any other symptoms, he never said.

"Good morning." A second nurse, a petite black woman, bustled up alongside Gordon's bed and expertly checked his monitors and IV drip.

Katrina responded softly, "Good morning."

"Are you family?" the nurse asked.

"I'm his wife." Katrina couldn't take her eyes off of Gordon. "And this is his daughter." Katrina didn't see the nurse arch her brow and stretch her eyes.

"He's not gonna die, is he?" Lorna asked.

The nurse adjusted the sheet on the bed. "Mrs. Dawson, have you spoken to your husband's doctor?"

"We just got in from New York a little while ago. Who is his doctor?"

"Dr. Pennington. He should be here any minute. I'll tell him you want to see him."

"Please do, because this doesn't make sense. I know Gordon has high blood pressure, but he's never had any history of diabetes, and certainly if it was just discovered, why is he in a coma?"

"Dr. Pennington will be able to answer your questions as soon as he gets here," the nurse said, hurrying away.

Katrina eased Lorna, still crying, over to a chair at the far side of Gordon's bed. "Get yourself together, Lorna. Crying isn't helping your father. We need to talk to that doctor."

Lorna sniffled, but she didn't stop crying.

Standing at Gordon's side, Katrina lay her hand on his chest as she had done so many times throughout their years together. There was no warmth there. The machine that was breathing for Gordon was pushing his chest up and down, but it wasn't warming his body. Gordon felt cold. Tears slipped down Katrina's cheeks.

At the nurse's station, Albert and the two nurses were in

hushed discussion when a young Trapper John-looking doctor joined them. After a minute, the doctor detached himself from the intimate circle and headed for Gordon's bed.

"Mrs. Dawson, I'm Dr. Pennington, your husband's doctor."

"Why is my husband in a coma?"

"Mrs. Dawson, your husband is an untreated diabetic. He's been a walking time bomb."

"Wait a minute. Gordon has no history of diabetes. I spoke to him just days ago, and he was perfectly healthy. How in the world can he suddenly be in a diabetic coma?"

Lorna stopped crying and waited to hear the doctor's answer.

Dr. Pennington lifted Gordon's chart off the foot of the bed frame. "Diabetes is a strange disease. Unless routine blood work is done or one is aware of the symptoms of the illness, diabetes lurks in the shadows, hiding in unsuspecting bodies, waiting to show its fangs. Your husband has adult onset diabetes mellitus. In laymen's terms, Mrs. Dawson, your husband's pancreas has stopped producing the protein necessary to regulate his glucose levels, which has affected his kidneys."

"I don't believe this. Gordon—"

"Mrs. Dawson, when your husband was brought into the ER, his glucose level was already dangerously high, along with his blood pressure, which is what brought on the stroke he suffered."

"No one told me he had a stroke!"

"I'm sorry, I thought you knew."

"Doctor, Gordon is only forty years old. You're talking about him like he's an old man. His condition is going from bad to worse."

"Mrs. Dawson, if your husband had been receiving treatment for his high blood pressure and the diabetes, he might not have suffered the stroke. Unless he had regular checkups—"

"Gordon hated going to the doctor, and yes, he knew about the high blood pressure, but he only took his pressure pills if he had a headache."

"Well, that's not how the medication is to be administered. Whether your husband felt well or not, Mrs. Dawson, he should have, daily, taken the dosage his doctor suggested. And if your husband had had regular physicals where his blood was tested for glucose levels, he would have known that he had diabetes," Dr. Pennington said. "The problem now is that your husband is non-responsive. The paramedics at the scene treated Mr. Dawson for heat exhaustion. He was given a saline solution to rehydrate him which complicated the diabetes."

"How could they *assume* that he had heat exhaustion and—"

"Mrs. Dawson, this area has been in the middle of a heat wave. Your husband had all the symptoms of heat exhaustion, and he was, in fact, overheated. Unfortunately, the underlying symptoms of diabetes manifested themselves at the same time. I'm sorry, but we've done everything we can—"

"But that's not enough. Isn't there anything else you can do to help him?"

Lorna pleaded, "Doctor, you got to wake my father up!"

Dr. Pennington rubbed his neck. He wouldn't look at Lorna. "Mrs. Dawson, your husband is not responding to the insulin treatments we've given him. His pancreas has completely shut down, his heart is weak from years of high blood pressure, and his kidneys have shut down." Skirting Katrina, Dr. Pennington went to Gordon's bedside. He glanced at the chart before checking Gordon's vitals. He jotted on the chart. "I wish I could give you better news. The best we can do right now is see that Mr. Dawson is comfortable."

Lorna went back to weeping.

"This isn't real." Katrina couldn't believe what the doctor was telling her. "Doctor, diabetes is a common disease. It's a manageable disease. My husband—"

"Normally, Mrs. Dawson, this is true. But that's only if the disease is treated timely and regularly," Dr. Pennington said. "Mrs. Dawson, your husband ignored the symptoms of diabetes that he had to have been experiencing. You said yourself he didn't take his blood pressure medicine correctly. And to be frank, Mrs. Dawson, your husband's diseases and his own negligence put him in this bed. At this point, we're doing our best to—"

"I know," Katrina said, "to make him comfortable."

Dr. Pennington replaced the chart. "I'm sorry, but I have other patients to see. If you need to see me later, I'll be back here around one this afternoon."

Katrina couldn't look at the doctor walk away. While her own tears fell, this time she did go to Lorna to hold her and comfort her.

"Excuse me, Mrs. Dawson," Albert said. "I have to speak to you. It's really important."

"I don't understand any of this. Diabetes? Gordon has always been a healthy man. I see him lying here near death, but I can't accept that it's really him. I know that sounds strange, but—"

"Not really. I've known Gordon for three years, and to see him like this is difficult."

"Yes, he—"

"What are you talking about!" a woman's loud voice asked, making Katrina look back toward the nurse's station. "What do you mean, his *other* wife is already here?"

It took only a second's glance for Katrina to see that no other visitors were in the ICU at that minute. Perplexed, Katrina looked back at the young, shapely blonde looking dead at her from what felt like a foot away.

"I'm Mrs. Gordon Dawson," the blonde said, "the *only* Mrs. Gordon Dawson."

Lorna's jaw dropped.

Katrina looked at Gordon. She looked at the blonde who was staring at her. She looked again at Gordon, but when she couldn't stand the sight of him looking old and sick a second longer, she closed her eyes and told herself that what she was thinking couldn't be true. That woman had to be talking about someone else.

"Mrs. Dawson, that's what I needed to speak to you about," Albert said. "Gordon's been married to Joan for a little over a year. He—"

Lorna quickly stood. "Oh, shit!"

Still with her eyes closed, Katrina began to slowly shake her head.

"Ma, did you hear what he said?" Lorna asked, shaking Katrina, forcing her to open her eyes to again look at Gordon.

"You bastard. I hope you die."

CHAPTER
13

If the heat from the late morning sun was any indication of the sultry day ahead, then Katrina had no doubt that she'd stroke out and end up in the bed next to Gordon—the lowlife. The sweat pouring from her face, however, wasn't solely due to the heat—she was smothering like a hot barbeque charcoal. The embarrassment of being hauled out of the ICU by hospital security and escorted out onto the sidewalk was nothing compared to the humiliation she'd felt when she was stared at by the nurses who'd known all along that there was another woman, a white woman, who was calling herself Mrs. Gordon Dawson. Now she understood the questions, the looks. That bastard!

"Did you see how they sided with that bitch?" Katrina shook in her rage that the nurses had protected that woman, Joan, from her by hustling Joan off to a room down the hall and slamming the door in Katrina's face. "Who's the wronged one here, me or Gordon's whore?"

"Ma, what're we gonna do?" Lorna matched Katrina's frantic pace, staying at her side. "That woman says she's Daddy's wife. Did he divorce you, Ma? Can he do that? Can he do that without you knowin' it?"

Katrina swallowed hard to keep her heart from squeezing all the way up into her throat. "I can't believe this shit!"

"Me neither."

"It's insane." Katrina turned first one way then the other, and not knowing which way to go, she stayed in front of the hospital. "I am going to kill Gordon! What the fuck did he think he was doing? Didn't he think I'd ever find out?"

"Ma, there's Albert."

Katrina rushed at Albert exiting the hospital. "You're the one who called me and told me to come here! You should've told me what was going on. Why didn't you tell me about that woman?"

Standing ramrod straight, Albert made no effort to answer Katrina's questions.

"Ma, maybe he didn't know how to tell you. Maybe he was scared to tell you."

"Scared? Fuck scared!" Katrina's voice boomed. She was oblivious to the passersby who came and went through the hospital doors. "If he was so scared, then he shouldn't have bothered to call me in the first damn place. You don't do shit half-ass, Albert. It—"

"Hold the fuck up!" Albert daintily held up his right hand, but there was no weakness in his voice. "I'm trying to give you all the respect in the world, Mrs. Dawson, but you're forcing me to come out of my bag."

"Hey, come the hell out! Don't hold back on my account."

"Maaa!" Lorna said, quickly stepping in front of Albert.

"Mrs. Dawson, calling you was the biggest favor you'll ever get from me, because I didn't have to call you at all."

"What am I supposed to do, kiss your ass?"

"Ma! What you doin'?"

"It's all right, Lorna." Albert stepped from behind Lorna. "I'm a big boy. I can handle irate wives with ugly mouths."

"You're a punk. You should've told me what was going on here."

"Did someone tell you I owed you something? If they did, they lied to you. I don't know you and you don't know me. So I'm not obligated in any form or fashion to you."

"You called me here, Albert! You could've told me about that ugly-ass woman."

"Speaking of ugly, Mrs. Dawson, what are you being?"

"Don't you—"

"I am not your husband. I will not take the blame for what just happened. And for your edification, I damn well don't have anything to be afraid of."

For some weird reason, Albert amused Katrina. He reminded her of a little boy. "How old are you?"

"What does my age have to do with anything?"

"Tell me and find out."

"Twenty-six, good and grown. Why?"

"At your age, hasn't anyone ever told you what happens to the bearer of bad news? Don't you know your history?"

"Ma, what's that supposed to mean?"

"It means," Albert said, "that I'm the one who told your mother about your father's betrayal, so I'm the one who should have my head cut off."

"Ma, that's foul. It's not Albert's fault that Daddy—"

"Shut up, Lorna."

Lorna sucked her teeth. "Dang! It ain't my fault either."

"Mrs. Dawson, this mess, this dilemma, belongs solely on Gordon's head. He should've told you himself that—"

"Which he didn't!" Katrina snapped.

"So you're the last to know, what else is new? The way I see it, this is not my problem," Albert said. "The blame you're trying to put on *my* shoulders, I'm not having it." Albert started walking away.

"Ma! See what you did. It's not his fault that Daddy cheated on you. Albert is trying to help us. Don't we need him to take us to Daddy's apartment?"

Katrina didn't have to be told that she needed Albert. "All right. It's not your fault."

Albert stopped, but he didn't turn back.

Katrina and Lorna both waited. Lorna finally nudged Katrina into saying, "I'm sorry."

Albert finally turned around, but he wouldn't lift one foot to go back to Katrina. Getting the message, Katrina, with Lorna at her heels, finally went to Albert.

"Mrs. Dawson—"

"Call her Katrina," Lorna said. "She don't like to be called Mrs. Dawson by grown people."

Katrina shot Lorna a reproachful glare.

"Ma, don't be so stiff. That's what you always say. Besides, Albert already calls Daddy Gordon. They're friends. He may as well call you by your first name, too."

Usually she didn't like to be called Mrs. Dawson by people over the age of eighteen; it always made her feel old. But right now, hearing herself called Mrs. Dawson was necessary.

"That's all right, I'm quite comfortable saying Mrs. Dawson," Albert said.

"Good," Katrina said coldly.

"Mrs. Dawson, you should know that I've often told Gordon that he was wrong. After he fell sick, I knew right away that this was all going to come to a head. I took it upon myself to call you so you'd know that Gordon was possibly going to die. I felt you had a right to see him. Although it's really not *my* place to divulge this kind of personal information, I knew I'd have to tell you something if Joan showed up at the hospital while you were here. This is why—"

"But you knew for a whole goddamn year that Gordon was guilty of bigamy—a goddamn crime! Since you took it upon yourself to call me, couldn't you have taken it upon yourself to tell me before I got on that damn plane that my husband had an illegal wife standing vigil at his bedside?"

"Ma, shouldn't we go somewhere else to talk?" Lorna eyeballed a middle-aged couple who were staring at them. "People are hearing your business."

"I couldn't care less. I am not leaving the grounds of this hospital until I get this mess straightened out. If Albert had told me—"

"You still on that? Gordon is my friend. My allegiance is to him, not you."

"Well, it must be wonderful to have such a loyal friend." Katrina wanted to punch Albert Waterman in his clean-shaven, nonsweating, unfazed mug.

"Gordon has been a good friend to me. He was my mentor

from the day I started working with the department. He also helped me through some very rough times in my personal life."

"Well, goody for you and fucking hooray for Gordon," Katrina said, unimpressed.

"Ma, he's trying to help us. Can't you—"

"Lorna, get off my back! I'm trying to understand this mess!"

Lorna's bottom lip and shoulders dropped as she started to walk away. Albert stopped her with a gentle touch on the shoulder.

"Lorna, your mother has every right to be angry. She—"

"Oh, I'm not angry," Katrina said. "I'm furious! I could kill Gordon." She started to pace.

"Ma, you're ballistic."

"Goddamn right I am."

"Mrs. Dawson, Gordon told me about you and his family in Brooklyn. I knew that he wasn't divorced from you, but I did think you were legally separated."

"Did Gordon tell you that lie?"

"Yes, but a year and a half ago I realized he wasn't legally separated from you when I overheard him speaking with you on the telephone. What he was saying didn't sound like a conversation that a man who was seeking a divorce would have, so I questioned him, and he told me the truth."

"Wow, what an interesting concept—he told you the truth. Isn't that something that he should have been telling me?" Katrina asked. "Oh, but his friendship with you was more important than his marriage to me."

"Like I said before, I'm sorry that you had to find out like this."

Katrina folded her arms tight and went to rapidly tapping her foot as hard as she could to distract her from the urge to cry. "Did he really marry that woman?"

"I attended the wedding."

"Oh, shit." Katrina stalked off, but immediately came back. "How in the world could he do this to me?"

"I can only tell you what I know. But, Mrs. Dawson, Gordon is a good man. He messed up and—"

"Spare me the bullshit." Katrina wiped away the tears that

spilled over. "A good man doesn't live such a vile lie. He's a snake!"

"Yes, Gordon was definitely wrong. There is no doubt about that," Albert said. "However, I know how much he loves you and his children. He just got caught up and—"

" 'Caught up' my ass, or should I say his white bitch's ass."

"Albert," Lorna said, "my father couldn't've loved us all that much if he snuck off and got married to another woman while he's still married to my mother. And I don't care if the woman he married was white or black. He shouldn't've done it."

"Okay, look, you're both right. I can't defend or explain why Gordon did what he did. I only know what he said. He said he asked you three years ago to move to Maryland and you refused."

"So it's my fault he stumbled into a church and got married to another woman." Katrina again began to pace.

"I don't think—"

"I'm going to kick his ass." Katrina suddenly bolted back through the hospital doors into the lobby. Both Albert and Lorna took off behind her.

"Mrs. Dawson, you have to calm down. You can't go back up to ICU when you're this upset."

"Watch me!"

Katrina marched across the lobby to the elevator bank. She could hardly catch her breath as she jabbed at the third-floor elevator button.

"Ma, maybe we should go for a walk or go have breakfast before we go see Daddy again." Lorna knew she was wasting her time. Katrina would hear no one, and she would listen to no one but her own mind.

"That's a good idea," Albert said. "It's still early enough to get breakfast. The cafeteria's in that direction." He nodded toward the right.

"Excuse me," Katrina said, "but does anyone else find it interesting that the other *Mrs. Dawson* hasn't come past us as yet?"

"Maybe she went out another way," Lorna offered.

"No, I believe they let her stay upstairs after they kicked me out, the racist bastards."

"Ma, you went ballistic up there. You started screaming at that woman, then you tried to slap her, and then you went after Daddy, and no telling what you would have done if they hadn't stopped you."

"I would have snatched that tube out of his nose and put my foot in its place."

"See, Ma, that's why they kicked you out."

"Mrs. Dawson, you're going to have to get control of yourself or you won't be allowed to see Gordon."

"I'll sue them so fast, they won't know what hit them."

"C'mon, Ma. Please calm down."

"Okay." Katrina took a deep lung-filling breath. "I'm calm." She held her steady hand out for Albert and Lorna to see.

"Good," Albert said.

"But you were right about one thing, Albert," Katrina said. "Gordon isn't going to make it. I'm gonna kill him—calmly."

Albert Waterman was keenly aware of the looks and whisperings behind them. "Mrs. Dawson, perhaps you should lower your voice."

"Fuck these people! I don't care . . ."

"Ma!"

". . . who hears what I have to say! My husband didn't just cheat on me; he went and married another woman. That bastard used to call me twice a day and tell me he loved me, yet, he was sleeping with his whore every night. He came home three weeks ago! He was in Brooklyn, in my face, in my bed. Nothing he did gave him away. If anyone should be ashamed of what people will think, it's Gordon 'stupid, lying-ass' Dawson."

Embarrassed, Albert glanced around to see who was looking at them, while Lorna slumped back against the wall. Her well of tears hadn't dried up yet.

Katrina jabbed harder on the elevator button. "Where the hell is that elevator? I'm not leaving this goddamn hospital until Gordon sits his ass up and tells me to my face what he did."

"Miss," a squat, middle-aged male security guard said, "I'm going to have to ask you to lower your voice or you'll have to leave the hospital." Two other men in similar blue uniforms came up and flanked the guard. With stern, disapproving faces, they stared at Katrina.

The show of force didn't faze Katrina in the least. She put her hand on her hip. "Look—"

Lorna suddenly pulled Katrina back. "She'll be quiet," Lorna said, stepping in front of an even angrier Katrina.

"Lorna, you don't speak for me." Katrina started nudging Lorna aside. "I—"

"Stop it, Ma!" Surprising even herself, Lorna grabbed Katrina by the arm and said steadily, "Chill out." She and Katrina locked eyes.

Katrina jerked her arm free of Lorna's hold and walked away.

"She'll be all right," Lorna said, rushing off behind her mother. Catching up with Katrina, Lorna tried to put her arm around Katrina, but Katrina rebuffed her, shaking Lorna's arm off of her shoulder.

At first undecided as to whether or not he should follow Katrina and Lorna, Albert stood watching them heading in the direction of the hospital cafeteria.

"Sir, if the lady creates a disturbance in the cafeteria, she'll have to leave the premises."

"She won't," Albert said, not believing his own words. "I'll talk to her." As much as he didn't want to, he went after Katrina. Gordon had been a good friend to him from the moment they had been introduced, so he would do his best to be a friend to his difficult wife. If Gordon died, there were things Katrina needed to know that only he could tell her.

CHAPTER
14

The beautifully lush white flowers of the gladiola stalks caught Celeste's eye. Admiring the garden, she saw that all the flowers were turning white. White gladioli filled her entire garden; no other flower, no other color could be seen anywhere. They were beautiful. Getting down on her knees, Celeste began to cut the stalks of gladioli when suddenly a single, blood-red rose was handed to her. It was strikingly beautiful. She reached for it. The hand that held the rose brushed the rose against her cheek. She looked up to see who it was that held the rose—it was Willie. He smiled and handed the rose to her again.

Celeste didn't take the rose. "Willie, where have you been? I've been looking everywhere for you."

Willie lowered his head in shame. Celeste started to stand just as the rose in Willie's hand was dropped in front of her. She picked it up. When she stood with the rose in her hand, Willie had vanished. He was nowhere to be seen. A single drop of water dripped onto Celeste's hand. She looked at the rose. It was dry, yet water dripped from its center.

Riiiiing!

The ringing telephone awakened Celeste. Groggily, she batted her eyes open and looked around the room. There were no gladioli, and no single red rose was in her hand. She had been dreaming, but it felt so real. Willie used to always give her red roses on their anniversary.

Riiiiing!

"Ah, damn." She glanced at the alarm clock—ten o'clock. It could only be Bryson or her father, and she already knew what they had to say. She had spoken to each of them twice since they'd left the house. She decided to not answer the telephone and had begun to roll over when she thought of Justine—it might be her calling.

Riii—

"Hello," she said sleepily.

"Good morning," Detective Vaughan said. "I hope I didn't wake you."

Celeste rolled onto her back. "No, I'm awake. I'm glad you called. I wanted to thank you for keeping me company until the locksmith left."

"I was glad to do it. I wanted to make sure everything was okay. So how are you this morning?"

"I'm fine. I feel so much better with all the locks changed."

"You did the right thing. I . . . my partner and I will be in touch."

"Great. Oh, by the way. Anytime you wanna try and win back your ten dollars, I'm game."

Detective Vaughan chuckled. "Please, don't tell anyone you beat me that badly. I won't be able to hold my head up."

"Don't worry, your secret is safe—no one need ever know that you're such a bad poker player."

Again, Detective Vaughan chuckled. "I was a little rusty. But before I sit across the table from you again, I'll sharpen my game a bit."

"Is that a challenge?" Celeste asked, smiling to herself.

"Maybe."

"Just name the place and the time." Celeste was enjoying this light banter with Detective Isaiah Vaughan. It was the most relaxed she'd felt since Willie died. Last night, after the crime scene unit had done its work and Celeste had put her house back in order with Detective Vaughan's help, she and the sexy detective had played poker for hours before the locksmith from ACE Security showed up at six-thirty. While the locksmith worked, they had shared an early morning snack of sharp cheddar cheese, crackers, and ginger ale that wasn't exactly appetizing, but it was filling.

"Are you there?" Celeste asked, realizing that Detective Vaughan hadn't responded.

"I'm here."

"I thought I lost you for a minute there."

"No, U'm . . . I . . . Look, I may as well just come out and say this," Detective Vaughan said. "Mrs. Alexander . . ."

Celeste raised her head off the pillow. Had she said something wrong?

". . . it might not have been such a good idea to sit with you this morning."

"Did I do something wrong?"

"No . . . but maybe I did. I'm working your husband's case. It's not a good idea to get too personal with a victim's widow."

"Is poker personal?" Celeste asked, knowing that she had felt something a little friendly developing between them the more they teased each other about who was losing.

"I guess it could be," he answered. "But here's the deal. Your husband's murderer is out there, and I intend to find him, or her if that be the case. I won't compromise this case. I enjoyed your company a little too much last night. It can't happen again."

Celeste smiled. It was a half-ass compliment, but she didn't mind. Whatever it was that had happened between shuffling hands of cards had done wonders to stop the wailing in her head. That alone, Celeste was grateful for.

"However, if I'm not being presumptuous, I'd like it if I could call you when the case is closed—that's if you don't mind. Of course, I'll understand if it's too soon for you to think about talking to anyone. I can respect that."

Easing her head back onto her pillow, Celeste thought about Willie. She once thought if he died while she was still young, if she ever looked at another man, it would be years down the line. Never in her wildest imagination would she have dreamed that Willie would have died the way he did, or that just weeks after burying him she'd be enjoying herself flirting with the lead detective on his case. Who would have ever thought that?

"I look forward to hearing from you, Detective. Have a good day." Celeste hung up with a smile and not a pang of guilt. Willie had come to her in a dream, and maybe the red rose was his way of saying that he was sorry, but she didn't know if she could ever forgive him. The hurt wasn't going to vanish like he had.

CHAPTER
15

The tightness in Katrina's chest wasn't letting up, although she kept telling herself to take deep, slow breaths. Even while she watched Albert Waterman top off his breakfast of pancakes and sausage with a large cold glass of milk, and Lorna finished her second apple danish, and that was after she had eaten an order of scrambled eggs and bacon, Katrina couldn't will herself to relax. How Lorna had an appetite at all was beyond Katrina; she hadn't even been able to drink the black coffee she'd ordered. Her nervous stomach couldn't hold a thing. How could Gordon do this to her? She had never even thought of . . . Well, she had gone out to lunch, several times, with Maurice Branch, an X-ray technician she had met at a sonogram seminar, but nothing that Katrina couldn't talk about in mixed company had happened. It could have, but she had put the brakes on more than once, although she had been quite tempted. Obviously, Gordon had never tried his brakes.

"How long ago did my father meet Joan?" Lorna asked.

"About two and a half years ago," Albert replied.

"Did he meet her on the job?"

"No, on the Metro. Like your father, Joan worked in Washington and lived in Silver Springs."

"How tacky," Katrina said, sickened at the thought of Gordon flirting with a young white woman sitting across from him on the subway. "So how long did it take for them to get together?"

"Mrs. Dawson, I don't know the intimate details. I just know that Gordon met Joan two and a half years ago. A relationship developed; they got married."

"A real fairy tale," Katrina quipped.

Albert glanced down at his wrist watch. Damn. It was only ten-fifteen. The whole day lay ahead. This scorned-wife drama was too heavy for him. If, by some miracle, Gordon made it, Gordon owed him big-time.

"So what kind of wedding did my husband give his fairy-tale bride?"

"You don't wanna know about that. You—"

"It was a big, fancy one, huh?"

Albert looked at Lorna, who shrugged her shoulders.

Katrina's leg went to swinging. "That bastard. When I married Gordon, we went down to City Hall in Queens. We honeymooned in Atlantic City for five rainy-ass days. Now, if I recall correctly, a year ago, Gordon went away. He said on business. That must have been when he was on his honeymoon. I bet he took his Barbie doll somewhere exotic. So, Albert, where did they go?"

Albert wasn't about to let himself be drawn into Katrina's lamenting. "Mrs. Dawson, wouldn't you like to go to a hotel to freshen up?"

"I'm staying here. As soon as Lorna finishes eating, I'm going to the administration office to make sure this hospital knows that I am the only, legal, Mrs. Gordon Dawson. Then I'm going back up to the ICU to see if Gordon's *play wife Barbie* is still around. As for going to a hotel, last I heard, Gordon had a one-bedroom apartment in Silver Springs. Does he still, or is that where he and his *play wife Barbie* live?"

Albert cringed, but he was going to have to tell it. "Yes, Gordon still has an apartment in Silver Springs, but it's a studio. He has a house in Upper Marlboro with Joan."

"Daddy's a dog." Lorna dropped the last piece of danish she was about to eat back onto her plate.

Resting her elbows on the table, Katrina closed her eyes and pressed her forehead to the balls of her hands. The more she heard, the worse it got. She felt as though she was trudging breathlessly through a mud pit that thickened the farther in she got. *Lord, please let Gordon pull through so I can kick his ass.* Katrina opened her eyes. She needed a miracle about now.

"So, if Daddy has a house, why is he keeping an apartment?"

"Why do you think?" Katrina asked.

"Oh, so you'd think he was living there."

Katrina pointed her finger in affirmation.

"Dang, Daddy is a big, scandalous dog."

Albert suddenly stood. "I'm going back up to the ICU to see how Gordon's doing. I'll speak to the nurse about letting you come back up, but, Mrs. Dawson, you have to promise to cool out."

Katrina softly sucked her teeth. "I'm out of promises."

"Ma, please."

"Mrs. Dawson, you have to remain calm or—"

"I'll try, damnit. But I am not about to take this shit lying down."

"But you—"

"She'll be okay," Lorna assured Albert, but as soon as Albert was out of earshot, "Ma, you have to take a chill pill. If we can't see Daddy, then his other wife will be all up in his business while we're down here wondering what's happening."

Katrina looked hard at Lorna. "When did you get so smart?"

"When I realized I had to keep up with you."

"When was that? This morning?"

"No," Lorna said seriously, "when I was six."

Katrina could only imagine that it wasn't easy being her daughter. She wasn't the easiest person to get along with, and she was hardest on Lorna. Patrice was stubborn and selfish, while Lorna was so giving and always trying to please. As opposite as they were, Patrice and Lorna got along fine with each other, but Katrina always found it strange that Patrice was the one that she was closest to. Perhaps that old adage, "like mother, like daughter," was their bond.

"Ma, why would Daddy do something so low?"

For lack of an explanation that she could sell to Lorna as well as to herself, Katrina shrugged. "You have to ask your daddy that."

"Well, is there anything we can do about it? Are you still his legal wife?"

"As far as I am concerned, Lorna, I'm your father's only wife. If he doesn't die, I will see him in jail. I guarantee you that."

Lorna gasped. "Granddad and Grandma aren't gonna believe what Daddy's done."

"Hey, I'm the one that doesn't believe what your daddy's done. Your grandparents won't have a problem."

"Shouldn't we call them and tell them what's going on?"

"I will, as soon as I know for sure myself." Katrina didn't look forward to calling home. It wasn't her father she was so much worried about; it was her mother. Stella hated Gordon. Years ago, Stella told her Gordon was no good and tried in vain to keep them from marrying. When that didn't work, Stella refused to contribute even a "rusty nickel" toward the wedding, which was how she and Gordon ended up getting married at City Hall. Stella always said there was something sneaky about Gordon. And damn if she wasn't proven right—literally overnight. Gordon had started cheating seven months into their marriage, but after that first time, she never told her mother another thing about Gordon's unfaithfulness, and that was because Stella had tried, like hell, to get her to leave Gordon—never mind that she was six months pregnant with Patrice. Throughout the years, Stella was cordial to Gordon, but she never did like him. Once she hears what Gordon's done, Stella is, no doubt, going to tell her how stupid she was to marry Gordon in the first place. Nope, she wasn't ready to call home.

"Here comes Albert," Lorna said. "That was fast," she said to him.

Albert said nothing as he sat.

"Well?" Lorna asked. "What did they say?"

Katrina could see that the troubled look in Albert's eyes was gone. Now he looked sad.

"Mrs. Dawson, you need to go to the administration office."

"So they're not letting us go back up to ICU?" Lorna asked.

"It's not necessary. Your father died ten minutes ago."

Lorna's eyes filled with tears while Katrina's remained unblinking and dry. She felt nothing but a belly full of anger. She wasn't going to cry over Gordon's passing. He deserved to die.

"I'll be back," Katrina said, standing.

"Ma, where're you going?"

"You stay here with Albert. I have to get Gordon's body released so I can burn his ass up."

"No!" Albert said, standing. "Gordon wanted to be buried. He's against cremation; he says it's barbaric."

"Yeah, well, I seem to recall something about that," Katrina said musingly, "but I can't be sure."

"Ma, you should do what Daddy would have wanted."

"Did your father do what I wanted? Did he stop cheating? And worse than cheating, did he stop himself from marrying another woman while he was still married to me? No, he didn't. He's gone. I have final say. I am going to do what I think best, and Gordon can't do a damn thing about it—dead people have no say."

"But, Mrs. Dawson, that's not right. It's sacrilegious or something, isn't it?"

"Albert, take note. There are harsh penalties for assholes who screw indiscriminately and hurt the ones they so-call love. They burn in hell and on earth." That said, Katrina hurried off past inquisitive glances to find the administration office before Gordon's Barbie lay claim to his body and his assets, whatever they may be.

CHAPTER
16

Celeste sped along Linden Boulevard into the tree-lined neighborhood of Laurelton, Queens. Her father's cryptic telephone call about a serious family emergency had her dressed and out of the house in fifteen minutes. Whatever it was, Richard wouldn't talk about it on the telephone. He ordered, "Get out here right away." It was probably about Justine, and her father didn't want her too upset to drive. If Justine was hurt, if something terrible had happened to her, she could only blame herself for sending her out there so she could be alone to wallow in her anger at Willie. Bryson was right. She wasn't being a good mother to Justine. She had been thinking only of herself. Justine needed her—

Justine wasn't hurt, and Justine wasn't thinking about her. Justine was chasing her cousin, Gordy, and the neighbor's son down the street, shooting a well-aimed, high-powered, shoulder-strapped water torpedo at them. She was having a good time. Celeste parked her car out front of her parents' home and watched Justine howl with pleasure when Gordy's water gun was suddenly turned on her.

She called, "Justine!" three times before Justine heard her.

"Hi, Mommy!" was her quick reply before she raced farther down the block. Celeste wasn't the least bit offended. In fact, she was relieved—the family emergency wasn't her child.

Before Celeste could make it all the way up the front walkway, her mother opened the door. Stella stood in the doorway in her usual summer wear—a loose-fitting, floral-patterned, cotton sundress down past her calves. As far back as Celeste could remember, every summer, her mother wore brightly colored, flowered cotton sundresses, many with thinner straps than the straps on the white bras she wore. When Celeste was a little girl, she thought her mother looked pretty. When she was really young, she thought her mother picked the flowers from her garden in the backyard and glued them to her dresses. Then when she was about seven, her mother started dressing her and Katrina in identical floral sundresses, which Katrina hated and Celeste secretly loved. They were so summery. But the other girls on the block made fun of them in their "old lady dresses," and she and Katrina begged their mother to stop dressing them in those "old lady dresses." To this day, Celeste believed her mother's feelings had been hurt, but that didn't stop Stella from wearing her favorite dresses herself.

"What took you so long?" Stella asked. "We've been waiting for you."

Celeste was puzzled by the angry glint in her mother's eyes. "What's wrong? Where's Dad?"

Stella lead the way into the dining room. Richard was sitting in his seat at the head of the table, steadily rolling a set of silver exercise balls in his left hand. The smooth, fluid rolling of the balls in her father's hand caught Celeste's eye. He had terrible arthritis and used the balls to keep his fingers flexible. He swore the balls worked, but he took a pain reliever all the same.

Neither Stella nor Richard spoke as Celeste sat in her old dinner space across from Stella. The sour looks on both their faces was disturbing.

"Daddy, are you sick?"

"It's not us," Stella said, "it's your sister. Katrina's in trouble."

"Don't tell me she's finally been arrested for being a bit . . . for being nasty?"

Stella and Richard both shot Celeste a warning glare.

"Yeah, well, she is."

"This is about Gordon," Richard said.

That quick, Celeste had forgotten about Gordon. This probably had something to do with him being in the hospital, but that was Katrina's problem. Yet she saw by the way her parents were looking at her, they were trying to make it hers.

"Don't you wanna know what kind of trouble your sister's in?" Stella asked.

Here we go! "Not really, Mother, but if you're gonna tell me, tell me."

"You tell her," Stella said to Richard. "I'm too disgusted."

"Gordon died," Richard said, with not an ounce of emotion in his voice.

Celeste almost shrugged. She caught herself, but the truth was, she felt nothing. In all the years that Gordon was married to Katrina, how well did she get to know him? Not well at all. She never hung out with Gordon because she didn't hang out with Katrina. What little Celeste knew of Gordon, she got from her mother and father, and to hear her mother tell it, Gordon was a dog. So was she supposed to feel something here?

"Katrina must be devastated."

"Not really," Stella said, flatly. "Gordon dying is the good part."

Celeste raised her brow. "Let's not be cruel, Mother."

"I hope his black soul rots in hell."

"What's that old saying? 'Don't speak ill of the dead'?"

"Dead or alive, Gordon was a bastard," Richard said.

"Okay. What's going on? Mother, I know you never liked Gordon, but, Dad, you at least tolerated him."

"That was for Katrina's sake," Richard said. "Gordon really was a bastard."

Celeste really didn't care to know what Gordon had done to warrant such disdain, but her curiosity was getting the better of her. "Are you people going to tell me what Gordon did or not? I know that's why you ordered me out here, so tell me."

The balls in Richard's hand stopped moving. "Gordon—"

Stella flat-palmed the dining room table. The sound was explosive. "I'll tell it!" she said. "The low-life, grass-rubbing bastard cheated on Katrina, big-time! He married a white girl who thinks she's his legal wife . . ."

Celeste's jaw dropped.

"The bastard should be stripped and fed to the buzzards!"

Celeste reminded herself to close her mouth, but she was also reminded of what Katrina had said to her about not taking care of Willie at home. What she wouldn't give to be inside Katrina's head right now, hearing what Katrina was saying to herself.

"I warned Katrina about Gordon. I—"

"Stella, no use bringing that up."

"Well, if she had listened to me, she wouldn't be in this mess. I knew Gordon was a dog ten minutes after meeting him. It was all in his eyes."

Richard slammed his silver balls back inside their red-velvet-lined box. "You've said that a million times, and a damn thing ain't goin' to change because you keep saying it."

"I don't care! I'll say it a million times more if I feel like it. Katrina should have listened to me, but nooo, she was grown and knew what she was doing."

"Mother, please, Dad's right. Talking about what Katrina should have done is a waste of time and energy. When did Gordon marry this person?"

"About a year ago," Richard said.

"Which he didn't bother to tell his wife and children about," Stella threw in.

"Seems they got themselves a sixteen-month-old baby, too."

"Oh, shit," Celeste said, forgetting that she didn't curse in front of her parents.

Stella gave Celeste a disapproving glare. "The woman was pregnant even before he *illegally* married her."

"Oh, my God. Katrina must be sick."

"But that's not nearly the half of it," Stella said. "The hospital won't release Gordon's body to Katrina because she has to prove to them she's his legal wife."

"Then she needs her marriage license," Celeste said. "She never got a divorce, at least that I know of, so there are no divorce papers for her to get. She needs her original marriage license, and maybe the kids' birth certificates with Gordon's name on them, and anything else she can come up with—insurance papers, tax returns, any and everything."

"That's what we figure," Richard said. "I want you to go over to Katrina's house and get all those documents together."

Celeste looked hard at her father. He didn't look like he'd lost his mind, but he had to be insane to suggest that she go to Katrina's house and search for her private papers.

"You heard me," he said.

"Then you must be insane, because I'm not—"

"Celeste!" Stella said. "Watch your mouth. You're not so grown that I can't put a belt to you."

At another time, that might have been funny, but it was far from funny now. "Why are you threatening me? This is Katrina's mess. I have nothing to do with it."

"Katrina needs help from her family. You—"

"Well, Katrina has other family members, Mother, including you and Dad."

"You're her sister," Richard said. "You will—"

"No, I won't. I'm not in this."

"This is a family matter, Celeste," Stella said. "You have to do this."

"What about Patrice? She can get those papers and take them to her mother. She's what? Eighteen? Nineteen?"

"Patrice is going to be upset enough about her father," Richard said. "Tomorrow, Patrice will meet up with her mother in Washington, and so will you."

Folding her arms, Celeste shook her head.

"Celeste, you have to—"

"No, Dad, I don't *have to.* The post office has overnight express service, and I'm sure UPS and FedEx can get it there, too. If anything, I'll deliver Katrina's papers to them."

"That won't do," Stella said. "Those papers are too important to put in the mail. Celeste, you have to hand deliver—"

"Why aren't you people hearing me? Am I speaking a language you don't understand? Why are you trying to involve me in Katrina's life? Didn't she tell you that we had a big fight the other night after *Dad* left her at my house?"

"That's not important."

"Yes, it is. Katrina said some terrible things to me."

"And I bet you said some terrible things right back to her."

"Mother, you have never seen my side of this crap between me and Katrina."

"Because it's all nonsense. Grow up, Celeste. You and Katrina are sisters. Act like it."

"Oh, so I have to act like I'm Katrina's sister, but she—"

"You're wasting time, Celeste," Richard said. "This has to be done."

"Yeah, but not by me. For one thing, I won't go rummaging through Katrina's house look—"

"Katrina keeps all of her important papers in a safe in the utility room off the kitchen," Stella said. "I have the combination and the key."

Celeste could feel her stomach churning. "You know why this is so sad, Mother? Katrina has never opened her house to me, and here you are about to give me the keys to her house and the combination to her safe. Do either of you understand that I can't do this? Katrina has never been nice to me, and in fact, she said she hates that she's even related to me. As far as I'm concerned, those ugly words nullify our familial connection."

"That's absolute nonsense," Stella said. "Katrina is your sister, your blood—no matter what spews from her mouth. And you two are going to start acting like you're sisters or I will knock both your stubborn heads together."

Celeste chuckled drily. "This is too weird. I'm being threatened because I won't let you force me to take part in Katrina's mess, when you both know how much Katrina hates me. Am I the one that's not thinking here? I'm not getting involved!"

"I told you we weren't gonna be able to make her go," Richard said to Stella. He went back to rolling his silver balls.

Ignoring Richard, Stella pointed her finger at Celeste. "I am going to say this to you one last time, and I don't expect to have to ever say it again . . ."

Celeste felt as if she was back in elementary school and was being scolded for some minor infraction that became monstrous once her mother found out about it. She quickly glimpsed her father slowly rolling those damn balls. Their motion was so fluid, so smooth, they made not a sound, but their movement irritated Celeste anyway.

"You and Katrina are sisters. Blood. Never mind that the two of you spent your entire lives fighting like hens in a barnyard over a cockeyed rooster."

"That's not my fault. Katrina—"

"Shut up!" Stella snapped. "I don't wanna hear a damn thing about fault, or about the stupid, petty fights that you and Katrina have waged for years. It's one thing to fight amongst yourselves, but it's another to stand back and let somebody from the outside hurt your sister."

"Oh, I get it," Celeste said. "This is about Gordon's money, isn't it? You don't want the other woman to get her hands on—"

"That's not the main—" Richard was about to say.

SLAM!

Again Stella slammed her hand down on the table. This time she hurt herself and began to immediately rub her hands together. "Damn right! This is about Gordon's money. But it's also about Gordon's lies, about his children, and about his wife, Katrina."

Richard tightly palmed his silver balls. "We're Katrina's family, Celeste, and you're her sister. If this had happened to you, and Katrina refused to help you, her ass would be sitting at this table getting the same damn lecture. Celeste, you will go to Washington. You will take care of your sister. You understand?"

Shaking her head, Celeste pushed herself up from the table.

"Yes, you will," Stella said. "I know you have your own troubles, and Katrina should have been there for you as well."

"But she wasn't, was she, Mother? In fact, you should hear the nasty things my dear sister said to me about how Willie died . . . By the way, Dad, thank you for leaving Katrina at my house. She really showed how ugly she can be."

Richard began rolling his silver balls yet again.

"Oh, and, Mother, remember when Katrina stole my boyfriend? You didn't even get on her this badly. Oh, you beat her butt, but that was it. You didn't—"

"Celeste, you weren't about to marry the boy! You probably never would have seen him past high school. You—"

"How do you know that, Mother? You don't know."

"No, but—"

"You let Katrina off easy. And you know something else? You've never gotten on Katrina for not being there for me."

"You don't—"

"And, if you're so concerned about this shredded sisterly bond between us, why is it that you've never gotten on Katrina about the way she's always treated me?"

"You don't know what I've said to Katrina over the years about her behavior. Katrina knows, but I'm not wasting time talking about the past."

"We don't have time," Richard said, those shiny balls rolling fluidly.

"Katrina can't straighten this mess out alone, no matter what she thinks. Katrina needs you, Celeste. You need to get yourself over to Katrina's and find the papers she needs."

"And if I don't?" Celeste surprised herself in how she was standing up to her mother. She had never defied either of her parents before.

Stella looked Celeste dead in the eye. "Do you dare defy us, Celeste, after all we've done for you all of your life? Have we ever asked you for anything in return? In fact, how often do we even ask you to do anything for us?"

"Celeste, if you can't do this for your sister," Richard said, "would you please do it for me?"

As much as she wanted to ignore the earnest gleem in her father's eyes, Celeste couldn't. He'd never asked anything of her before that she couldn't do.

"Fine! You want me to go to Katrina's and get those papers? Done. No problem! But I am not going to Washington. I have a daughter to take care of."

"Justine will be fine right here, just as you planned for the rest of the summer," Richard said.

Celeste felt herself losing ground. "But, Dad, I have to be here in case the police have questions about Willie's death."

"Another maggot," Stella mumbled.

"Wait a minute! You always liked Willie."

"That goes to show you how wrong I can be about a person."

"Whatever Willie may have done to me, Mother, he was always respectful and kind to you. Why would you—"

"Let it go, Celeste," Richard said.

"No, Dad. I wanna know—"

"I said let it go!"

Celeste hushed up immediately. Since Willie died, everything seemed so off center, but why the hell was she getting the brunt of it?

"Celeste, no need of fighting amongst ourselves over this mess," Richard said.

"I can't go anywhere. Did you forget that my house was just burglarized?"

"You changed the locks. Leave me a set of keys and I'll check on your house every day."

"Dad—"

"Celeste, in life, we do what we have to for family. No matter how we feel about each other, we're the only ones we have to depend on. You have to go to Washington; your sister needs you. Give that detective working Willie's case our number. If something comes up, he can call us, and we'll tell you."

"But, Dad, I need to speak directly to the detective. I—"

"Celeste, we know just as much as you know about Willie's death—which is nothing. And since you said you don't give a damn who killed Willie, and I don't blame you, it's not like you have to be here."

"So now you're throwing that in my face?"

"Celeste. I'm trying to tell you that we all have to help each other."

"That's right," Stella said. "We want you to understand that if one of us in this family has a problem, we all have a problem. Right now, you and Katrina's lives are messed up because of the men you chose to marry."

"So what Willie and Gordon did is our fault?"

"I'm not saying that. I'm saying your husbands, on their own, were not men of honor. They're nothing like your father. Your husbands soiled your beds. I thank God they're gone . . ."

"Amen to that," Richard said.

". . . but they've left you a whole lot of filthy laundry to do. Right now, we have to clean up Katrina's mess. After that, we move on."

Celeste felt sick. "So you all want me to drop whatever I'm doing to go to Washington to help a woman who can't stomach the sight of me?"

"Celeste," Stella said, "what are you doing that's so very important right now?"

"I . . . I'm—"

"Exactly. Nothing. Celeste, you took time off from work, but you hardly go out. Last I saw, you were moping around your house growing bitter over what Willie did. Maybe going and helping Katrina is what you need to pull yourself up out of the hole Willie dropped you in."

"Thanks, Mother, and you, too, Dad. You've both made me feel so good. Don't either one of you give a damn about what I'm going through?"

"We care, Celeste, and you know it. I agree with your mother. I think you and Katrina can best help each other. Your problems are about the same."

"Dad!"

"He's right," Stella said. "No matter how you look at it, you both got dead, cheating husbands."

Snatching her pocketbook, Celeste started to stalk off.

"You get back here, Celeste Louise!" Richard's voice boomed. "And I mean right now." Richard returned the silver balls to their box. For the first time since Celeste arrived, he got up out of his chair.

Celeste didn't make it out of the dining room. She stood with her back to her parents. Angry, near tears, she hated that they had ganged up on her to make her do what she didn't want to do.

"Sweetheart," Richard said, going to stand behind Celeste. "Look at me."

She refused to turn around.

Richard stepped alongside Celeste and put his arm around her. "Katrina needs a strong, powerful ally."

Celeste pulled herself out of her father's hold. "That's not me! You and Mother—"

"Yes, your mother and I could very well go and help Katrina, but you, Celeste, equal us in every way and more."

"Save it, Dad. I'm not buying it."

"I'm telling you like it is, Celeste. You're a strong woman. You're smart, you're resourceful, and—"

"And you're level-headed and tenacious," Stella said, rubbing Celeste's bare arm. "Katrina's very emotional. She needs you to be the voice of reason and to watch her back. Celeste, we're trusting that you won't let Katrina get hurt, no matter how ugly she is to you, and yes, we know how ugly Katrina can be."

"We're counting on you, Celeste," Richard said. "Don't let us down."

Celeste fought back the tears. "I'm not strong enough to do this. In case you hadn't noticed, I've been kind of emotional myself lately."

"We're aware of that, but you've handled yourself like a queen. And with Katrina, you'll do the same."

"But—"

"You'll surprise yourself," Stella said.

"And if Katrina starts—"

"Call home. We'll set Katrina's behind straight right quick."

"Oh, wow. I'm sure a tongue-lashing over the telephone will set Katrina straight right away. Mother, wake up and take a good look at your other daughter."

"I know who Katrina is. I've been with her from the start. Don't sell us short, Celeste. We still have some power to back up our threats."

It was slow in coming, but Celeste started to chuckle. Her mother had finally said something funny. Celeste looked at the bespectacled little five-foot-nothing woman who used to always back up her threats with a quick, hard swat across the behind with a twenty-four-inch ruler. The last time Celeste got hit with that horrid thing, she was fifteen and back-talked her mother over staying out past one in the morning. If her mother got her ruler now, Celeste would probably take it from her. But the thought of it was kind of funny.

"Did I say something funny?" Stella asked.

"Funnier than you'll ever know. Let's get this over with."

"That's my girl," Stella said. "Now, don't you worry about Justine or Gordy; we can take care of them just fine. Katrina's keys are on the hall table. Your father wrote down the instructions and the combination for opening her safe. The safe is in the pantry behind an empty cardboard box. Most everything should be there. Make sure you get something current, to show that the marriage never ended. Then go home and pack your bags. You have an eight-thirty flight to Washington tomorrow morning."

Celeste gasped. "You already bought me a ticket?"

"An E-ticket. All you have to do is pick it up," Richard said. "I'll take you to the airport. Bring your car back out here and park it in the garage so you don't have to worry about getting a ticket on the wrong side of the street."

"So this is a fait accompli? I have no say about any of this?"

"Of course you do, honey," Stella said, "just not at the moment. By the way, you have a room at the Best Western on New Hampshire Avenue, the same hotel Katrina and Lorna are staying at."

Oh, shit!

"We think having your own room is best."

"There should be a law against busy-body, old parents manipulating grown children."

"Well, dear," Stella said. "Before you petition for that law, consider the fact that you'll be an old parent yourself one day."

What could she say to that besides, "I just don't believe you two."

And from the uncompromising look in her mother's eyes and the firm set of her mouth, together, the message was, believe. That was the same look Stella had given her when Celeste was fourteen and wanted to wear a blue halter dress to her junior prom. She bought the dress herself from the money she had saved, but Stella refused to let her wear it. "It shows too much cleavage," she said. Well, hello! Celeste was real proud of the cleavage she thought she'd never get. She was a late bloomer and wanted to show off what she had. "Either wear something else or forgo the prom," Stella said. There was no compromise—Celeste couldn't wear a shawl to cover herself. Stella knew that she'd lose the shawl the minute she was out of sight. Celeste missed her junior prom, and the dress hung in her closet until it was too small to ever be worn by her.

"I tell you what, Mother. I'll go to Washington, but when I come asking for your blood, I want no excuses."

Stella held out both her wrists. "How much do you need!"

It was no use. Disheartened, Celeste sighed. "How long will I be gone?"

"How ever long it takes to make sure that Katrina comes out on top."

"Oh, brother. Who'd ever think I'd be trying to make sure Katrina won the day? By the way, does she know I'm coming?"

"She'll know within the hour," Stella said.

Celeste gawked at her parents.

Stella did not smile. "We love you."

The kiss that each of her parents planted on her cheeks sent Celeste angrily on her way. It wasn't a kiss she needed to fight Katrina's battle; it was a sword—a double-edged sword. While doing battle with Gordon's other family, Celeste had no doubt that she was going to have to do battle with Katrina. No way was Katrina going to hold her tongue and be nice. *Why me?* was the question Celeste kept asking herself.

CHAPTER
17

The streets were unfamiliar, and so were the houses that Katrina passed along the way. Some of the houses were grand, some were modest, but in none of these houses did Katrina know a living soul. Sitting in her car, she felt lost. She knew no other direction to drive but straight ahead. At the corner, at the stop sign, a man crossed in front of her. Katrina knew him.

"Gordon! Gordon!"

Gordon did not turn around. He continued across the street. Katrina jumped from her car and ran after him, but Gordon outdistanced her, although he seemed to be walking at an unhurried pace.

"Gordon! It's me—it's me!"

Gordon disappeared into one of the grand houses, the one at the corner. Katrina ran up to the house. She began banging on the front door. No one answered, no one came.

"Gordon! Gordon, open the door." Katrina continued to bang, and bang, and . . .

"Ma! Ma! Ma, wake up."

Batting her eyes open, Katrina slowly focused on the face above her.

"Ma, you okay?" Lorna anxiously dabbed a cool, damp washcloth to Katrina's forehead. "Albert! She's waking up."

Albert rushed back into the room and immediately put his fingers to Katrina's wrist.

"Is she okay?" Lorna asked.

"Be quiet a minute." Albert began to count Katrina's pulse beats in his head.

Katrina thought about her dream. She had never been good at interpreting dreams, but this one wasn't difficult to figure out—Gordon couldn't face her. He was in that house, a house she didn't know, and he wasn't coming out. According to Albert, Gordon had a house in Upper Marlboro. God, how could he do this to her?

"Well? Is she all right?" Lorna asked.

"You made me mess up." Albert let go of Katrina's wrist. "I guess she's okay; she's awake."

"What happened?" Katrina sat up with Albert and Lorna's help.

"You blacked out, Ma. Are you all right?"

"Hell no."

"Get her some water," Albert said.

"I don't want any damn water. Get me a ginger ale and an Alka Seltzer—I feel queasy."

"Actually, Mrs. Dawson, you need some food in your stomach. I'll call down for room service. What would you like?"

"An Alka Seltzer and a ginger ale."

"Mrs. Dawson, the bile in your stomach has got to be eating you up. You were up most of the night damning Gordon to hell, ranting about your sister, bitching about Joan, whom I really wouldn't be blaming and—"

"Why not? She calls herself married to my husband."

"Yeah, but she couldn't be calling herself married to Gordon if he didn't marry her. And your sister, you should be glad she's coming. You need help here. Joan isn't going to deal with you alone. She'll have her family and her attorneys. You should probably get an attorney yourself, but for now, if you don't eat something, you won't be able to take care of business later if you're fainting every two minutes."

"Ma, Albert's right. You should eat something, and I'm glad Aunt Celeste is coming."

"You would be." Katrina let herself fall limply back onto the bed. She didn't have the energy to curse Lorna out about Celeste.

No way in hell did she want Celeste in her business, and if she could have stretched her arms across state lines, she would have strangled both her parents for sending Celeste to Washington. Celeste was the last person she wanted or needed to see on top of the headache and runaround she was getting from the hospital because of the road blocks Joan had already begun to put in place. She certainly didn't need Celeste to complicate her life any further.

Last night after she slammed the telephone down on her parents for the third time, she wanted to stick her head out of the window and scream at the top of her lungs, but the hotel windows were unopenable. She'd gone into the bathroom instead, turned on the shower, and screamed until she felt her own heart racing inside her chest, and a sharp pain at the back of her neck. Then came the light-headedness that blackened her mind and her eyes. That was the first time in her life she'd ever blacked out. This morning was the second. Maybe she did need to eat something.

Albert sat on the side of the bed. "Mrs. Dawson, you're letting yourself get too worked up."

"That's a stupid thing to say, Albert. You'd be upset, too, if you found out your husband was a bigamist and he'd just had a baby with that other woman."

"You might be right about that, but I wouldn't be wasting my energy throwing hissie fits and not taking care of myself. You need to channel your energies in a more direct, more positive way and not scatter them all over the universe. Nothing is getting accomplished here."

Katrina raised her head and looked at Albert. "Where are you from?"

"California. Why?"

"Figures." Katrina's head flopped back onto the pillow. She closed her eyes as much to rest them as to block out Albert's cosmic babble. "Lorna, call room service and order me anything with chicken. You know what I like. No fries. A salad on the side and don't forget the ginger ale and the Alka Seltzer."

"They're probably still serving breakfast; it's only ten forty-five," Albert said.

"I don't want breakfast. Lorna, order the chicken. The hotel probably has a twenty-four-hour menu, and make that two ginger ales, and see if they have any kind of antacid tablets. Order something for yourself, and . . . oh, Albert, too."

"I had a big breakfast before leaving home this morning."

"Lorna, order from the outer room. I need to speak to Albert."

"I know you're just getting rid of me," Lorna said, "but it's cool. Albert, tell me what she says."

Albert smiled. He and Lorna had become fast friends.

"Close the door," Katrina said.

As soon as the door was closed, Albert asked, "What do you want to know?"

Katrina sat up. "More about you."

"You know my name, you know that I worked with Gordon, you know we were friends. What else do you need to know?"

"Why are you helping me?"

"Gordon was my friend."

"Yes, but maybe he would have wanted you to help Joan. You knew her, not me."

"True, but I always thought Gordon was wrong for marrying Joan. Don't get me wrong, Joan is a nice enough person, but she has funny ways I could never get with."

"Like?" Katrina asked. She wanted the dirt.

"Well, she didn't like me hanging around and would tell Gordon that I was bad for his image."

"Oh, so you being gay was not acceptable in her circle?"

"Joan is a Yallie. She works for the Department of State and thinks she's all that; image is everything."

Katrina digested Joan's resumé on a sour stomach. She wanted to throw up. Gordon's body had to be released to her—she needed to know that his ass was roasting. "I would think marrying a married man, a black man at that, would be bad for that perfect image of hers."

Lorna opened the bedroom door. She stood listening.

"Oh, the black man part wasn't a problem. Gordon was well-received."

"Probably because of his job and his title."

"Perhaps," Albert said, "but the married man part is definitely a problem."

"Yeah, she was married to a bigamist."

"Which is why I'm thinking that Joan may not have known, which works in your favor. Joan is not going to want anyone to know that she was married to a bigamist, so she probably won't give you too hard a time."

"Like I'm worried about that. Her dumb ass needs to be exposed."

"But, Ma," Lorna said, standing in the doorway. "Suppose Joan didn't know Daddy was married?"

Albert answered, "Then your father wronged her, too. Although I must tell you, I'm not altogether convinced that she didn't know."

"And why is that?" Katrina asked.

"Well, several months after Gordon and Joan were married, Joan found a picture of you and your kids in Gordon's wallet. She questioned Gordon, and he said you were his ex-wife. Keep in mind, at this point, supposedly, Joan didn't know there had been a first Mrs. Dawson. This is when Gordon convinced her he was divorced."

"And she bought it?"

"She stayed with him."

"Stupid. I would have had a private detective on his behind so fast I'd know the next time he wiped his ass."

"She was a newlywed, Mrs. Dawson. She was in love."

"No, her ass was in denial, but enough about her. I'm tired of talking about her." Katrina looked at Lorna. "I thought you were ordering."

"I am. I wanted to know if you wanted dessert?"

"No, and close the door."

Alone with Albert again, Katrina said, "You didn't answer my question. Why are you still here?"

Albert got off the bed. "Are you saying I've outstayed my welcome?"

"Sit down, I didn't say that. In fact, I'm grateful you've been helping me, but I'm curious. Albert, how close were you and Gordon? And to be blunt, were you more than just friends?"

"Why would you ask such a question?"

"Need you ask? After finding out about another so-called wife, I think the question has to be asked. So?"

Turning his body sideways to face Katrina, Albert crossed his legs. "Actually, maybe I shouldn't be surprised you asked."

"So what's the answer?"

Slightly tilting his head, Albert looked unblinkingly into Katrina's eyes. He had told himself if she asked about his relationship with Gordon, he'd lie, but now he wasn't so sure.

A flash of heat crept up Katrina's neck onto her cheeks.

"Gordon and I, we—"

"Never mind. I don't wanna hear it."

"It only happened once. I swear, just once."

On the other side of the door Lorna stood frozen with her hands covering her mouth.

"Oh, God," Katrina said. "Once, twice, it doesn't matter. Gordon slept with you!"

"Gordon was curious. After that one time, it—"

"You're disgusting!" Katrina shot up off the bed. "He's disgusting. I wanna kill him. I hate him, I hate him!"

Lorna's tears fell onto her hands still covering her mouth.

Albert uncomfortably tugged on his left earlobe. He said softly, "I should have never said anything."

"Oh, God! Oh, God!" Katrina gasped for air. Tears filled her eyes. She snatched one of the pillows off the bed and flung it across the room. She couldn't understand how her marriage to Gordon had been a lie for so long. His vows meant nothing.

Albert thought Katrina was throwing the pillow at him. He had ducked. Still, he was watchful of Katrina as she took off prowling wildly around the room.

"What the hell is going on?" Katrina pressed her hands to her aching head. "Who the hell was Gordon Dawson? How could I be married to a man for twenty damn years and not know he was a faggot? Why didn't I see that he was capable of having such disregard, such disrespect for me and his children that he'd lie, cheat, commit adultery with men and women? I hate him! I hate him!"

Lorna quietly opened the door to the bedroom. She had dried

her eyes, but her timid presence told Albert and Katrina that she had heard everything.

"Don't hate your father, Lorna. It was only once."

"Don't talk to her!" Katrina grabbed Lorna, holding her, clutching her with all her might.

Lorna hugged Katrina just as tight, letting her cry herself out.

Again tugging on his ear, Albert hated that Lorna had to learn about her father's deceptions from him.

Katrina's arms suddenly fell from around Lorna and dangled at her sides as she began to sink to the floor. Albert and Lorna both caught Katrina and helped her to the bed. The floodgate of tears that Katrina had slammed shut since hearing of Gordon's betrayal gushed open with a plaintive wail, tearing at her throat, scaring Lorna.

"Ma, you don't have to cry over what Daddy's done. He's gone. He can't lie to you anymore."

Katrina couldn't hear Lorna; she was lost somewhere in a dark pit of despair.

CHAPTER
18

Lord, please, give me the strength to deal with Katrina's mess and mine, too. With the hope that God was listening, Celeste let the elevator door close on the fourth floor, the floor her room was on, and pushed the button for the seventh floor. She had gone to her room to drop off her luggage, but she hadn't sat down for fear she'd procrastinate about meeting with Katrina. *One more thing, Lord. Please let Katrina be civil, because if she's not, I'm liable to kick her ass.*

Celeste glanced down at the large manila envelope in her hand as she prepared to get off the elevator. She couldn't help wondering if the angst she was feeling since the plane lifted off from LaGuardia was a warning of trouble. That angst settled on her like a bad cold, filling her chest and head with anxiety as thick as mucus, leaving her stuffy and irritable. In the seconds it took for her to get to room 723, she hadn't figured out an immediate cure for her apprehension beyond turning and high-tailing it back to Brooklyn, but she hadn't come all that way to run like a scared rabbit. Taking a deep breath, Celeste knocked at Katrina's hotel room.

The door opened right away. "Oh, you must be Mrs. Dawson's sister," Albert said.

"Yes, I—" Celeste could hear Katrina crying out, "I hate him! I hate him!"

"Come in." Albert opened the door wider. "I'm Albert Waterman."

Celeste had expected that Katrina would be upset, angry, bitter, but crying? Celeste hadn't prepared herself for that. She glanced around the room. Katrina had a small suite. She was back in the bedroom crying, "Why is this shit happening to me?"

"Has something else happened?" Celeste asked.

"Maybe you should just go on into the bedroom."

The last thing Celeste wanted to see was Katrina in the broken-down, tearful state she was in—she had never seen her so. *God, give me strength.* The sight of Lorna and Katrina sitting on the bed with Lorna holding Katrina's head in her lap, stroking her hair while they both cried, threw Celeste for an unexpected emotional loop. There was a tiny stinging in her nose. Going on into the room, she went to Lorna and immediately began to rub her back. She kissed her on the forehead.

"Oh, Aunt Celeste." Lorna slumped against Celeste, crying.

Hearing Celeste's name, Katrina sat up. She turned her face away and tried to get control of herself, wiping hastily at tears that defied being wiped away. Like the ache in her soul, Katrina's tears could not be shut off. In the presence of the sister she despised, Katrina cried deep, painful sobs that tore at her throat and closed her eyes.

Comforting Lorna was easy to do, but doing the same for Katrina was foreign to Celeste. Still, she had to do something. Getting Lorna to move over, Celeste sat between the two. She put an arm around Katrina and an arm around Lorna, drawing them both close. While Katrina wanted to pull away, she had no strength. Like her daughter, she slumped against Celeste and let her sister's unfamiliar embrace remind her that she wasn't alone.

"We'll get through this, Katrina. Don't worry. Everything's gonna be all right." At least Celeste prayed that all would turn out as she said—all right. But she prayed also that she could shoulder the weight of Katrina's and her own problems without crumpling under the strain. She had never been down this road before.

CHAPTER
19

In the twenty minutes since she stopped crying, Katrina had spent much of that time in the bathroom where she splashed cold water on her face, first to cool down, and then once she got a good look at herself, to lessen the puffiness around her eyes and nose. The tap water wasn't cold enough to do any good, and the wet washcloth pressed to her eyes did little to get rid of the redness. What did it matter, and who the hell was she trying to look good for anyway? She dropped the washcloth into the sink, took a seat on the closed toilet bowl, and began staring at the bathroom door through which she'd eventually have to go. As hard as she tried, Katrina couldn't quell the quiver in her gut or muster the courage to face Celeste. She had never wanted Celeste to see her this weak, this beat down.

"Katrina, may I come in?" Celeste asked from the other side of the door.

Damn! Katrina wanted so badly to vanish into thin air.

"Ma, you all right?" Lorna asked.

"Would you stop asking me that? Hell no, I'm not all right, and I'm not going to be all right for a hell of a long time."

"Dang, Ma, I was just askin'."

"Katrina, she's concerned about you. Can we come in?"

Katrina tightly crossed her legs and folded her arms. She grumbled, "Can I stop you?"

"Ma!"

"Damnit, come in!"

Celeste entered the small bathroom as cautiously as a mouse enters an unfamiliar room. Lorna was close behind. Albert stayed outside the bathroom door.

Katrina kept her eyes lowered, but Celeste didn't have to look into Katrina's eyes to see her shame or her embarrassment; she felt it. Wasn't this the state of her own existence? "Lorna, maybe you should let your mother and me talk alone."

"No. Lorna knows what's going on. I need her here."

Lorna settled back against the sink.

Katrina fixed her eyes on Albert's woven tassel slip-on tan loafers. "Close the door," she said, speaking to no one in particular. She didn't care who closed the door as long as the door was closed.

"I got it," Albert said, "but, Mrs. Dawson, you and I need to speak further. It's imperative."

Katrina turned her head toward the wall. She had no intention of ever speaking to Albert again.

"Ma."

"Close the door."

Celeste wondered about the dynamics between Katrina and Albert Waterman.

"I'll be out here if you need me." Albert pulled the door closed.

"Ma, how come you gotta be like that?"

"Lorna, I'm worried about you. You're too trusting of people."

"I just don't judge people."

"I give up." Katrina couldn't help but shake her head. The rose-colored glasses Lorna was born wearing didn't come from her. Sure, she had sense enough to know she shouldn't be angry with Albert—he wasn't her husband; he owed her nothing—but just knowing that he stuck his . . . Wait, maybe it was the other way around. Maybe Gordon stuck his . . . *Oh, God!* Grimacing, Katrina shivered at the thought of Gordon and Albert doing whatever it was they did and then Gordon having the nerve to crawl into her bed in between his sexual romps with Albert and with his white wife. How messed up was that? Now she was going to have to get herself checked. God knew what else or who else Gordon had been doing.

Celeste felt as if she'd entered a room where everyone was speaking in code, leaving her out of the conversation.

"Ma, Aunt Celeste thinks we should call a lawyer."

Who gives a damn what Celeste thinks? Katrina steadied her gaze on Lorna while her mind's eye was on Celeste. *How in the world did Mom and Dad get Celeste to come to Washington? Oh, wait a minute. Maybe it wasn't difficult after all. Maybe Celeste is here to gloat. Yeah, that's it. Damn, payback certainly is an ugly bitch!*

Celeste sat on the side of the foot-high bathtub with her knees up in her chest. *I should have told Mother and Dad to go to hell. I should have taken Justine and hauled my ass back to Brooklyn.*

"Ma, shouldn't we call a lawyer?"

"I don't know." Katrina was too tired and too angry to think strategy.

"But we can't let that woman think she's Daddy's real wife."

"That's not going to happen," Celeste said. "Katrina, I brought all the proof you need to verify that you're married to Gordon. Oh, and before I left home, I went on the Internet and pulled down some information on the bigamy laws in the United States, and in particular in New York, D.C., and Maryland. I have that material with me, too. I think you'll find the antibigamy laws are quite interesting. For instance—"

"The last thing I need is an armchair lawyer who got a crash course in antibigamy laws off the Internet."

Celeste felt the sting of Katrina's rebuff, but then, what had she expected? Katrina was never going to pat her on the back and say, "Job well done."

"Ma, maybe what Aunt Celeste found can help—"

"Lorna, if Celeste had all the answers, people would stop going to law school."

"You're right, Katrina," Celeste said. "You should get a real lawyer, one who's been to a real law school. But first, we need to go to the hospital to see if we can get something done on our own. If not, then we should think about contacting the District Attorney's Office here in Washington to—"

"What for?" Katrina still would not look at Celeste. "The District Attorney's Office is for criminal matters."

"Bigamy *is* a criminal matter, Katrina. In fact, in most states, it's a felony."

"I knew that."

"Ma—"

"But there is a problem," Katrina continued. "The last time I checked, the *criminal* was dead. Who are we supposed to be filing a complaint against, Gordon's ghost?"

"Look, I'm not about to pretend I know exactly what to do, but something legal needs to be done, which is why we need to consult an attorney before Gordon's second wife—"

"Correction! *That* woman is not his wife."

"Okay, but *that* woman probably has papers just like you, which is why you should file before she gets a chance to—that is, if she hasn't done so already. Katrina, you need to be the one initiating the investigation."

Should . . . need. You're not my mother!

"You do not want to be shut out of any of the findings that the DA's office comes up with. The second wife can file also, but I don't think she'll be able to exclude you from anything she's doing."

"How do you know?" Katrina shifted sideways on the toilet seat to face Celeste. "You don't know what the DA's procedure is."

A warning bell went off in Celeste's head. She could see the scorn in Katrina's eyes and hear the agitation in her voice. She looked at Lorna, but it was to Katrina she spoke. "I guess I don't really know for sure. We're brainstorming here, right?"

"That's right," Lorna agreed. "Right, Ma?"

"Celeste seems to be the only one brainstorming," Katrina said.

"Then you tell me, Katrina, what should you be doing?"

"How the hell do I know? I've never had to deal with this bull-shit before."

"And neither have I, which is why I believe the DA's office is our best bet if we want to keep that other woman from claiming Gordon's body."

The tightness across Katrina's shoulders began to ache. "Albert said this Joan person may already have an attorney, and that attorney probably has friends in the DA's office, which might well be a problem for me."

"Yeah, 'cause some people stick together," Lorna said sarcastically.

"Let's not assume, Katrina." Celeste said. "Attorneys, friends, it doesn't matter. None of them can stop you from filing a complaint. I think you should file the complaint, claim Gordon's body so that you can arrange for the burial, and be the one to receive the death certificate. And, Katrina, you will need that death certificate to lay claim to anything Gordon has."

"I know that! You act like I don't know a damn thing!"

"Ma! Aunt Celeste—"

"Who put you in charge of my damn life, Celeste? I didn't. I don't even want you here!"

"Ma, truce out. Aunt—"

"Shut up, Lorna! I'm not talking to you!"

Lorna's bottom lip shot out as her arms wrapped tightly around her body.

Celeste stood. "I didn't come here for this shit."

"You didn't have to come at all."

"Ma, you wrong! Until Aunt Celeste got here, all you was doing was bitchin' and cryin'. Aunt Celeste is tryin' to help you. How come you don't let her?"

Celeste laid her hand lightly on Lorna's arm. "Lorna, your mother doesn't need my help, and I don't need the aggravation. I'm going home."

"Maaa!" Lorna said reproachfully, holding Celeste back from leaving. "Would you please be nice?"

"Damnit, Lorna! I'm your mother; you're not mine. Stop telling me what to do." Katrina flopped forward, resting her elbows on her knees. She started massaging the back of her neck.

"I ain't trying to be your mother, Ma. But you wrong. You keep jumping all over us. I'm used to you, but Albert ain't. He didn't do nothing to you, and neither did Aunt Celeste. Man!"

Katrina could not believe that she was sitting on a toilet in a hotel room being scolded by her damn daughter and being forced to listen to Celeste tell her how to solve her problem. Life was such a bitch.

"Ma."

Katrina wouldn't lift her head.

"Ma!" Lorna shouted, forcing Katrina to look up. With her eyes, Lorna tried to tell Katrina to say something to Celeste.

Holding her lips tight, Katrina rolled her eyes away from Lorna. The moment was irritably tense in the small, white-tiled bathroom. Celeste read clearly the plea to stay in Lorna's eyes, but she wasn't about to hang around if Katrina was going to dump on her every chance she got. Celeste put her hand on the doorknob.

Lorna clutched Celeste's arm tighter. "Aunt Celeste, please don't leave."

Lorna's firm hold told Celeste how desperately Lorna wanted her to stay. At that moment, she told herself she'd try to hang in there for Lorna. Besides, she hadn't come all that way to let Katrina's nastiness send her running with her tail tucked. She was there, so she may as well stay. Letting go of the doorknob, she briefly squeezed Lorna's hand just before she again sat on the side of the tub. It crossed her mind that perhaps she was a bit of a masochist.

"Ma, you okay?" Lorna began to massage Katrina's shoulders.

Letting her hands drop from her neck, Katrina took a minute to allow Lorna's hands to relax the muscles in her neck and shoulders.

"Okay, Aunt Celeste, what should I do?"

Oh, no, sweetie. It won't be me telling you what to do, especially not in front of your mother. "It's up to your mother. Whatever she wants you to do is on her."

"Ma, what do you want me to do?"

"Give me a minute. I'll think of something."

"Yeah, 'cause this is a family matter. We got to all do something, right?"

It was obvious to Celeste that Lorna had been speaking to her grandparents.

Katrina couldn't wait for Patrice to get there. Lorna was driving her insane. Lorna was weak just like her father. She was easily fooled, so unlike Patrice. Patrice was headstrong and determined. Patrice didn't like Celeste and would have gotten Celeste out of there so fast her head would still be spinning.

"Ma, we can all work together, right?" Lorna continued massaging Katrina's shoulder. She stopped when she heard the knock on the hotel door. "That's probably room service. Ma, you need to eat something."

Katrina didn't bother to look up or respond.

"Aunt Celeste, Ma hasn't eaten anything since we got here." Lorna opened the bathroom door just as Albert was signing for the food.

"Go set up the food," Celeste said. "We'll be out in a minute."

"Okay." Lorna was mindful to softly close the door behind her.

Neither Katrina nor Celeste had words to begin the discussion that was inevitable. Katrina closed her eyes and tried to will away the stiffness in her neck. God, how she wished she could tell Gordon to his face how much she hated him.

Celeste's behind was starting to burn from sitting on the hard, narrow porcelain. She tried squeezing her butt cheeks together and holding them to relieve the burn, but that didn't work. She felt strange pumping her ass up and down, so grunting once, she pushed herself up off the tub. She squeezed her cheeks as tight as she could before letting go. *Whew!*

It was obvious to Katrina that Celeste was uncomfortable in the bathroom with nowhere to sit, but she wasn't ready to go out into the room and look at Albert. For the moment, staying in the bathroom with Celeste was the lesser of the two evils, although she had no desire to be with either.

Celeste glimpsed herself in the bathroom mirror. Boy, did her face look gaunt. *Damn, how much weight did I lose?* Through the mirror she could see that Katrina was looking at her.

"I see you still like looking at yourself."

"Don't you? At least you used to."

Katrina sneered and looked away.

On the other side of the door, both Lorna and Albert had their heads pressed to the door.

"Look, Katrina. I know you don't want me here, and it goes without saying I didn't want to be here. We can both thank our bossy, manipulative parents for finagling me into coming here, but they are right about one thing—we both have problems, just that yours is more pressing at the moment."

Katrina mumbled, "I wouldn't be so smug."

"Damnit, Katrina, don't start! I didn't come here for this pettiness."

"I didn't ask you to come."

"Hey, if you want me to leave, just say so. I know how to get to the airport."

Goddamnit, go! Itching as she was to tell Celeste to get the hell out, Katrina didn't say so. "Why did you come? And don't tell me it was because Mom bullied you."

"Well, that would be the truth. But look, Katrina, I'm not here to fight with you. I'm here to do whatever you need me to do to get Gordon's body released. However it's done, we need to try and get along to get it done. We don't have to kiss each other's ass, but we certainly don't have to kill each other either. For both our sakes and Lorna's, and as she's said, we have to truce out so that we can attend to the business at hand. Can we try and do this peacefully?"

For a very tense, breath-holding moment, Celeste and Katrina locked eyes. Celeste refused to blink first.

Katrina sat back. *I can't stand to look at you; how am I going to work with you?* "If you stay, you stay because you want to."

I could kill Mother and Dad!

"I don't need you here telling me what to do."

"I'm not—"

"I'm not stupid, nor am I so distraught that I can't think for myself. I . . ."

"Katrina, I didn't say any of that."

"can take care of this bullshit that Gordon dumped on me without . . ."

Celeste threw up her hands. "I'll never learn."

"your supercilious, know-it-all attitude lording it over me."

"Oh, the hell with this. I won't put myself through this."

"Then don't. I don't need you looking down your nose at me, thinking that you're better because your husband didn't do something so underhanded to you. Oh, then again, Willie did do something just as bad. He died getting his last fuck on."

Celeste could see herself ramming her fist in Katrina's ugly mouth. The only thing stopping her was the good sense she was born with. She yanked the bathroom door open, startling Albert and Lorna. "You know something, Katrina? I don't blame Gordon for marrying another woman behind your back. Being married to you must have been a nightmare."

"Fuck you!" Katrina shouted at Celeste's back.

"Aunt Celeste! Aunt Celeste, don't go!" Lorna caught Celeste before she could get out of the suite. "My mother's really upset. She—"

"She's her same old *sweet* self."

Albert stood aside, quietly watching. Like Lorna, he'd heard Celeste and Katrina's brief but contentious discussion which didn't surprise him. Gordon had told him that Katrina's mouth and attitude were as nasty as a junkyard dog.

"Aunt Celeste, she didn't mean what she said. Please, don't go."

"Lorna, I love you dearly, but your mother and I will never be able to work together."

"Yes, y'all can. Y'all just gotta cool out and forget that y'all got issues."

"Yeah, that's a good way of putting it. Lorna, I have my own issues, and being treated like a hated stepchild by your mother isn't what I need right now. I'm going back to New York."

"Please, Aunt Celeste. Just wait one minute. Pleeeze!"

"Don't beg, Lorna." Celeste and Lorna had always gotten along in spite of the bad relationship that she and Katrina shared. How had someone as nasty as Katrina given birth to such a sweet child, or sweet children—Gordy was an angel, too. Neither had ever acted ugly toward her because of the nasty things they had to have heard Katrina say about her. Patrice, on the other hand, was Katrina through and through. Even as a small child, Patrice would never speak whenever they did meet and would suck her teeth and roll her eyes if Celeste dared speak to her. It was obvious that Patrice was influenced by Katrina. She was moody like Katrina and definitely had a touch of Katrina's evilness in her, but that had never bothered Celeste; she didn't have to be around her.

"Aunt Celeste, can you wait till I talk to my mother? Just a minute, okay?"

Relenting, Celeste said, "You get one minute." She let Lorna pull her to a chair and practically push her down into it. Katrina was getting one last chance.

"Albert, talk to my aunt, okay? I'll be right back." Lorna marched into the bathroom, slamming the door behind her. Katrina was at the sink running her fingers through her damp hair from splashing water on her face. Through the mirror, she looked at Lorna.

"Now what?"

"Ma, why you gotta go get nasty with Aunt Celeste? She came here to help us."

"Did she say I got nasty with her?"

"I'm not deaf, Ma. I heard what you said."

"You're never gonna pay attention to what I say about her, are you?"

"Not when you're wrong."

Katrina narrowed her eyes threateningly. "I keep telling you, Lorna, I'm not one of your little girlfriends. Watch your mouth."

Although she stood only a few feet from Katrina, Lorna didn't fear being that close. "Ma, you act like Aunt Celeste is your worst er emy when she's not. That woman Daddy married is who you need to be fightin'. Aunt Celeste—"

"Lorna, this is none of your business. You need to get outta my face—"

"It is my business, Ma! My father just died and my mother is actin' like she's bingeing on a quaalude-crack cocktail. Ma—"

"What do you know about quaaludes and crack, Lorna? Are you doing drugs?"

"No, but you act like you do."

Katrina raised her hand. "Girl, I'll—"

Lorna flinched, but she wasn't silenced. "Ma! You been buggin'. Nobody can talk to you."

Katrina lowered her hand.

"C'mon, Ma. You've been messed up ever since you found out what Daddy did. That's why we need Aunt Celeste here. She's calm, she's smart, and—"

"What am I, stupid?"

"See, Ma, there you go again. This ain't about who's smarter, you or Aunt Celeste. This is about how are you gonna handle your business when you're so upset? Aunt Celeste could help you talk to those people. She's a lot calmer than you are right now."

"You're calm, Lorna. Aren't you going to help me? You, me, and Patrice—when she gets here—can do whatever needs to be done. We don't need Celeste."

"Ma, you trippin'. I can't help you and neither can Patrice, at least not in the way you talkin' about. Yeah, me and Patrice can go up to that woman's house and beat her down, but we can't make her get up offa Daddy's house or whatever else she got that's his, 'cause she know we're just kids and she's not gonna take us serious. Plus, I know me and Patrice are too young to do a lot of other stuff you gotta do. We can't go to a lawyer. We can't go to those people at the hospital. Ma, I'm tellin' you, you need Aunt Celeste to watch your back or you're gonna get burned in all this."

Leaning on the sink, Katrina let her head drop forward, her chin to her collarbone. As much as she hated to admit it, Lorna was right, and so were her parents. She did need a second set of ears, eyes, and hands to get through this mess.

"Ma, you gotta let Aunt Celeste help you. You gotta be nice to her."

Katrina reluctantly raised her head. "I didn't say anything really mean to Celeste. She's just sensitive about how Willie died."

Lorna gave Katrina a knowing look. "Ma."

"Well, I spoke the truth."

"Ma, I heard you say Uncle Willie was gettin' his last—"

"Don't you dare say it."

"See, Ma. You know you wrong. You need to get up offa Uncle Willie 'cause Daddy did much worse. He married that woman and got a new baby behind your back."

"Don't remind me. Where's Celeste?"

"She's in the front room. Should I tell her you wanna talk to her?"

"No. What you can do is tell Albert to leave. I can't look at him and deal with Celeste, too. I might throw up."

"Dang, Ma, it's not Albert's fault what Daddy did. Daddy—"

"I don't wanna hear it. Tell him, Lorna, or I will. And I guarantee you, you won't like the way I tell him to get the hell outta here."

Lorna didn't waste time thinking about what Katrina meant. "I'll tell him to come back later."

"No. Tell him we'll call if we need him, which I doubt."

"But, Ma, Albert's been good to us, and you said—"

"I know what I said, Lorna, but that was before I . . . Look, just get rid of him, or—"

"Okay . . . okay." Lorna hurried out of the bathroom.

In the mirror, Katrina saw the tiredness in her own eyes. Lorna was right—Gordon was to blame for this whole ugly mess, not Celeste. It was Gordon who had deceived her, and it was his death that exposed him. Balling up her fist, Katrina brought it down hard on the sink, hurting herself. As God was her witness, she was going to see Gordon's ass burned to ashes. The bastard!

Lorna stuck her head in the bathroom. "Ma, a lady named Miss Woodard is calling from the hospital. She wants to speak to you."

"It's about time." Katrina was ready. At least she hoped she was.

CHAPTER
20

If Katrina didn't have the good sense to be embarrassed for herself, Celeste did. She was plenty embarrassed for the both of them. Neither Mr. Mortimer, the hospital's legal counsel, nor Miss Woodward, the hospital administrator, could look Katrina in the eye for more than a hot second before they'd have to look away. Who could blame them? It had to be unsettling to have to speak to a wife, a widow at that, about the adulterously clandestine behavior of her husband. This, too, Celeste knew about first hand. Miss Woodward, in particular, seemed to be more comfortable talking to her. Humph, if she only knew. Detective Vaughan had a hard time looking her in the eye when he had to talk about Willie's last hour with whomever he was with—perhaps he didn't want her to see the pity in his eyes. As long as Detective Vaughan didn't have to talk about that part of the investigation, he could look her in the eye. But unlike Detective Vaughan, Mr. Mortimer and Miss Woodward had been eager to get out of the room, away from Katrina.

"Ma, what you think is taking them so long to come back?"

Celeste had been wondering the very same thing herself. Miss Woodward and Mr. Mortimer had taken Katrina's original papers—they didn't want the copies—and gone, they said, ". . . to consult with other counsel."

"Who knows. But, what I do know is that they had better bring back all of my papers."

Celeste had tried to say very little so as not to irritate Katrina, but the overly long absence of the administrator was worrying her as well. "I wonder if they're meeting with the attorneys for Gordon's other wife?"

"Yeah, Ma. What if they are. I wonder what they're saying?"

"I can tell you that," Katrina volunteered. "They're saying that Gordon was a low-life, toe-sucking, bigamistic bastard."

Frowning, Lorna dropped her gaze. She began picking deliberately at a hangnail on her left thumb. Her trembling chin signaled how close to tears she was, and to Celeste, that was understandable—this situation had to be painful for her. Especially having to stand with her mother against the father she'd adored. Celeste could only wonder if Katrina had allowed Lorna to shed a single tear for Gordon. Katrina's anger, Celeste understood also—she was living that nightmare herself. But Katrina should be cognizant of Lorna's conflicted feelings about Gordon. Bigamist or not, Gordon was forever Lorna's father.

Celeste patted Lorna on the arm. "Would you like something to drink?"

"Oh, please!" Katrina exclaimed, noticing Lorna's long face. "Girl, I know you're not upset about what I said. Your father wasn't Pope John Paul, and you know that. He was a liar, a cheater, an asshole of a bisexual bigamist who apparently cared very little for me and even less for the children he had with me. How else do you explain the lie he lived? If he cared about you, Lorna, if he loved you or Gordy or Patrice, he would not have put any of you in this god-awful situation."

Lorna sniffled, but said not a word, while Celeste couldn't hold still.

"You're right, Katrina, but go a little easy with what you say in front of Lorna."

"Don't tell me what I should or shouldn't say around my daughter!" Katrina glanced back at the door. She lowered her voice. "Whether you like it or not, I am not censoring a single, damn word I have to say about Gordon. Gordon was scum. I have to deal with it, and so do my kids."

"Yes, but be a little more sensitive to—"

"I got this, Celeste. I can mother my daughter without your help." Katrina took a tissue from her pocketbook. "Lorna, sit back, dry your eyes, and never, ever shed another tear for a man, any man, who doesn't give a good goddamn about you. You are never to trust any man unless you can carry his penis around with you in your pocketbook and reattach it when you want him to use it. Do you hear me?"

I know that's right, Celeste almost said out loud.

Lorna sat back. She dried her eyes, but she didn't look at Katrina or Celeste. She fixed her gaze on nothing in particular on Miss Woodward's desk while she tried to pull herself together.

Celeste thought of the irony of the moment. She and Katrina were actually in agreement about something—those were the exact reasons she hadn't shed a tear over Willie. Yet, she would never bad mouth Willie in front of Justine. Justine could never fully understand her mother's anger at her father, and although Lorna was older, it would be a while yet before she would fully understand, too. Plus, Celeste had to be cognizant of raising a young woman who wouldn't be biased against men based on her mother's bad experience, so she could never let her anger at Willie taint Justine.

"Where the hell are they?" Katrina sprang out of her chair. "Somebody had better get in here and tell me something. This is ridiculous." She began to pace with her arms folded high and tight across her chest. "I'm the legal wife. What else do they need to prove that?"

While Lorna slumped in her chair and went back to pulling on her hangnail, Celeste watched Katrina angrily prowl like a lion with a thorn stuck up its ass. It seemed she was born with that thorn up her ass. Celeste couldn't fathom how she and Katrina could be so different in their attitudes, their temperaments, their personalities, yet end up in the same marital bed of infidelity, and in the same hole of darkness about who their husbands really were. How in the world had that happened? In essence, how had they ended up with the same man? Both were as two-faced as a double-sided quarter. *Hell, if a woman can't trust the man she sleeps with and bears children for, who can she trust?*

"That's it!" Katrina flung her pocketbook over her shoulder. "I'm outta here."

Celeste and Lorna hurried to catch up with Katrina, who had bolted from Miss Woodward's private office into the outer office area where her secretary sat. The middle-aged woman's gray-green eyes were as big as saucers as she stared up at Katrina suddenly looming above her. Her red blotchy cheeks stood out on her peach pale skin.

"Call your boss and tell her I want my papers, I want my husband's body released to me, and I want outta here—now."

"She . . . Miss Woodward will be back at any moment."

"I do not have one more moment to spare. I've been sitting in that office for nearly an hour, waiting, with no word from a living soul as to what's going on. I've had it. Where is Miss Woodward, and where the hell are my papers?"

"Ah, Mrs. Dawson, Miss Woodward will be right with you. She—"

"Where is she?"

The secretary picked up the telephone. "I'll—"

"No! Just tell me where she is. I will go to her."

"Mrs. Dawson, if—"

"Point me in the direction your boss went. I will find her myself. I'll be damned if—"

"Katrina!" Celeste pulled Katrina aside. "You're not getting anywhere like this."

"Don't pull on me!" Katrina yanked her arm free.

The secretary quickly punched in an extension.

"Katrina, you have got to calm down."

"No the hell I don't! I'm tired of this. I want my papers, I want Gordon's rusty-ass body, and I want out of this hospital. These people have been giving me the runaround ever since I got to Washington. It ends now, Celeste, and if you're planning on being more of a hindrance to me than a help, then I don't need you here."

"Tell me something I don't know, Katrina. But I'm telling you, getting loud and being impatient won't get this settled any faster. We have to wait and see what these people can do."

"No *we* don't. You and Lorna can go back to the hotel. I am going to settle this today, come hell or high water."

"Ma, chill. We're staying. So calm down."

The secretary finished talking on the telephone. "Mrs. Dawson, Miss Woodward will be right here."

Katrina set her face in a stern mask of contempt.

"Thank you," Celeste said to the secretary. "Katrina, let's go sit down."

Ignoring Celeste, Katrina headed for the hallway. She was too angry and too hyped to sit.

"This situation has been very trying," Celeste said to the secretary before following behind Lorna. She stepped out into the hallway in time to see Katrina barreling down on Miss Woodward, who had just stepped outside of an office a distance down the hall.

"Oh, shoot." Celeste took off at a trot.

"I couldn't stop her," Lorna said as she and Celeste scampered after Katrina.

"Where are my papers?"

Miss Woodward pulled the door to the office she had exited closed behind her. "Mrs. Dawson, we have your papers. If you'll—"

"I want my papers—*now!*"

"Mrs. Dawson—"

"Are they in there?" Katrina pushed past Miss Woodward into the office.

"Mrs. Dawson, please! We—"

"Oh! So this is what's going on." Katrina now understood the long wait. Seated in the office was the woman—Joan—she had seen the first day at the hospital. With her were two white men who looked as if they ran a Fortune 500 company or something. Mr. Mortimer sat stiffly behind his desk. All eyes were on Katrina.

Celeste and Lorna slipped into the office before Miss Woodward could close them out.

"I get it," Katrina said. "She gets to see my papers, but I don't get to see hers."

Mr. Mortimer stood. "Mrs. Dawson, we were about to—"

"So this is how the game is to be played? Me in the dark, *her* in the know."

"I'm Joan Dawson," Joan said, standing. "I—"

"You think you are." Katrina never looked Joan's way. "Where are my papers?"

Joan exchanged an uneasy glance with the older man next to her as she sat again.

"They're right here." Mr. Mortimer gathered up the papers and started around the desk. "Mrs. Dawson, we had to compare the papers and make some calls to—"

"To prove their authenticity?" Katrina snatched the papers from Mr. Mortimer's hand. "Believe me, these papers are very, very real." She checked the papers to see that they were all there and unaltered. "Just as my children are."

"I didn't know about you," Joan said softly.

Katrina ignored her. She continued checking her papers.

Curious, Celeste crept farther into the room until she had a better view of Joan. She studied her. Joan could not have been older than twenty-six. Shoulder-length, straight blond hair, medium height, slim, attractive but not gorgeous. There was something so familiar about this Joan Dawson that Celeste stared harder at her. Then it dawned—except for the pink skin, the sharp nose, and the straight hair, Joan Dawson was a lookalike for Katrina. Gordon had gone and married himself a younger Katrina—in a pastel shade of pink.

"From the start, Gordon told me he was never married, that he had no children . . ."

"Well, he lied."

". . . but when I became suspicious, he admitted that he had once been married, a long time ago, but that he was divorced. How was I to know?"

Tears streamed down Lorna's face. "How could my father say that he had no children? I'm his daughter! How could he deny any of us?"

Celeste stepped back to stand next to Lorna. She put her arm around her. She couldn't tell her that it was all right, because it wasn't. Gordon had been dead wrong.

"I swear, I didn't know," Joan said, more to the man next to her than to Lorna or Katrina.

"Tell us another one," Katrina said, not believing the lie.

"Mrs. Dawson," Mr. Mortimer said, "we—"

"Yes," both Katrina and Joan answered.

"No, I . . . I mean Mrs. Katrina Dawson."

"There's definitely a distinction, isn't there?" Katrina said.

Embarrassed, Joan brought her hand to her mouth and turned to the man next to her, who put his arm around her shoulder and whispered to her, "Pull yourself together."

Mr. Mortimer continued. "Mrs. Dawson, we were discussing possible solutions. Perhaps we can come to terms."

"Terms? Am I supposed to be negotiating here? I don't think so. I *am* Gordon Dawson's *legal* wife. I have been *legally* married to him for twenty years. I have three children that are *legally* and *biologically* his. I have no divorce papers, and I have no notice of a divorce being rendered without my knowledge. My last discussion with *my husband*"—Katrina glanced pointedly at Joan—"Gordon Dawson, was a week ago when he told me that he was coming home for the weekend. The fact that he committed adultery and that he neglected to mention that he had been shacking up with another damn woman does not in any way change the status of our marriage. His so-called marriage to another woman isn't something that a husband shares with his wife—it's not pillow-talk material. So these *terms* that you're speaking of, I'm not willing to discuss. I don't have to. I *am* the legal wife."

While no one said anything, the silence was static and deafening. Celeste could swear that she could hear every pulse beat and every breath that was taken.

"It's not as cut and dry as that," the man to the left of Joan said, drawing everyone's attention. "My daughter has legal papers, too. In a court of law, she could be ruled the legal wife."

"That is correct," the man seated on the other side of Joan said. "In the District of Columbia, where Joan and Gordon Dawson were legally married before a justice of the peace, the law recognizes her as his legal wife."

"I don't care what the fucking District of Columbia recognizes,

I'm from New York, and Gordon and I were *legally* married there twenty years ago. We've never divorced. If you goddamn people think you can bully me, think again. I will not . . ."

"Katrina."

". . . roll over and—"

"Katrina!" Celeste shouted, letting go of Lorna.

"What?"

"Settle down for a moment."

Her chest heaving, Katrina had been about to spew forth every four-letter word she had ever heard. Momentarily locking eyes with Celeste, she used the time to try and catch her breath. Her throat was so dry it was sore.

With her back to Joan and her father, Celeste mouthed softly to Katrina, "Please," while pleading with her eyes for Katrina to let her speak. Katrina got the message and remained silent.

"If I may," Celeste said, not really asking permission of Joan, of her father, or of the man she assumed was their attorney. "Who are you?"

"I'm Jonathan Ashfield, attorney-at-law."

Under her breath, Katrina mumbled, "Oh, shit." She immediately recalled Celeste's insistence that they get a lawyer. The quick look Celeste gave her said, "I told you so."

"Well, Mr. Ashfield, I'm Mrs. Katrina Dawson's sister, Celeste Alexander, and if I'm not mistaken, in this country there are laws against bigamy in all fifty states. In fact, while some states levy only a misdemeanor against the offending spouse, most states, including New York, the District of Columbia, and Maryland, consider bigamy a felony and will lock a bigamist up for as many as seven years. Of course, Gordon can't be locked up; he's dead. However, Gordon Dawson's first, legal marriage to Katrina was never severed by a valid decree because a divorce was never sought. That marriage supercedes any subsequent, illegal marriage that Gordon entered, rendering the subsequent marriage not only illegal but nonexistent. Now—"

"That's not totally true," Mr. Ashfield said. "If the first married parties were apart for a number of years, as many as five, then—"

"Which is not the case here," Katrina said. "Gordon and I lived apart for weeks at a time because of his job, and nothing more."

"Exactly," Celeste said. "They were not separated legally or otherwise. Couples live apart all the time because of careers in this country, which does not free them to take another spouse in another state. Now, my research tells me that Gordon's marriage to your client does not legally exist. In fact, their so-called marriage is in violation of the antibigamy laws of the state where they were married and in the state in which they live. Gordon's death leaves Katrina a widow, not your client. In fact, again if I'm not mistaken, your client may have to get an annulment, because a legal marriage never did exist between them, and legally, her name is not Dawson. Now, this entanglement would be interesting fodder for the *Washington Post* or any local or national newspaper, don't you think?"

Joan, her father, Jonathan Ashfield, Mr. Mortimer and Miss Woodward all looked anxiously from one to the other. Jonathan Ashfield had nothing to fire back with.

Katrina was impressed. She almost wanted to shout out, "That's my sister!" but didn't. "It sounds to me like Gordon used you," she said, speaking directly to Joan for the first time. "Is it true that you have a baby by him? Does the baby look like him? Are you sure Gordon's the father?"

"How dare you talk about my baby!"

"You have no right to defame my daughter's name!"

"Please! Please!" Mr. Mortimer shouted. "Mrs. Dawson, this kind of talk only serves to incite the situation. It won't get us anywhere."

Joan began to weep.

Celeste shot Katrina a reproachful glare. Her being mean wasn't necessary.

Jonathan Ashfield immediately began consulting with Joan and her father. Joan's head went to shaking. "No . . . no. This isn't right." Her father put his arm protectively around her. Her tears continued to flow as he tried to hide her face with his large hand.

Katrina gave Celeste a boastful nod. Miss Woodward and Mr.

Mortimer whispered between themselves. Lorna stood with both hands over her mouth. She was no longer crying.

"Are we done here?" Katrina asked. "I have a cremation to arrange."

Uncertain, Miss Woodward and Mr. Mortimer looked questioningly at Jonathan Ashfield, but he was still busy conferring with his clients.

"Well, I'd like to suggest," Celeste said, "that we waste no more time haggling over who has a legal right to claim Gordon's body. My sister has that right; her papers prove that. Mr. Ashfield, as a lawyer, you know that your client doesn't have a legal leg to stand on. Let's end this now."

The fact that Joan was still crying could only mean that Katrina had won. It seemed Albert was right—Joan wouldn't want to draw attention to her predicament. While Celeste couldn't help feeling a bit full of herself, she hoped it didn't show on her face.

Mr. Ashfield suddenly stood. "The body is yours."

"Forgive me if I don't say thank you," Katrina said sourly. She turned to Miss Woodward. "Where do we go from here?"

"I can better assist you from my office."

"After you."

"Mrs. Dawson," Mr. Ashfield said, stopping Katrina at the door. "You get nothing more from my client. Any assets she accumulated with Gordon Dawson remain with her."

"That remains to be seen. If Gordon's name is on anything, I might just have rights to all or part of those assets."

"No!" Joan shot up out of her chair. "You will not touch my home or anything else I acquired with Gordon. You have his body; that's all you're getting. Everything else belongs to me."

Cooly looking Joan up and down, Katrina smirked. "That's where you're wrong, sweetheart. I have Gordon's name, something that you will never have. And I have three of his children who carry his name. All you have is a bastard."

Joan's father exploded, "How dare you!"

Gasping, Joan screamed, "You bitch! How dare you call my child a bastard!"

"Believe me, he's going to be called a whole lot worse in his lifetime. In case you didn't notice while you were screwing Gordon, he was a black man."

Again, a loud, startled gasp gushed from Joan as if someone had put an ice cube down her back.

"Katrina," Celeste urged, "let's go."

"Ma, come on."

Katrina wouldn't let herself be pulled out of the office.

"Mrs. Dawson, there is no cause for you to be disrespectful and rude to my client."

"You should have told her to not disrespect me by playing house with my husband."

"I didn't know!"

"You knew. You had to know. Gordon wore a wide, gold wedding band for twenty years. On the rare occasion that he took off that ring, there was a permanent impression on his finger. You had to have seen it. It was clear as the nose on your lying face. Tell me, honey, did he fulfill your fantasy?"

"Shut up!" Joan's father roared. "Don't you ever say another word to my daughter, you filthy woman!"

Katrina said, cooly, "Fuck you and fuck your daughter."

Together, Celeste and Lorna hastily hustled Katrina out of the room and practically pushed her down the hall toward Miss Woodward's office.

"My God, Katrina, that was just plain ugly."

"Ma, you didn't have to say that about her baby."

"You certainly didn't, Katrina. That baby is related to your kids."

"No, he isn't."

"Yes, he is, Ma. We have the same father."

"It's not the father's line that counts, Lorna. It's the mother's. That child doesn't have the same mother, therefore, you're not related to him."

Celeste couldn't believe what she was hearing. "Biology 101, Katrina. Genetically, half of that baby is Gordon, just as half of each of your children is Gordon."

"Yeah, well, that's the bad side. Personally, I'll never accept that child into my family."

"Humph. I don't think you have to worry about Joan begging you to accept her child. After what just happened back there, she'd rather see her child carried off by a pack of wolves than acknowledged by you."

"Believe me, I'm real hurt."

Miss Woodward entered her office minutes behind Celeste, Lorna, and Katrina. Her face was as red as a pock-marked strawberry.

"It's about time," Katrina said. "Let's do this. Gordon is waiting to be sent to hell."

CHAPTER
21

Katrina got what she wanted—she got Gordon's body released, and she got the satisfaction of proving to Gordon's bitch that she was his one and only legal wife. Still, she was angry. She was angry at the hospital administrator for trying to keep her in the dark, while trying to help Joan and her father claim Gordon's body. Katrina was of a mind to sue the hospital, but Celeste argued she didn't have a case. "The hospital can't be held liable for Gordon's lies." Celeste was probably right, but Katrina continued to entertain the idea anyway; she was that pissed off at the hospital for giving her the runaround.

Whether what she'd told Katrina was true or not, Celeste didn't care. She was just glad it was over. She had done what she had been forced to come to Washington to do. Now she could go back home and deal with her own mess.

"So whata we do now, Ma?" Lorna asked upon following Katrina and Celeste out of the hospital.

"Find a funeral home that will cremate your father's cheating ass ASAP."

"Ma! You're really gonna cremate him?"

Even Celeste was taken aback. "Aren't you taking Gordon back to New York and maybe take a day to think about how you want to put him away?"

"No, I'm not taking him back to New York, and no, I don't need time to think about how I'm gonna put him away. I'm burning his ass up. Let's get a cab."

Lorna stopped walking. "Ma, you for real?"

"Do I look like I'm kidding."

"But, Ma—"

"Lorna, as soon as I find a funeral home that will arrange an immediate cremation, I'm sure as hell doing what I said."

"Maaa."

"Don't start with me, Lorna, I'm not in the mood. Cremation is legal and the way many people choose to leave this earth. I might wanna be cremated my damn self. Personally, I don't like the idea of being put in a box six feet underground just to become maggot food and eventually a toothy-faced skeleton in rotten clothes."

"That's gross, Ma, but I know Daddy didn't want to be cremated. We talked about that after Papa died. Aunt Celeste, talk to her."

"No. Uh uh. I have no say in this."

"You sure don't," Katrina said, "and besides, you wouldn't know how Gordon wanted to be put away anyway."

"No, I don't, but maybe you need to discuss this with all three of your children before you decide this, Katrina. Gordon is their father."

"Yeah, Ma, don't we—"

"No! Neither you, your brother, your sister, nor anyone on Gordon's side of the family have any say as to how I choose to dispose of his body. I'm his wife. I have the only say. Now, can we go? I think I've discussed my personal business two times too many in front of this damn hospital to last a lifetime."

Katrina went immediately to the curb and hailed a cab. Having no other choice, Celeste and Lorna followed, but Celeste felt she needed to say something to Lorna.

"Don't worry, Lorna. Your father's life force, his spirit, is long gone. His body is just a shell. Whether he's in the ground or burned up, he won't feel it."

"And that's too bad," Katrina said. "He got off easy."

The ride back to the hotel was quiet. Lorna sniffled a few times, Katrina kept shaking her foot, and Celeste closed her eyes when unexpected thoughts of Willie kissing her kept invading her mind. The memory of his long, tender kisses made her feel as if she was floating outside of her body.

Lorna tapped Celeste. "We're here, Aunt Celeste."

Falling back to earth, Celeste hated that she missed Willie's kisses so. It wasn't fair that such sweet memories continued to sneak in and pain her mind and soul.

"You coming to our room, Aunt Celeste?"

"Actually, I'm pretty tired, but I also need to see if I can get a flight back to New York tonight."

"Oh," Katrina said, "so you're not gonna help me find a funeral home?"

Now that surprised Celeste. "I didn't think you needed or wanted my help with that."

Katrina was the first off the elevator. "Why half step? You played a role in getting the body; why not play a role in getting it roasted?"

Slack-jawed, Celeste stared at the back of Katrina's head as Lorna pulled her off the elevator. *Damn, that's cold!* But then again, who was she to talk? Hadn't she wished worse for Willie? Damn, it was like looking in the mirror. She was just as bitter as Katrina, and that wasn't a pretty thing to look at. Yep, it was time to go home.

"Why don't I join you all later. I have to go to the bathroom."

"You can use our bathroom, Aunt Celeste."

"I think I'm gonna need some privacy."

"Aw, c'mon, Aunt Celeste, we all cop a squat. Ma, can't she use our bathroom?"

"I don't see why not." Katrina slipped her key card into the door lock. "If Celeste wants to leave, let her."

"But she's staying, right?"

Praying that she wouldn't regret it, Celeste went on into the room. When was she ever going to be able to say no to Lorna or even to her parents and stick by it? Willie used to say that it was her need to please her family that she allowed them to manipulate her. These last two days just may have proven him right.

"Somebody's been in here," Katrina said, looking around the room.

Celeste couldn't tell if anything was out of order. "It was probably housekeeping."

"They were here earlier, before we left." Katrina spotted the black carry-on suitcase against the side of the sofa. "Oh, it's Patrice. That's her bag."

Lorna hurried off toward the bedroom. "It's her. She's sleeping." Lorna flopped down hard on the double bed, shaking Patrice awake. "It's about time you got here."

Yawning, Patrice turned onto her back. "Where have y'all been? I've been waiting for hours."

"We were at the hospital. Aunt Celeste got them to release Daddy's body."

Slowly sitting up, Patrice looked around Lorna toward the door. Her voice hushed, she asked, "She's here?"

"Who? Aunt Celeste?"

"Shhh! Yeah, her! She here?"

"Yeah, and don't go messin' with her."

Patrice sprang up off the bed. "I can't stand her."

"Leave her alone, Patrice."

"And if I don't?"

Out in the front room, Katrina cut her eyes at Celeste. Lorna was right—it was Celeste who had gotten those fools to release Gordon's body. If it wasn't for Celeste, they might still be at the hospital arguing.

"How did you know all that stuff about antibigamy laws?" Katrina asked.

"The Internet. I did a quick search before I left home. That's what I was trying to tell you before we left for the hospital. You have everything I found in the manila envelope I gave you."

"I guess I better look it over." Of course, Katrina realized a thank-you was in order, but she didn't feel like saying it. "Patrice, get out here. What time did you get in?"

Oh, well. Celeste sat back and crossed her legs. So much for appreciation.

"In a minute. I have to go to the bathroom." Patrice hurried into the bathroom and locked herself in.

"Well, hurry up. Celeste has to use it, too."

Celeste really didn't have to use the bathroom. It was an excuse that hadn't worked.

"I need a drink," Katrina said, going to the desk by the window. "But I better get started looking through the yellow pages for a funeral home. I wanna get this over with."

"Ma," Lorna said, coming back into the room. "Why don't we just call Albert? He lives here. He probably knows who to call."

"I bet he does, but I have no intention of looking at Albert's face."

"You don't have to see him, Ma. Just ask him, on the telephone, who to call."

"I pass."

"Then I'll call him."

"Girl, aren't you bothered, in the least, by what you know about your father and Albert?"

"We can't do nothin' about what they did, Ma. Daddy's dead. It's over—permanently. Besides, Albert's cool."

"Damnit, Lorna! You're so goddamn naive. Patrice! Patrice, get out here and talk some sense into your sister."

"Will someone clue me in?" Celeste asked. "I met Albert. What about him and Gordon?"

"Albert's a friend of Daddy's."

"Friend and lover," Katrina added. "Patrice!"

Celeste raised her brow questioningly.

"That's right. Gordon was not only a bigamist; he was a faggot."

"What did you say?" Patrice asked from the doorway of the bedroom. "Daddy was a what?"

Everyone looked at Patrice. "A faggot," Katrina answered.

"Ma!" Lorna said. "Dang."

"Hi, Patrice," Celeste said. "Girl, you're all grown up. If I'd passed you on the street, I probably wouldn't've recognized you. You look great."

"I know. Ma," Patrice said, dismissing Celeste. "Ma, Daddy was no faggot."

Oh. Excuse me. Celeste knew a slight when it was thrown up in her face. *Okay, just be cool.*

"Yes he was," Katrina said, "and *that* his lover told me from his own mouth."

"But, Ma," Lorna said, "Albert said it only happened once."

"That's what he *said.* Do you think he'd tell me everything?"

"He didn't have to tell you that, Ma. So why would he lie about how many times they did whatever they did?"

"Wise up, Lorna. Albert told me that he was Gordon's lover. Once is never enough for most people. Now—"

"But, Ma—"

"Lorna, for all I know, Gordon may have slept with men we'll never know about. In fact, I wouldn't be surprised if he was a pedophile, too."

"Ma!" Patrice and Lorna said at the same time.

Celeste rolled her eyes at Katrina's wild assumptions. Of course, she was right in that no one knew all that Gordon was involved in, but now she was really stretching.

"Don't *Ma* me. Look at all the things your father's done behind my back—your backs. He could be into bestiality for all we know."

"What's that?" Lorna asked.

Celeste cringed at the thought. "You don't wanna know."

Looking at Celeste, Patrice sneered at her, but Celeste didn't see her.

"I don't wanna hear no more bad stuff about Dad," Lorna said.

"Me neither," Patrice said, still standing in the doorway. "I might have nightmares."

Celeste again looked at Patrice. *Okay, I'll try again.* "Patrice, it's been a while since I've seen you. How have you been?"

Huffing, Patrice rolled her eyes. "I'm cool."

Fuck it. That's the last time I put myself out there. Celeste was used to Patrice's nasty, standoffish ways, but damn.

"Don't be antisocial, Patrice," Katrina said.

"Yeah, Patrice," Lorna said, opening the small glass cabinet where the hotel had a well-stocked stash of goodies. "You low on sugar or something?"

"Katrina"—Celeste was two seconds from bolting—"shouldn't we be searching for a funeral home?"

"I'm just about to start." Katrina began pulling out first one desk drawer then another, looking for the local telephone books.

"Patrice, they have your favorite candy in here." Lorna pulled out a jumbo Snickers candy bar. "You want it?"

"Bring it to me."

"Patrice!" Katrina snapped. "Get your lazy ass in here and get it yourself!"

"Dag, Ma, why you sweatin' me?" Patrice strutted into the front room, eyes fixed on the candy bar Lorna held out to her. Snatching it from Lorna's hand, Patrice wasted no time unwrapping the chocolate log filled with peanuts. Her first bite was big and chewy. Smacking loudly as she chewed, she kept her back to Celeste.

"Dang, Patrice," Lorna said, disgusted, "get some manners, will ya?"

"Leave me alone, Lorna."

"I'm not botherin' you."

"Both of y'all cut it out." Katrina pulled out the middle drawer. "Where the hell are they hiding the telephone books?" The books were there.

Celeste watched Patrice chew hungrily. She hadn't seen Patrice in about two years and was struck by how pretty she was. She had a nice, shapely figure that she showed off in her tight red capri pants. Too bad her nasty attitude didn't match her pretty face.

Still eating, Patrice went and stood next to Katrina and busied herself looking through the telephone book with her.

Celeste ached to escape to her room.

"Ma," Patrice said, "whatcha looking for?"

"Finally you say something to me?"

"Ma, we just talked this morning."

"So, you still say hi to me when you see me, with your moody self."

"I'm upset about Daddy. I have a right, don't I?"

"Yeah, but hurry up and get over it. He's not worth it."

"Ma, how can you—"

"Look, I understand how you and Lorna feel, but y'all got to understand how I feel. Your father didn't just cheat on me; he married another woman while he was still married to me. I hope and pray that nothing like this ever happens to either one of you. Your father could not have hurt me more if he had put a knife in my gut and rammed it through to my back."

"Man." Patrice's mouth went dry. The once sweet chocolate tasted like plastic.

Lorna opened up an expensive jar of cashews and began plopping them in her mouth.

To Celeste, the air in the room felt like the calm before a storm. She glanced longingly over at the door. Any minute she was going to be on the other side of it.

Katrina finally got to the funeral home section of the yellow pages. "Celeste, what's your bet that Joan person knows about bestiality? No telling what she and Gordon were into."

"I wouldn't wanna know."

"I would. It would be more to hate Gordon for. I know you felt that way when you found out about Willie's other life, right?"

Lorna and Patrice both waited for Celeste to respond.

"Don't remind me." Celeste suddenly stood. "It's been a long day."

"What in the world were Gordon and Willie thinking?" Katrina asked. "Didn't they think they'd ever be found out?"

Celeste was being drawn into a conversation she did not want to have with Katrina. "If they thought that, they would never have cheated, but cheaters and liars, stupidly, don't ever think they'll be caught."

"Yeah, but didn't they think that if they died—which their asses did in a hot second—that they'd leave all this ugliness for us to discover?"

"Maybe they didn't give a damn. They were about self-gratification and nothing more."

"They were bastards," Katrina said.

"Yeah, but the women bear some blame here. The one that was with Willie was a slut. That Joan woman might not have known about you, Katrina, but the woman with Willie had to know that he was married. Why else would she steal away to a cheap-behind motel with him?"

Katrina shrugged. "Oh, I don't know. Maybe the motel was all Willie could afford."

Celeste knew that she was standing on shaky ground. "Oh, no. Willie could've afforded a whole lot better. Maybe a sleazy, transient motel is all his slut was worth."

"I gotta go to the bathroom." Patrice rushed to the bathroom, slamming the door hard.

"What's wrong with her?" Lorna asked.

Katrina sat at the desk and began moving her finger down the list of funeral homes. "Like you, she was crazy about her daddy."

"How stupid of us, huh, Ma?" Lorna went off into the bedroom, slamming the door behind her.

Katrina shouted, "You and Patrice had better watch how you're talking to me!" Katrina flipped a page hard enough to tear it. "And stop slamming doors around here!"

To Celeste, it was kind of funny that Katrina, with all of her mouth, had girls whose mouths were just as smart as hers. "I guess everyone is a bit on edge. Maybe I should check on Lorna."

"Leave her alone." Katrina picked up the receiver and began punching in a telephone number. She sensed that Celeste was watching her. "I guess one place is as good as the next. As long as they cremate, I don't give a damn. Celeste, you have a red dress with you? We should all dress in red when Gordon is cremated. It's a most fitting color for a bigamist. Actually, you should have worn red at Willie's funeral. He was no better than Gordon."

If Celeste had to say who was better or worse, she couldn't. Neither Gordon nor Willie had wings on their backs. They were both bastards for what they had done, but at least Katrina knew what took Gordon's life. Now, for the first time, she was curious about who was responsible for taking Willie's. Now she wondered where Gertrude's daughter, Naynay, was the morning Willie was killed. Gertrude said Naynay had snuck out of the house early that morning. That day, she thought Naynay had snuck out to be with her boyfriend, Melvin, but now that she thought about it, Naynay had always been sweet on Willie. Even as a little girl, Naynay had greeted Willie with a big "Hi, Willie!" and just a half-hearted hi for her. Willie used to think it was funny and cute that little Naynay had a crush on him. When Naynay had turned fifteen and her body blossomed, it wasn't so cute to see this flirtatious young thing with cleavage and behind grinning in Willie's face all the time. Could it be that it was Naynay that Willie had slipped away with in the early morning hours?

CHAPTER
22

"What's *wrong* with you people? If a Jew can be buried within twenty-four hours of death, so can a black man!" Katrina slammed the telephone down.

Lorna came back into the room. "But you want Daddy cremated," she said, picking up Patrice's half-eaten candy bar and a bottle of water.

"It's the same damn thing!"

"Not really." Lorna gave Katrina a wide berth and slipped back into the bedroom.

"This is insane!" Katrina shrieked. "Why is this happening to me?"

That was Celeste's question for herself. "Katrina, it may have to take a few days. Call one of those funeral homes back and schedule for the earliest possible date."

"I want it done now—today, tomorrow!"

"Yeah, but—"

"I should call a synagogue and tell them Gordon was Jewish."

"You can't do that."

"Why not? There are black Jews, you know. Wasn't Sammy Davis, Jr., a Jew?"

"Converted."

"Jew nonetheless."

"Was Gordon circumcised? Because if he wasn't, that might give him away."

Katrina thought for a moment. "I'll cut off his dick, and they won't have to worry about it."

"You're losing it. Besides, it's too late for that."

"Not if I ask for some time alone with my *dearly* departed. I know how to use a knife. Celeste, you could distract them while I—"

"Get serious. What're you gonna do? Walk out with his . . . his thing in a sandwich bag?"

Katrina thought about it. "I'll have my pocketbook with me. There's plenty of room in there, or I could flush it."

"Why am I humoring you? You know something like that would be missed when they're preparing the body."

"True. Oh, I could say, quite innocently mind you, that his *thing* was stuck up Joan's ass, or maybe better, it got lost up in Albert's ass and he's keeping it as a souvenir."

Celeste exploded with laughter, doubling over. Seeing how hard Celeste was laughing, Katrina realized what she'd said, and her slow snicker built to a belly-jerking, open-mouthed howl. Celeste clutched her chest, and while her and Katrina's eyes filled with tears, their laughter grew louder. Both Celeste and Katrina were keenly aware that this was the first time they'd laughed together in God knew when.

Lorna and Patrice hurried back into the room. "What's so funny?" Lorna asked.

Wiping at her eyes, it took a while before Katrina could tell them what she'd said. Lorna and Patrice exchanged quizzical glances. Neither laughed.

Katrina dismissed their deadpan stares with a flip of her hand. When she and Celeste could stop laughing, although a smile remained on both their lips, Katrina closed the telephone directory and slammed her hand on top for good measure.

"Call your pal, Lorna."

Lorna immediately pulled the piece of paper with Albert's telephone number on it out of the pocket of her jeans. She got

Albert right away. Her articulation of the problem to Albert impressed Celeste. Not once did Lorna confer with Katrina.

"He said he'll take care of it," Lorna said as soon as she got off the phone.

"We'll see." Katrina checked her watch. "We should order something to eat. I'm starving. Patrice, you look kinda tired. What's up with you?"

"Nothing."

"Have you been partying down there in Chapel Hill instead of taking care of business for the fall?"

"Ma, why you stressin' me? Get off my back."

The warning look Katrina shot Patrice was hard and threatening.

Slowly rolling her eyes, Patrice turned away.

"Young lady, I'd check my damn attitude and shut my mouth if I were you."

Patrice quietly sucked her teeth.

Katrina eyed Patrice until she was sure Patrice would keep her mouth shut. She opened the room service portfolio. "Now, what do you wanna eat?"

"Nothing."

"Suit yourself."

"Well, I'm hungry," Lorna said. "I want a juicy fat cheeseburger with lots of fries."

"I think we should all eat a little something," Celeste said. "We might feel better."

Patrice glared at Celeste. "Who asked you?"

Stunned, Celeste froze.

"Patrice." Katrina shook her head.

There was a nervous thump in Celeste's chest. "Were you talking to me, Patrice?"

"Do I need to call your name?"

Lorna exclaimed, "Oh, no she didn't!"

Celeste didn't blink; she didn't move a muscle. That air of thick, simmering tension she had sensed since she spoke to Patrice the first time lay on her like the dense hot air of a sauna.

"Mind your business, Lorna!"

"Damnit, Patrice." Katrina wanted to grab Patrice and shake her. "Shut your mouth."

"You buggin', Patrice. Ma, you hear what she said to Aunt Celeste?"

"I'm not deaf, Lorna. Patrice, cut it out." Katrina went back to looking at the menu.

Patrice glowered boldly at Celeste, but she kept her mouth shut.

To Celeste, it was obvious that Katrina had no intention of making her nasty daughter apologize, but that didn't mean that she wouldn't.

"You don't like me very much, do you?"

Patrice sucked her teeth. "I don't like you at all."

Katrina slammed the menu down. "Enough, Patrice! I told you about that damn mouth of yours. Don't start no mess up in here."

"Well, I'm tired of people gettin' all up in my business."

"First of all," Celeste said, putting some attitude in her voice, "I wasn't *all up in your business.* I simply made a suggestion that we all eat something. I didn't, specifically, call your name, but even if I had, you don't talk to me like that. I'm not a child. You better check yourself."

"Tella, Aunt Celeste!"

Katrina pointed at Lorna. "Stop instigating."

"Ma, I'm not the one—"

"Shut up, Lorna!"

Lorna's bottom lip shot out. She folded her arms high and tight across her chest. "This is foul."

"That's right, brat," Patrice said. "Shut up and mind your business!"

"You should take your own advice," Celeste said, standing. "I'm outta here."

"I said be quiet, Patrice! What's wrong with you?"

"Better a brat than a bitch," Lorna retorted.

"Lorna!" Katrina exploded.

"It takes a bitch to know a bitch," Patrice said, determined to not let Lorna get the last jab.

"Shut the hell up—both of you. Patrice! Goddamnit, cut it out! If I have to tell you again—I'm gonna kick your ass myself."

On her way to the door, Celeste stopped. "Really nice seeing you again, Patrice."

"Don't leave because of her, Aunt Celeste."

Patrice defiantly rolled her eyes, rolled her neck, and sucked her teeth all at the same time.

"Do that again," Katrina dared, "I'll pluck your eyes, snap your neck, and knock all the damn teeth outta your mouth in two seconds, and still have fifty-eight seconds to kick your ass. Don't believe? Try me."

Her face tight, Patrice went to rapidly tapping her right foot.

Looking at Patrice and Lorna, Celeste was reminded of her own warring childhood with Katrina. How strange to be on the outside looking in at her own past in the present. "I've definitely outstayed my welcome," Celeste said.

"You girls are acting like you don't have no damn sense up in here."

"Ma," Lorna said. "Why you puttin' me in it? I didn't do nothin'."

"Then keep doing nothing and be quiet."

Lorna flopped down in the desk chair and, pushing off with her feet, turned the chair so that her back was to Katrina, but then she picked up the television remote, turning on the television. She grumbled inaudibly as she began channel surfing.

As much as Celeste didn't like that Lorna was getting the fallout from Patrice's vicious assault on her, she wasn't about to stay and be her ally.

"Brat," Patrice said under her breath.

"Shut up, Patrice!" Katrina shouted.

"Well, she was all up in my business, too, Ma."

That did it. Celeste put her hand on her hip. "Let me tell you something, Patrice."

Lorna turned back expectantly.

"You can't tell me nothing," Patrice said.

"You sure about that? You sure I can't tell you that your smart-ass mouth is about to get your behind kicked."

"Uh oh," Lorna said, excitedly.

"Celeste, let me handle my child," Katrina said, looking hard at Patrice, "who'd better keep her big mouth shut once and for all."

Patrice again rolled her eyes.

"Patrice," Celeste said, disregarding what Katrina had said, "you're in for a rude awakening one day."

Patrice huffed her disgust at Celeste speaking to her.

"You're not so special or so pretty that people will kiss your ass and take your shit. You—"

"Listen, bitch—"

"Patrice!" Katrina rushed at Patrice and shoved her hard in the direction of the bedroom. "Shut the fuck up!"

"I can't stand her, Ma, and neither can you! How you let her come here?"

Celeste wasn't surprised that those words were spoken, and now that they had been, she had most certainly outstayed her uninvited welcome.

"Patrice, get your ass into that bedroom. I don't need this. I have enough crap to deal with without you showing your tail. I don't need you fucking with me or Celeste. Celeste is here helping me. You don't talk to her like that. Now, you take your narrow ass back in that room and cool off before you and I get into it. And you know, you *will* come out the loser."

Blatantly sneering at Celeste, Patrice rolled her eyes before going off into the bedroom.

It wasn't anger that Celeste felt as she stared at the empty doorway; it was total dislike for her niece. What a nasty girl Patrice was.

Katrina pretended to study the menu. "Damn, I'm hungry. Celeste you're gonna stay and eat, right?"

"Ma, you know that was cold. Patrice really dissed Aunt Celeste."

Celeste could feel the vein pulsing in the side of her neck. "Real sweet child you have, Katrina."

"I'll deal with Patrice, Celeste, don't worry about it. What do you want to eat?"

"Katrina, you and I have our history, so I know the deal with us. But your daughter? I've never done a damn thing to that girl. I'm not gonna let her disrespect me like that again."

"Ignore Patrice, Celeste. She gets a thorn up her ass when her hair doesn't look right, so you know she's worse now after hearing about Gordon."

"Ma, Patrice—"

"Be quiet, Lorna. I don't need your two cents."

Lorna stormed off into the bathroom and slammed the door.

"Celeste, after we eat and as soon as we find out about the arrangements for Gordon, you call Mom and Dad. I'll call some of Gordon's people, but I'll be damn if I'll wait for any of them to get here. I wonder if any of them knew about his marriage to that woman?"

"I'm going up to my room."

"Well, okay, but you could wait until we hear from Albert."

Riiiiing!

"I hope that's him. Lorna, get out here and answer this phone!"

Lorna didn't answer.

"Lorna!"

Riiiiing!

Lorna yanked the bathroom door open. "How come I gotta answer the phone?"

"Why do you think? Answer it!"

Riiiiing!

Lorna grabbed the telephone. "Hello!" She listened. "Yeah." She listened. "No, I'm not okay."

"Who is it?" Katrina asked.

"Albert." Lorna turned her back to Katrina. "Yeah. Where?"

Celeste smiled. Lorna had gumption, and Celeste liked that.

Katrina was too through. "I'm gonna kill these drama queens up in here."

Opening the door, Celeste was about to step out of the room when Katrina asked, "You can't wait one more minute?"

Not really. "It seems Albert solved your problem."

"Okay," Lorna said, "I'll tell her. Thanks, Albert." She hung up.

"When? Where?" Katrina asked.

"Daddy can be cremated at noon tomorrow. Where, I don't

know. Albert's gonna take us there. He'll be here in forty-five minutes."

"Well, bless his little gay soul."

"Ma! Would you please be nice to Albert? He's cool. You don't say vicious things about that fag hag, Robert. He's *too* gay, and you talk to him all the time like he's your best girlfriend."

"As far as I know, Robert never slept with your father. Now, if I find out otherwise—"

Celeste stood at the open door. "I'm going up to my room."

"Aunt Celeste, you're goin' with us, right?"

"I'll skip this outing, thank you. Call me when you get back. I'm up in room 723."

"Tell Mom I'll call her later," Katrina said.

Only after she was up in her own room, away from the nasty, disdainful attitude of Patrice, did Celeste unclench her jaw and her fist. She had wanted badly to reach out and touch Patrice— with a hard right. What in the world had she ever done to that girl?

"Not a damn thing!" Celeste answered her own question. "That little witch's hate for me has to come from Katrina and her nasty mouth. Why else would she hate me so? And the one damn time, in all these years, that Katrina and I actually laughed together, that damn Patrice ruined it with her nasty-ass mouth. What the hell am I doing here taking this shit? I'm going home. I don't need to be here for no damn cremation. I don't need to pay any damn respects to Gordon. I haven't seen him in years, we weren't buddies, he didn't attend Willie's funeral, and I have no great love for Katrina, and absolutely none for Patrice. Shoot! I'm going home."

Riiiing!

Snatching up the telephone, Celeste shouted, "Hello!"

The caller hesitated.

Celeste exhaled impatiently. "Hello."

"Is this Mrs. Alexander?"

"Who is this?"

"This is Detective Vaughan calling from Brooklyn, New York. Is Mrs.—"

Celeste dropped her hand with the telephone in it to her side. "Damn."

She took a deep breath before bringing the receiver back to her ear. "Detective Vaughan, I'm sorry. It's me. I . . . ah . . ."

"You sound like you're having a rough day."

"If you only knew. How can I help you?"

"Your father gave me your number. I wanted to bring you up to speed on the investigation."

"Do you know who killed my husband?"

"Not yet, but we went to your husband's office at Dialacom. We spoke to several people who worked closely with him, but none had any information specific to his murder. However, they did speak about something that was going on in your husband's office."

"And what was that?"

"A mail clerk, a Tyrel Johnson, was arrested just before your husband's murder for grand larceny."

"What does that have to do with Willie?"

"According to some of your husband's coworkers, Johnson and your husband were friends."

"I don't know if I'd call them friends; they weren't hang-out buddies. I know they went out to a club one time after work. I believe it was someone's birthday. Willie spoke about Tyrel, yes. He said he was a nice guy, but that's about it. I doubt if Willie stole anything with this guy."

"We don't believe he did. Following a hunch, we paid Johnson a visit at the Brooklyn House of Detention, where he's waiting to be brought before the grand jury. Seems your husband called Johnson's mother late on the evening of July fifth. Are you aware of that call?"

Celeste had to sit down. "No. Why did he call her?"

"According to Johnson, your husband told his mother he had something that would get Johnson out of jail, just that he couldn't explain it to Johnson's mother right then. He told her to tell Johnson that he'd take care of it when he got back from his vacation, and not to worry."

"What could he have meant?"

"I was hoping you could tell us. Did your husband tell you about any problems that Johnson was having on the job?"

"No."

"Are you sure?"

Celeste answered irritably, "I'm damn sure." The dead silence that filled her ear told her that her harshness had offended Detective Vaughan. "Look, I don't know anything about this situation."

"I see."

"Willie didn't tell me anything about Tyrel's problems. Like I said before, the night before Willie died, I had only one thing on my mind, and that was the vacation I ended up not taking. We didn't talk about any job-related issues."

"Okay. This is our thinking," Detective Vaughan said. "Your house was burgled. Nothing appeared to be taken. We're thinking that the intruder was looking for whatever it is your husband told Johnson's mother he had that would get Johnson out of jail."

"Are you serious? You think whatever that something is, is maybe still in my house?"

"That we don't know. If it was a tape, then your husband may have recorded something that could clear Johnson. Without that tape, we don't know. We checked your husband's workspace. His desk has been cleaned out, there's nothing in the workplace that remains that's his personally, and he spoke to no one there, that we know of, about whatever evidence he may have had."

Celeste began rubbing her forehead. "So there are no answers."

"Not at this time, but we plan on subpoenaing the telephone company for the phone logs of your incoming and outgoing calls for the night of July fifth and the morning of July sixth. If your husband made that one call to Johnson's mother, then he might have made other calls. In addition, if he received calls that you don't know about, then we might have a lead on what took him to the location where he was murdered."

Celeste hadn't thought about phone calls. She never checked the caller ID box for numbers and had, in fact, cleared all the numbers from the box after Willie died without looking at a single one.

"Mrs. Alexander, don't worry yourself at this point. We'll let you know what we find."

"You'll tell me everything?"

"Of course I will."

Now Celeste wanted to know everything. Willie had obviously kept a lot from her.

"I won't keep you any longer," Detective Vaughan said, yet he didn't say good-bye.

"Thank you for keeping me in the loop."

"Just doing my job."

A few breaths of uncertain silence. Celeste didn't know if she should say more. The flashing red message light on the telephone base caught her eye. The only ones besides Detective Vaughan who knew she was in Washington were her parents and Bryson. It had to be one or the other.

"So, how's the weather there in Washington?"

"Hot. How's it there in Brooklyn?"

"The same."

"Thank God for air-conditioning." It dawned on Celeste that Detective Vaughan didn't act like a man in a hurry to get off the telephone. "So, Detective. Are you taking a vacation this summer?"

"I'm scheduled for the fall. I'd rather go away when everyone else is coming home."

"Reverse traffic, huh?"

"Something like that. So when will you be back in Brooklyn?"

"Hey, if I could sprout wings, I'd be on my way back right now. As soon as I get off the phone with you, I'm calling the airport. I'm done here."

"Your father told me about your sister's husband. My condolences to her."

Yeah, right, I'll tell her. "Thank you."

"So, I'll let you go. Give me a call when you're back."

"I will," Celeste said, smiling to herself. "You have a good day."

"I will now."

Even after the phone was silent at her ear, Celeste still held it there. "I will now," he'd said. How could she not read something into that? Detective Vaughan's deep voice sounded like velvet when he said those words. A smile tickled Celeste's lips. How could such simple words sound and feel so good? Hanging up the telephone, she settled back and smiled to herself. There was nothing overtly suggestive in what Detective Vaughan had said, yet his words put a smile on her lips, and a warm tingly feeling filled her belly. She could almost feel her blood flowing from all directions to her g-spot. Whew. It was getting mighty warm down there. Could this mean that she was ready—

Knock . . . knock . . . knock!

Hanging up the phone and sucking her teeth, Celeste was annoyed that her one good thought of the day had been dashed by a knock at the door.

"Yes?"

"It's me—Lorna."

The door wasn't open all the way before Lorna said, "Aunt Celeste, my mother and Patrice are screaming their heads off at each other. Patrice is all up in Ma's face, and Ma's so mad, I know she's gonna punch Patrice out."

"Oh, well."

"But, Aunt Celeste, you gotta go down and stop them—"

"The *only* thing I *gotta do* right now, Lorna, is call the airport. Your mother and sister can kill each other for all I care. You coming in?"

"But, Aunt Celeste, you—"

"Lorna! My name is Bess and I'm staying out of that mess. If I see your sister again, I'm liable to kill her myself. So, stay or go, you and I are friends either way. Your choice."

CHAPTER
23

For the third time Katrina apologized to the hotel manager, who could easily double as a stand-in for Laurence Fishburne, for all the shouting she and Patrice had been doing. "It won't happen again."

"We'd appreciate that, Mrs. Dawson. Our other guests are quite upset. The Best Western prides itself on—"

"You have my word, it will not happen again." Katrina quietly closed the door on those brown piercing eyes. She could about guess what he was thinking—*Some of our people just don't have any class.* She was embarrassed, but she was twice as angry. She headed straight for the bedroom. Patrice was stretched out as stiff as a board on her back on the bed. Her arms were crossed over her chest. Her eyes were wide open.

"*You* are going to get us kicked out of this hotel."

"It was just me in here yelling, right, Ma? You weren't yelling back at me, huh?"

"Patrice, you might be nineteen, but that don't make you pain proof. You can still feel the sting of my hand. You will not keep talking to me any ol' way you want. I won't have it. And that goes for the way you spoke to Celeste, too."

"You defendin' her?"

"No, I'm stating facts. Celeste is *my* sister, not yours. I don't care how you feel about her; you do not have the right to disrespect her the way you did."

Patrice stiffly crossed her ankles. "So now she's your best friend?"

"Hell no, but she's not to be talked to like that by you."

"Oh, just you, huh?"

"I can tell Celeste to kiss my ass and drop dead if I care to, but that's *my* prerogative as her sister, not as her niece."

Patrice turned onto her side and got up on her elbow. "You know something, Ma? You're such a hypocrite. You have never liked Celeste, you have never said one kind word about Celeste, and for the most part, you never even see Celeste. From the time I knew who Celeste was, you drummed it into my head that she was a conniving, manipulative little bitch that made your life miserable when you were a kid. Until today, you never said anything about the way I treated Celeste, and now, all of a sudden, you want me to respect her, be nice to her, give her a kiss on the cheek and say, 'I love you, Auntie.' Are you for real?"

"I'm not asking you to love the woman, Patrice, because I don't give a good goddamn about her my damn self, and that's not being hypocritical. But I am asking you, no, I'm *telling* you to cool out, to harness your big mouth. The last thing you need is for Celeste to look too hard and too long at your hatred of her and think that there is something more than my feelings about her rubbing off on you."

Patrice and Katrina locked eyes. What Patrice saw in her mother's eyes deepened the furrows in her brow. She sat up all the way. "What do you mean, 'something more'?"

"Just that you've come out *aggressively* strong against Celeste for no reason at all. In truth, Celeste has never done anything to you, Patrice, just to me. But you really laid into her earlier like she'd done something personal to you. I know you, Patrice. It was as if you had a reason, beyond defending me, to attack Celeste. Do you have such a reason, Patrice, that you haven't talked about that you need to be telling me about?"

"Why you askin' me that?"

"Because I wanna know what you're thinking, Patrice. Do you have something else to hate Celeste for?"

"This is stupid." Patrice slipped off the bed and went into the front room. Katrina followed.

"Has Celeste ever done anything to you?"

"I don't wanna talk about it."

"Talk about what, Patrice? What about Celeste?"

"Would you please drop it, Ma? I'm getting nauseous." Patrice took a pack of chocolate chip cookies from the snack chest.

"If there's nothing, Patrice, then I want you to leave Celeste alone. Do you hear me? Stay out of her way, because she will jump all over you, and I don't wanna have to kill her over you."

"Screw Celeste. I ain't scared of her. That stupid bitch can't get close enough to do anything to me."

Katrina jerked Patrice around, knocking the open pack of cookies out of her hand. Cookies lay broken on the floor. "Ma! Look what you did."

"You're not listening to me, Patrice."

"I told you, Ma. I ain't scared of Celeste. She ain't shit. She's a stupid bitch."

Katrina flat-handed Patrice hard on the forehead, snapping her head back.

"Whatcha do that for?" She rubbed her forehead.

"I'm trying to knock some sense into your stupid head. And I told you before, watch your mouth."

Patrice started to move away, but Katrina yanked her back and then pushed her against the snack chest, rattling it. "Listen to me. Celeste is not stupid. I have never said that she was stupid. If I didn't hate her so much, I'd tell you how smart she is. Just like I know that something's not right, she knows something's not right, too. And believe me, Celeste will be trying to figure you out."

"Well, she can't. I'm just as smart as she is, if not smarter."

"You think so?"

"I know so. I know something Celeste will never know. And, actually, if she keeps getting on my nerves, I just might give her the shock of her life."

Katrina didn't like the smug look on Patrice's face, nor did she like the false security her child was wallowing in.

"Whatcha lookin' at me like that for?"

"My stupid, stupid child."

"I'm not stupid! Why you saying that?"

"Patrice, if Celeste ever figures out what I know about you—"

"What's that, Ma? You don't know nothing."

"Don't bet your life on that, Patrice." Now it was Katrina's turn to be smug. "I know who it was you were sneaking around with."

Patrice drew back against the small snack chest, pushing it tighter against the wall. Her eyes bugged out of her head.

"I know who you were sleeping with that you should not have been sleeping with. I know that you've gotten your little young ass in a whole heap of trouble that I may never be able to get you out of."

"Ma, what—"

"Oh, yes, Patrice. I know who you were sleeping with, and I've known for months. You had better pray that Willie never told a living soul about his affair with you."

A horrible, deep-throated gasp erupted from Patrice's mouth just as a dam of torrential tears flooded her cheeks. Her legs gave way. She fell to the floor, crying harder than she'd cried the morning Willie died.

Katrina didn't try to comfort her child. She stood over her, unmoved. "You were stupid to get involved with Willie. I should have confronted you the first time I saw you get out of his SUV, two blocks from the house. I was at a stop sign across the street, watching him kiss you. I saw the way he touched you. You don't know how close you both came to getting rammed with my car. But in that briefest of moments, I thought of Celeste. I hated her so much, I almost cheered when I realized that you, my daughter, were screwing her husband. I have to admit, I felt empowered. Through you, I had gotten something over on Celeste. I know I was wrong to say nothing, but it was empowering nonetheless. I felt like I had personally brought her down a peg—hell, a whole lot of pegs.

"Celeste thought she had everything—that house she thought was so grand, a job she bragged about, and a man she thought *loved* her, and only her. She was so smug in her marriage to Willie, and I wanted so many times to burst her bubble. I would have never wanted you to be with Willie, but I figured you would have the pleasure of sticking the pin in Celeste's ass when Willie left her for you. But then his ass got killed, and assuming that you didn't do it, with your stupid self, you were with him."

"Oh, God," Patrice sobbed. "Ma, somebody killed Willie while we were doing it. It was awful. He was so bloody."

Katrina listened to Patrice's gut-wrenching sobs. She had planned to never talk to Patrice about Willie, but her dumb-ass attacks on Celeste had to be stopped.

"Did you see who killed Willie?"

"I couldn't see who it was, Ma. I was . . . Willie was . . . Me and Willie were—"

"I don't need to know what you and Willie were doing. It'll disgust me."

"Ma, I loved Willie."

"Don't be stupid. You didn't love Willie. You screwed Willie because you hated Celeste."

"No, I did love Willie. He loved me, too—he said so. He was gonna leave Celeste for me."

"You believed him, which is why you were trying to get out of going away to college. I knew that."

"We were gonna be together."

"If that had happened, Patrice, you would have, in time, grown very tired of Willie. He was too old for you, he was too ugly for you, and he was a nothing, a nobody. He wasn't good enough for you, and if the truth be told, he really wasn't good enough for Celeste. She just deserved a lowlife like him."

"Ma, Willie was better than Celeste."

"See, Patrice. You're stupid, or rather stupidly naive."

"I wish you'd stop saying that! I'm not stupid. I—"

"Patrice, you were with Willie, how long? How many months?"

Patrice said barely above a whisper, "Eleven."

"In all that time, Willie never left Celeste for you. Did you ever wonder why?"

"He was going to, Ma. He said so."

"Oh, his word. Willie gave you his word. Of course, we'll never know now, will we?"

Patrice began crying again.

"Do you need more proof of your stupidity, Patrice? What about you being in the same room, in the same bed with Willie, wide awake when he got killed, and you didn't see who killed him. Need I say more?"

Patrice stared at her mother. "How did you know I was with Willie that morning?"

"I saw you when you came home. You weren't in bed when I got up, and you were nowhere to be found, so I figured you had sneaked out to see Willie. You see, Patrice, you weren't as slick as you thought. I overheard you, a few times, talking to Willie on the telephone."

Patrice covered her mouth in disbelief.

"That's right. One time you were in the bathtub with the shower door closed. You must have thought that cloudy glass was sound proof—it wasn't, stupid. You didn't hear or see me when I stuck my head in the bathroom because you were giggling with your lover, but I heard you. In hindsight, maybe I should have said something then, but again, it was Celeste's face that I saw. So that morning when you came home looking scared out of your mind, and your eyes were red from crying, I thought maybe Willie had broken off with you. You locked yourself in your room, so I left you alone. All that morning I thought of ways to get back at him for hurting you, when your grandmother called and told me that Willie had been killed. Then I understood why you were crying."

Fresh tears flowed under Patrice's hands covering her face.

"Again, I'm assuming, no praying, that you didn't kill Willie. Patrice, did you kill Willie?"

"Ma! How could you ask me that?"

Tired, Katrina sat heavily. "Let's just hope I'm the only one that ever asks you that question."

Scared, Patrice asked, "Are the police going to come after me?"

"Believe me, Patrice. I pray the police never come knocking at our door. They must never find out that you were in that motel room. You didn't leave anything there, did you?"

Patrice nodded timidly.

"What did you leave?"

"My panties."

"Oh, God. Where?"

"Under the pillow."

"How could you be so stupid? God, if they ever connect them to you, you—"

"Ma, my name wasn't written inside my panties. If they . . . Wouldn't the police have come after me by now if they knew the panties were mine?"

Katrina thought about it. "I guess so. Thank God you don't have fingerprints on file anywhere."

Patrice wiped her face. "Yes, I do."

"What?"

"A week ago, I was fingerprinted for my school ID down in North Carolina."

"Damn, Patrice. Let's just hope those prints aren't put in the national database anytime soon. We don't need that hassle."

"Maybe we can try and find out what the police know."

"I say leave it alone. Asking questions can open up a can of worms. So far, what I know about Willie's murder, I found out from your grandparents. I'd never ask Celeste; she knows I never cared for Willie."

"Ma, you won't ever tell anyone that I was with Willie when he got killed, will you?"

"Patrice, do I look like I'm stuck on stupid?"

"Ma, I . . . I just don't want anyone else to know."

"They won't if you keep your mouth shut and stop trying to pick fights with Celeste."

"I won't say nothing to her ever again."

"Good. Because if this affair with Willie ever comes out, Celeste won't be the only one hurt. You will be dragged, kicking and screaming, through a cesspool of gossip and the legal system. It won't be pretty, Patrice. So please, *please*, practice being inconspicuous around Celeste and anyone else that knew Willie. All you need to do is slip up one time."

"What about the police? What if they come asking questions?"

"Patrice, if the police had anything that pointed them in your direction, they would've questioned you weeks ago. Apparently, your panties haven't given you away. So don't worry, don't give anyone cause to look your way."

"Okay, Ma." Patrice got up and hugged Katrina. Their embrace was a commitment to keep Patrice safe. Katrina knew that her child had not killed Willie, and she would never allow the police or Celeste to point the finger at her. She was glad that Willie was dead; it was just desserts for screwing her child.

Abruptly ending their embrace, Katrina pulled Patrice down next to her. "I want you to tell me everything, from A to Z, about your affair with Willie. How it started, where it started, and goddamnit, why it started. Don't leave out a single detail. If he farted, I wanna know when and where."

Patrice began rubbing her hands as if they were cold. Again the tears started.

"There's no time for tears, Patrice. You—"

Knock . . . knock . . . knock.

Katrina started for the door. "Go wash your face." She waited until Patrice closed the bathroom door before she opened the door to Albert.

"Are you ready?" Albert's voice was as strong and as unwavering as his gaze.

Katrina put out her hand. "Let's be friends, Albert. After all, we both loved Gordon, no pun intended."

Albert glanced down at Katrina's hand and then squinted at her. "Are you palming a cherry bomb?"

"No, silly, an olive branch."

After a second's hesitation, Albert shook Katrina's hand. He didn't trust her; her moods were too unpredictable. She didn't trust him—he had been Gordon's lover—but he was as close to an ally as she'd get in Washington. Besides Gordon's arrangements, she still had to get to his apartment and his house, and there was no one better than Albert to show her the way.

CHAPTER
24

Other than a good-bye to Lorna, who thought she'd still be at the hotel when they returned, Celeste left no message when she dashed to catch a hastily booked flight out of DCA. She had no illusions that she'd be missed by anyone but Lorna. And now that she was back home soaking in her own tub, cleansing herself with her favorite mango butter and shea body wash from her favorite store, Nubian Heritage, Celeste could almost feel the slime of Katrina's demon seed slush off her body to the bottom of the tub. In fact, the weight of the stress and strain that had been her constant companion since Willie died seemed to let up. Perhaps it was because she forbade herself to take any blame for Willie's cheating—she had been a good wife to him—and she had made up her mind that she wasn't taking any crap from Patrice or Katrina ever again. As far as she was concerned, they'd seen the last of her. She was done. That vicious sneer on Patrice's lips and the venomous hate in her eyes was forever seared in Celeste's mind.

Thoughts of Patrice sickened Celeste and tightened her brow. So much for her relaxing bath. She got out of the tub and quickly dried off.

Bzzzzz!

"Not tonight," she whined. She didn't feel like seeing anyone.

Celeste wrapped her light cotton robe tightly and hurried to the window in her cool, air-conditioned bedroom at the front of the house. With a single finger she held aside one narrow slat of the vertical blinds so that she could peek out onto the dimly lit stoop a floor below. It was Bryson and Erica. *Damn!* She had called Bryson to let him know that she was back home, but that call wasn't an invitation to come rushing over.

Bzzzzz! Bzzzzz!

Celeste pulled the blinds aside and opened the closed window. "Get off my bell!"

"Then open the damn door!" Bryson shouted back.

"Stop yelling at her," Erica said.

"I didn't yell at her."

"Yes, you did."

"Both of y'all stop fussing on my stoop." Closing her window, Celeste pounded barefooted down the wooden stairs to let Bryson and Erica in.

Erica hugged Celeste. "I know it's late, but *Bryson* insisted."

"Figures. Control freak that he is."

"So I'm controlling because I wanted to see for myself how you were doing?"

"I told you on the telephone that I was fine."

"Well, I wanted to see for myself."

"Wouldn't you call that controlling, Erica?"

"Don't involve me. This is between you two."

"Baby," Bryson said to Erica, "you could defend me."

"No, baby, I could mind my business and let you do what you need to do."

"And what is that?" Celeste asked.

"Aw, nothing. Nothing urgent," Bryson said, sweating. "Damn, it's hot in here. How come you don't have the air conditioner on?"

"It's on in the bedroom. Why are you here, Bryson? And why did you leave four messages in my hotel room? Man, I was only there one day, and not even overnight."

"I told him about that, Celeste, but he—"

"I thought you were gonna mind your business, Erica."

Erica pressed her lips together and then mimed zipping them.

"Celeste, maybe if you had returned one of my calls, I might nct have had to call four times. You wanna sue me for that?"

"I need to, Bryson, you're getting on my nerves."

"How?"

"Bryson, ever since Willie died, you've been trying to control my life. You act like I need a baby-sitter."

Erica loudly cleared her throat.

"I'm grown, Bryson. I don't need a sitter."

Shaking his head, Bryson said, "That ain't how it is. I'm trying to be here for you."

"But, Bryson—"

"Excuse me, can I say something?" Erica asked.

Celeste and Bryson both looked at Erica as if to say no.

"Okay, I'm gonna say it anyway. Celeste, Bryson is just worried about you."

"Why? I'm fine."

"You don't get it, Celeste," Bryson said, lightly punching the palm of his left hand. "I love you like blood. You didn't sound good on the phone, so I came over to make sure everything was copasetic."

Erica cupped Bryson's chin. "Isn't he sweet?" She pecked him on the lips.

"Oh, please," Celeste said. "Look, I appreciate you, Bryson. No, I didn't sound good. You wouldn't sound good either after spending time with Katrina and Patrice. I felt like I was sipping tea with the devil while he ripped out my heart with his bare hands."

"Patrice was there?" Erica asked. She and Bryson exchanged furtive glances.

"Yeah, and her ass was ugly. Excuse the French, but that little witch was in all her vicious glory. She is Katrina incarnate."

"What did she say to you?"

"Nothing I care to repeat."

Bryson went and sat in the lone armchair. "Was that the first time you'd seen Patrice since Willie died?"

"I hadn't seen Patrice for a few years before Willie died. And I can tell you this, it will be decades before I see her ass again. She was vicious."

Celeste bent to pick up the television remote. She didn't see the wide-eyed look that Erica gave Bryson, or the fearful look he gave her back.

"Celeste," Erica said, "I don't know why you'd put yourself out and go to Washington to help Katrina when—"

"Because my parents twisted my arm." She clicked on the television.

"Humph," Erica said. "They would have had to break my arm because I would not have gone."

"Yeah, well, never again."

"I hope you mean it, because your sister hates you, Celeste. And when people hate like that, they have no problem killing the object of their hatred."

"Katrina wouldn't kill me."

"Humph," Erica said again. "I don't know how you're so sure about that, considering the history you have with her. And God knows what her demonic daughter might do."

"C'mon. Erica, aren't you being overly dramatic?"

"Actually, she's not," Bryson said. "We both believe Patrice hates you more than Katrina."

"But how would you know that? I didn't tell you what happened." Celeste saw the sheepish look exchanged between Erica and Bryson. "Do you know something I don't?"

Erica looked pointedly at Bryson. Bryson knuckled-rubbed his nose.

"Well?"

"Celeste," Bryson said, "Willie told me how much Katrina and Patrice hated you."

"Did he happen to tell you how much he hated me?"

"Willie didn't hate you, Celeste. He lo—"

"Spare me. Willie was a liar, and if I get started on him, I'll just get upset and I won't be able to sleep. Anyway, how long are you people planning to impose on me?"

Erica chuckled.

"Damn, throw us out, will ya?" Bryson said, wiping his sweaty brow with his hand.

"Stay too long and I will. Look, I'm going up to put something on. You both know where the kitchen is."

Fifteen minutes later, Celeste joined Erica and Bryson in the much cooler living room. The air conditioner was running. They were sitting close up on each other on the sofa watching Denzel Washington's movie, *John Q.* Each had a tall glass of the instant iced tea Celeste had made earlier. A third sweaty glass of iced tea was waiting for Celeste. As late as it was, Erica and Bryson were too comfortable when Celeste really wanted them to go home so she could go to bed. After watching the movie for a few disinterested minutes, Celeste couldn't hold back a second longer.

"Bryson, you've seen that I'm okay. I love you both, but why are you still here?"

Erica softly elbowed Bryson in the rib cage.

He nudged her back with his knee. She elbowed him again. Harder.

Something was definitely up, and Celeste was out of patience. "Spill." She was looking at Erica.

"Not me. Bryson has to tell you."

"Well, someone better tell me. I've had it with the secrets."

Again Bryson nudged Erica. This time, harder. "If I was on the run," he said, "and hiding in your basement, you'd give me up, wouldn't you?"

"Depends," Erica said. "Would you be making mad passionate love to me down in that basement?"

"Damn right." Bryson kissed Erica lightly on the lips. She kissed him back.

"Okay, stop it. You two perverts are trying to distract me—which isn't working. One of you had better tell me what's going on."

Again Erica deferred to Bryson. "Get it over with."

"Straight out, Celeste," Bryson said, "have you gone through Willie's things yet?"

That question threw Celeste. "Why?"

"Have you?"

"A few things, important things—the insurance, Willie's bills, whatever needed immediate attention. Why?"

Bryson looked uncertainly at Erica. She gave him a nod of encouragement.

They were scaring her. "Okay, you two. What's going on?"

Bryson bent forward, resting his elbows on his thighs. He clasped his hands together. "I think you need to go through everything Willie had."

"What am I looking for?"

"Pictures. I think you'll come across pictures that'll show you who Willie went out to see that morning."

Celeste gawked at Bryson as he pulled his sweaty shirt away from his chest. The cool air was doing nothing to cool him down. He wouldn't look her in the eye. A lump caught in her throat. She swallowed hard, but that lump wouldn't move.

Bryson kept his eyes on his hands.

"You knew!"

"I—"

Quick as a cobra, Celeste crossed the few feet that separated her and Bryson.

Slap! The slap caught Bryson off guard, turning his head to the side. Other than his eyes closing briefly from the assault, he took the slap without reacting.

Bryson glanced at Erica, but Erica had lowered her eyes.

With her hands covering her mouth, Celeste backed away from him.

"You lied to me!"

"Willie was my brother, Celeste. I loved him. I wanted to protect him, but I didn't want you to be hurt either. Right now, the important thing is to find his killer. Willie—"

"You said I was like blood to you."

Erica looked up just as tears began rolling down Celeste's cheeks. She looked at Bryson, and his eyes were glistening.

"Okay, Bryson, *my brother,*" Celeste said. "Tell me, *your sister,* who Willie was seeing."

Bryson's chin began to quiver. His eyes filled with tears. Erica put her arm around him. She squeezed him to show that she was there for him. Bryson clasped his hands tightly. When he raised his eyes to look at Celeste, that lump grew bigger in her throat. All the shame and pain in the world was in Bryson's eyes.

"Bryson didn't wanna hurt you," Erica explained. "A lot of nights he couldn't sleep because of what he knew."

"What about you, Erica? You're supposed to be my friend and never told me what you knew."

"I didn't always know, Celeste. I found out the day Willie died, and I couldn't tell you that day; you were hurting too bad."

"I'm hurting now, goddamnit! How could you—"

"I asked her not to," Bryson said. "It's not her fault."

"Then you tell me, Bryson. Tell me who Willie was seeing."

Bryson raised his eyes to the ceiling as if he were seeking guidance from a higher power. "Celeste, Willie really did want to stop. He—"

Celeste started to cry.

Erica went to Celeste and held her, rubbing her back.

"I swear," Bryson said. "Willie didn't know who she was when he met her. She didn't use her first name. She used her middle name, and Willie didn't know her by her middle name. Celeste, Willie didn't recognize her when he first met her, he hadn't seen her since she was a little girl. He said—"

"Oh, God. Just say her name."

"Patrice. It was Patrice, Celeste. Your niece, Patrice."

All sound around Celeste vanished. Her ears stopped hearing. The walls closed in around her. Her eyes closed, her mouth opened. Her head exploded. "Aaaaaaaa . . . Aaaaaaaa . . . Aaaaaaaa . . ." She couldn't stop screaming.

CHAPTER
25

As much to get Patrice and Lorna off her back as to half-heartedly attempt to do what was right, Katrina begrudgingly relented and gave Albert permission to preside over a very private, very brief funeral service for Gordon in the smallest chapel Erskine Memorial Funeral Home had available, and that chapel would have held fifty people. There were only three people in attendance to mourn Gordon—Katrina refused to play the grieving widow. Gordon's family was screaming mad, but that was too bad. Not a thing any one of them said or threatened put enough fear in Katrina's heart to make her hold up the cremation, nor was she willing to bite her tongue and hide her true feelings about Gordon's betrayal to any one of them. Dorothy, Gordon's sister, the very person that Patrice was going to be staying with while she was away in college at Chapel Hill, was the most understanding of the bunch.

"I love my brother, but he was wrong. Do what you have to do."

Katrina needed no one's blessing, but she liked Dorothy all the more.

While Albert eulogized Gordon, Katrina sat out in the lobby of the funeral home, thinking only of the many things she had to do, and one of those things had to do with Patrice. As soon as she was finished with her business in Washington, she was sending

Patrice back down to Chapel Hill—she was going to school there anyway in the fall. Whatever Patrice needed, Katrina would ship when she got back to Brooklyn herself. There was no need to tempt fate and have Patrice and Celeste cross paths again, and that—*Oh, no she didn't!*

Katrina couldn't believe her eyes. Joan, her lawyer, Jonathan Ashfield, an older woman who looked too much like Joan to not be her mother, and a younger woman, who looked like nei-ther—she was African American—had all just come into the fu-neral home. How in the hell did they find out about the funeral?

"This is a private service, *family* only," Katrina stood and in-formed Jonathan Ashfield as he, alone, approached her, leaving Joan and her pitiful entourage at the door.

"Mrs. Dawson, your claim as the lawful wife has been estab-lished and is, therefore, not in dispute. However, a funeral home is public domain. You cannot stop my client from entering these premises, and by law—"

"Oh, yes, the law. As the *lawful* wife, I can keep her, *and you*, out of a private service that I arranged."

Jonathan Ashfield presented Katrina the letter he carried in his hand. "You don't own these premises, Mrs. Dawson, and by law the only individual who can bar us from entering any area therein is the owner, Mr. Archibald Hickson, who, by the way, has given us written permission to enter his place of business."

Katrina didn't bother to read the letter. She let it drop to the floor.

"Your feelings are well understood, Mrs. Dawson. However, we'd appreciate it if you would allow my client to pay her last re-spects."

Katrina glanced at Joan, who looked beat down tired. Her eyes were red and puffy, her long blond hair was pulled back in an ex-tremely tight ponytail, and her pale skin showed no signs of a tan even as hot as it was.

"Hey, if she wants to waste her tears crying over a man who she says lied to her, who tricked her into an illegal marriage, and then died, leaving her with an illegitimate baby, let her. She has my blessing." Katrina stepped aside. "Go on in. I don't give a damn. Gordon is dead, and none of your legal maneuvers or her sorrowful tears can wake him up."

Jonathan Ashfield beckoned to Joan. Katrina watched as all three women paraded past her into the chapel as if they wore blinders. It didn't bother her in the least that Joan was going in to see Gordon. It wasn't like he could cheat anymore. The funny thing was, she felt a sense of satisfaction about that. Tiptoeing to the door, she peeked in just as Joan went to stand at Gordon's open coffin. The other two women took seats, far away from Patrice and Lorna. Katrina slipped into the room and moved along the back wall to get a better view of Joan. She wanted to see if, indeed, Joan would cry for Gordon.

Patrice and Lorna whispered between themselves while watching Joan. Albert, who had been standing at the foot of the coffin finishing up his eulogy, had stopped in mid sentence. He, too, watched Joan, who suddenly hawked and spit a wad of phlegm onto Gordon's lifeless face. Albert dropped his head. A startled gasp exploded from Patrice and Lorna. The two women who had come with Joan were unfazed. Jonathan Ashfield, however, was shocked and sat with his mouth open.

Katrina saw the humor. Hadn't Gordon spit in her face?

Albert folded the sheet of paper he had been reading from and tucked it inside his jacket.

It took a second for Patrice to get over her shock. "What the hell you think you're doing? Bitch, you don't spit on my father!"

Uncharacteristically quiet, Lorna sat and cried.

Katrina raced to the front of the room and grabbed Patrice before she could go after Joan. "Leave it alone," she said, holding her back, secretly pleased that Joan had spit on Gordon.

"Let me go, Ma! She spit on my father."

"Actually, Patrice, your father spit on her first."

Calmly, Joan walked away from the coffin to her waiting friends. As they passed, Katrina could see that her cheeks were wet. She was amazed that the woman could still cry for a man who hurt her like that.

"Should we go on?" Albert asked.

"No. I think we're done here," Katrina said. "Albert, why don't you ask the director or whoever is around to close Gordon up."

"Isn't there something else we should do?" Lorna asked.

"Say your last good-byes, Lorna. Your daddy is out of here."

Lorna and Patrice went to Gordon's side, touching him, crying for him, wiping the spit from his face with a tissue. While her daughters' crying saddened her and tugged on her heart, Katrina willed her heart to harden as far as Gordon was concerned.

"Go ahead," Albert said. "I'll take care of them."

"Thanks." Katrina was all too happy to leave. Not one of her tears would be shed in that chapel.

"Mrs. Dawson," Mr. Ashfield said, just as Katrina stepped outside the chapel. "Fair warning. My client will be suing for her son's share of Mr. Dawson's estate."

"What else would she do? Bring it on."

CHAPTER
26

Six thirty-three-gallon-sized black plastic garbage bags filled to bursting with Willie's clothes—some shredded with a good pair of scissors, and some not—and any and everything else that was Willie's that Celeste could get her hands on now sat discarded out in the front yard waiting for garbage day on Thursday. Watches, cufflinks, suits, coats, shoes, and anything else Bryson wanted, he had taken with him. Yet again, the house was torn up, and several desk drawers were broken in her insane search for Willie's private stash of pictures. She needed to see for herself what Bryson had said was true. Even knowing what she knew, Celeste's mind resisted wrapping itself around the concept of Willie having an affair with Patrice. Just the thought of it was too ludicrous, too outrageous. It just couldn't be.

Last night after she had finally stopped screaming and found herself on the sofa between Bryson and Erica fussing over her, pressing an ice-filled washcloth to her forehead, she thought that maybe Bryson had lost his damn mind or something. That was, until she saw his bleary, red eyes. He had shed some tears of his own. Bryson and Erica both were swollen with despair over having to be the ones to tell her about Willie and Patrice. God, how Celeste didn't want it to be true. Willie could not have been that low of a dog. Wouldn't she have known that about her own husband?

Nothing made sense, and as tired as she was from not sleeping, from being emotionally drained and from searching feverishly for pictures of Willie with Patrice, Celeste refused to lie down. At three in the morning, minutes after Erica and Bryson had reluctantly gone home driving a car loaded down with garbage bags, she continued to look for the pictures. She found nothing in the basement, nothing in the bedroom, nothing in Willie's empty closets, nothing in his den, nothing anywhere that smacked of his impropriety with Patrice or anyone for that matter. The pictures she did come across were mostly of her, Justine, and Willie when they were blissfully happy.

At six-fifteen in the morning when her tiredness came down on her as though she'd suddenly been covered with an oversized leaded radiation smock, and her head pounded, and her sore, tight calves threatened to buckle under her, Celeste gave up. Too tired to take off her clothes and too weak to pull back her spread, she fell out on top of her bed, bone-tired, but still too stressed to sleep. It was her mind, her worry, that would not let her rest. Bryson had to be wrong. He had to have gotten the name wrong. Maybe Willie had told him he was seeing someone named Patricia. That's an easy mistake to make; the names were so similar. But Katrina's Patrice was never called Patricia because her name was Patrice, and Bryson had said that Patrice had called herself Renee. Yet, Bryson was sure that it was Patrice.

"Willie said he was partying at this club with some coworkers when this young girl asked him to dance. He asked her her name, and she said it was Renee. He said she was all over him from the start, dirty dancing and hugging up on him. Then Willie said, before he knew it, they were kissing, and things got so hot they ended up out in his SUV getting it on."

Hugging herself, Celeste began rocking. "Oh, God, I'm gonna be sick."

"Don't tell her any more," Erica said.

"I think Bryson had better tell me whatever the hell he knows."

Bryson was hesitant. "Celeste, you don't need to—"

"The girl said her name was Renee. That sounds nothing like Patrice."

"It was Patrice, Celeste. Willie said, after they'd . . . you know . . . done it and they were talking, Renee said, 'You're married to my Aunt Celeste, you know.' Willie said he jumped off top of her so fast he hit the back window of his SUV with such force he cracked it."

Celeste slumped into an emotional stupor. She remembered a year ago when Willie had come home with a cracked rear window and said he'd come out from the club and found it that way.

"You remember that cracked glass, don't you?" Erica asked.

Celeste didn't confirm what she and Erica knew to be true. She'd told Erica about it at the time.

"Well, that's when this Renee said her name was Patrice. She said she told him her middle name, Renee, because she didn't want him to know who she really was. That's how much she supposedly wanted to be with him."

"Conniving little bitch," Celeste said. "She's probably the one that killed Willie."

"We thought of that," Erica said. "That's why we came over."

"Then we need to tell Detective Vaughan what we know."

"Hold up," Bryson said. "Celeste, we only know that Willie and Patrice were having an affair. That doesn't mean that she killed him, but she might know something."

"I think she's the killer," Erica said.

Celeste agreed. "She's certainly mean enough and conniving enough to be a murderer."

"She tricked Willie into an affair, at least that's what he said," Erica said. "She gotta be conniving for that."

"Yeah, but no matter what name Patrice used, Willie should not have been open to having an affair with anyone."

"Amen to that. Right, babe?" Erica said to Bryson.

"I'm not my brother. I know not to put my meat in someone else's sandwich."

"Keep remembering that."

"This isn't about me, Erica. This is Willie's mistake."

Celeste cringed at that word—"mistake." She'd always hate that word.

"Look, Celeste," Bryson said. "Willie said he asked Patrice why she tricked him like, you know, changing her name, and she said because she wanted to have sex with him and knew that he wouldn't if he knew who she was."

Erica was disgusted. "She's a snake. Willie should have cut and run right then."

"Well he didn't, did he?" Celeste said.

"I can't believe he didn't know," Erica said.

"Well, I asked Willie how is it that he didn't know, right off, that he was dealing with Patrice?"

"Yeah, and he said?"

"He said he didn't recognize her. He said the last time he'd seen her, Patrice was about ten, if not younger. At eighteen, he said he didn't have a clue. She looked like two different people."

"That's a stupid-ass excuse!" Celeste said irritably. "Willie probably knew who Patrice was the minute he saw her."

"Celeste, you just saw her in Washington. You don't see her that often, did you know her?"

Celeste remembered how different she thought Patrice looked. "She looked older, she was older, but I knew who she was."

"That's because you're a woman," Bryson said.

"What the hell does that have to do with anything?"

"Celeste, men don't see detail or colors; the women do. Women notice haircuts, a new tie, weight gain. Men don't. We see much of our lives in black and white."

"That's true, Celeste. Bryson doesn't see paper on the floor or dust on the table. He only sees the floor, and he only sees the table. He probably can't even tell you what color they are."

"That's because it's not important. Damn. As long as they function, I don't care what color they are."

"I know men are like that," Celeste said. "But Willie could not have been fooled by Patrice if he hadn't wanted to be fooled."

"Okay, Celeste," Bryson said, "for argument's sake. Do you know Patrice's middle name?"

After thinking about it, Celeste had to admit that she didn't.

"See," Erica said, "that's what happens when families aren't close. This is really sad."

"I believe his meeting with Patrice happened just as Willie said," Bryson concluded. "Most kids do look different from age ten to eighteen."

"Nah," Erica said. "That's still no excuse. Willie shouldn't've been on the prowl. His zipper should have been welded shut."

"I'm not disputing that, Babe. I'm just saying he didn't know who this girl was."

"I still don't get it," Celeste said. "Why would Patrice wanna have sex with my husband? Especially knowing who he was. For God's sake, why?"

"You're not gonna like this, Celeste, but according to Willie, Patrice has a serious hate on for you. He said she couldn't stand you, and the way I see it, sleeping with your husband, maybe even breaking up your marriage, would make her day."

The tears came. "I saw how much she hated me in Washington. I've never done a damn thing to Patrice."

"Oh, sure you have," Erica said.

"No, I haven't!"

"Yes, you have. Celeste, you're probably everything Patrice might wanna be but can't."

"She's nineteen. I'm more than a decade older than her. Patrice has time to be greater than me."

"With her attitude, do you think she'll have a very successful life? Celeste, you have a beautiful home. You have a wonderful child, you have a great job, and before Patrice came along, you had a great marriage. And above all that, you're nice. You're a good person; people like you. I doubt Patrice will ever have a personal resumé like that."

"Then, if anything, my life should have encouraged Patrice to be a better person."

"You don't get it, Celeste. You're everything her mother isn't, and her mother hates you, so she hates you, too. Imagine all the horrible things Katrina has said about you over the years."

Celeste didn't have to imagine; she'd gotten a taste of it.

"Get the connection?" Erica asked. "Patrice hates you as if she were hating you for her mother. Plus, she hates you because her own mother isn't as nice as you, as pretty as you, as—"

"Erica, the first part of your analysis I agree with, but the second part is bullshit."

"Okay, so you don't see it, you're too close to the situation, but I'm telling you, Patrice has serious issues with you."

"I got that. Then why go after Willie? Why not attack me, head-on, like she did in Washington?"

"Because that attack was just words. Going after Willie and succeeding was tangible. Something she could feel, something solid she knew would devastate you."

"I can get with that, Celeste," Bryson said. "That's why I know Willie was set up. He—"

"Willie was weak! He wasn't supposed to be tempted or otherwise open to getting into an affair with anyone. It wasn't a one-night stand; it was a year-long affair. And even if Willie couldn't help himself because his brain got infected by some unknown virus, and he could no longer think about the consequences of his actions, he should have cut off his dick to protect himself from what he had no control over."

"Damn." Bryson eased his thighs together to still the weird tingling in his groin.

"That works for me," Erica said, "but, Celeste, it seems your niece would have done anything to hurt you. It's like Katrina's hatred of you was passed on to her daughter."

"Fuck 'em." Celeste wiped her face of the tears that seemed to have no end. "Bryson, what about the pictures? Have you seen them?"

"Celeste, I don't wanna keep—"

"Oh, just tell me!"

"Damn, I didn't wanna be involved in this mess."

"Well, you are," Erica said, "and you have your brother to thank for that. Tell her."

"If Willie was here, I'd strangle him," Bryson said. "Okay, Celeste. Willie asked me to hide the pictures for him . . ."

"Asshole."

". . . but I refused. I told him to burn the damn pictures and end the affair with Patrice, which he said he would. If he kept the pictures, he never told me where he hid them, and I wasn't interested in finding out. I told Willie he had too much to lose if you ever found out, and he said he was aware of that. Celeste, Willie cried over what he was doing. I just don't understand why he kept it up."

"I do," Erica said. "That little slut gave Willie her tail to eat out of. I'd bet my last bottom dollar on it."

"How do you know that, Erica?" Bryson asked. "You weren't there."

"I know men. You guys lose your minds over a piece of tail."

Bryson's face fell. "I'm beginning to worry about you. I never thought you were a man hater."

"I'm not, and you know that. I just don't trust blindly. I think most, if not all, men—gay or straight—are weak when it comes to a piece of young tail—male or female."

"I hope you don't see me that way."

"Are you a man?"

Bryson gawked at his wife. "I don't believe this. You don't trust me."

Erica shrugged.

"Erica—"

"Can we get back to Willie?" Celeste said, annoyed with Bryson and Erica's prelude to an argument.

"But, Erica—"

"Bryson," Celeste said, "let it go. Don't make this about you and Erica. This is about Willie and he was no naive little boy who didn't know how to put his penis to bed without dessert."

"That's right," Erica agreed, while ignoring the frown on Bryson's face. "Once Willie tasted that slut, he forgot about you, Celeste. He forgot about Justine, and he sure as hell forgot he wasn't a cat. He had only one life to lose, and he lost it in that damn motel room. Willie was a man who didn't think he'd ever get caught."

Celeste wiped away her tears. "He was stupid."

"I'm learning a lot about you, Erica," Bryson said. "I didn't know I was married to such a flaming sexist."

"Yes, you did. Babe, you know how I feel about rapists and adulterers—they should all be castrated."

"What about women? Y'all can be adulterers, too."

"Yes, and we can be rapists. But we have nothing to cut off that would augment our personalities. Babe, we come from a more emotional viewpoint. And really, sex doesn't rule our existence as it does men."

"Aw, man. This is male bashing. I can't believe you're saying all these things."

"You can thank your brother; he brought out all of my sleeping demons."

"Willie's not to blame for everything, Erica. He didn't do anything to you."

Half listening to Bryson and Erica, Celeste almost wanted to laugh at the appalled look on Bryson's face. He seemed to be hurt that Erica was lumping him with guys who lied and cheated on their wives. By the time they left, he still hadn't gotten over Erica's remarks and said very little to her. Their ride home was probably, at the very least, tense.

Finally left alone, Celeste climbed into bed. She couldn't get her mind off of the way Patrice had acted in Washington. Now it all made sense. How could Willie allow himself to carry on an affair with Patrice, of all people? If what Bryson was saying was true, Celeste didn't need pictures, but she wanted them for proof. She still couldn't imagine Willie with Patrice. If the pictures existed, Celeste wanted them. But if they were anywhere in the house, after searching all night, she would have found them. She knew every nook and cranny, from the basement up, because of the renovation work they had done years ago, and there was no space left un—

Celeste sat straight up in bed. The attic space! The one place in the house that she never foraged was the dark crawl space up in the attic. No one but a midget could stand tall and walk up there; it was too low and unstable. That space was always left to Willie and workers hired to clean out the attic and insulate it, and Willie had never bothered to install a light fixture up there. Celeste never went up there herself because not only was it dark and tight, but the only way to get up there was through a narrow, dark hall closet on this rickety wooden ladder that led to the roof past this small black opening to the attic. She had attempted to go up to the roof once and had abandoned the idea when her phobia kicked in at the attic space level. The opaque blackness at which she instinctively squeezed her eyes shut unnerved her—too spooky. God knows what mutant bug or rat was lurking in all that darkness. With cobwebs made by unseen spiders and layers of dust all around her, Celeste had begun trembling and sweating while clinging to the ladder. Once she'd returned to the solid flooring below, she vowed she'd never go up there again. Willie had laughed at her, calling her a chicken for being afraid to go up into her own attic or onto her own roof. Going up there had been a lark for him. At the start of every season, Willie had climbed up to check the roof for damage caused by the weather. What if—

With flashlight in hand, her fear in check, Celeste wasted no time ascending the ladder through creepy silken webs to the dark attic space. She'd worry about what was in her hair when she was all done. Two-thirds of the way up the ladder, at the opening to the attic space, she stopped. As determined as she was, she still wasn't about to crawl up in there, so she perched herself steadily on a rung of the ladder and shone her flashlight's narrow beam into the attic opening. The light bounced off the labyrinth of cobwebs and settled on the thick layers of dust coating the cross sections of beams filled in between with faded, fluffy pink insulation throughout the low, tight space. Nothing else was visible. Disappointed, Celeste was about to descend the ladder when the angle of light caught the corner of an object to the right of the attic opening. Slightly leaning into the dark opening and shining the flashlight up against the inside wall onto the object, she could see a gray, rectangular metal strongbox hugging the wall. Only a very thin layer of dust coated its surface. Her hands trembled as she pulled the box out of its hiding space. She lifted the not too heavy box and clutched it to her chest as she shakingly descended the wobbly ladder to the second-floor landing.

Celeste cautiously carried the box as if it would detonate if she shook it too hard. In the rays of the bright morning sun shining through her bedroom windows, she sat on the floor with the box in between her outstretched legs. With her fingers she tried to raise the lid—the box was locked. Of course, it would be too easy if the box was unlocked. Without a moment's thought, Celeste got up off the floor and hurried off to get a hammer, a screw driver, a chisel, and a pair of pliers. One, if not all, of those tools might be needed to open the box. Again in her bedroom, Celeste sat on the floor, her hands trembling, her heart pounding, and her eyes filling with angry tears as she went about demolishing the front of the box where the keyhole was. When the box finally yielded its secrets, Celeste wailed from the core of her belly. Pictures showing Willie and Patrice, naked, making love, kissing, hugged up, having fun, enjoying each other, laughing as if they knew that she'd one day see these pictures and realize that they were laughing at her, that the joke was on her, sickened her. There was no question who the girl overexaggerating her sexy poses in the pictures was—it was Patrice, bold and sassy to the point of ad nauseam.

Painfully horrific cries tore from Celeste's throat. She began tearing the pictures, while wishing that it was Willie and Patrice she was clawing at. *Stop it!* a voice shouted in her head. *You will need these pictures.* In an instant moment of clarity, Celeste stopped ripping the pictures. She stopped crying. Yes, she needed the pictures. She needed them to destroy Patrice. No wonder the little bitch was all up in her face in Washington—her hatred was all too real. Oh, but that was okay. Payback was a serious bitch, and Patrice was going to pay for sleeping with Willie and for killing him. The vicious little slut didn't know who she was fucking with.

CHAPTER
27

*B*uzzzz!
The doorbell startled Celeste. Yet, she welcomed the inter-ruption from her one-woman tirade. She rushed to answer the door, hoping that it would be Bryson and Erica. When they had left earlier, they left because they had to—Erica's mother was baby-sitting the twins and had to get up and go to work in the morning just as Bryson and Erica had to do. Without asking who it was, Celeste opened the door and was disappointed to see that it was Gertrude.

"Are you all right? No, you aren't. You've been crying."

Celeste touched her face. She hadn't washed her face of the tears that streaked her cheeks. With her hands, she tried to wipe away the ashy stains that surely had to be there.

"Oh, honey, I know you're still having a tough time. I heard you scream, so I rushed over. No one broke in here again, did they?" She looked past Celeste into the house. "I kept a lookout while you were away."

"Everything's fine. I was just having a moment, but I'm okay now."

"Are you sure? I can come in and sit with you a while. I'm not doing anything."

"Oh, no, Gert, thanks but I'm fine. Really. Ah . . . I had a bad night. I'll be fine." *I shouldn't've ripped up those pictures.*

"Are you sure, Celeste? You don't have to deal with this alone."

"Thanks, Gert, I know. I'm just tired right now." *I wish you'd go home.* "My brother-in-law and his wife were over last night, I didn't get much rest. I was just about to lie down." *So, please, leave!*

"Yes, you should rest. You'll feel better."

Not in a million years. "Gert, thanks for checking on me. As soon as I'm up to it, I'll come next door for a visit."

"That would be fine. I could use the company myself. My daughter's been away for a while. She went south to Jacksonville with that idiot, Melvin, to visit his mother."

"Uh oh. That sounds like marriage."

"Not if I can help it. That child's too young to be thinking about marriage, and it would kill me if she married *Melvin.*"

"Oh, I don't know, Gert. Melvin doesn't seem so bad. He seems to really care about Naynay."

"Melvin's lazy. I already got three lazy men laying up on me. My house is full. I don't need another man-child."

You raised them. "How's Walter? Is he taking time off for the summer?"

"He's off now, but he sleeps most of the day."

"Then go wake him up, Gert. Make him take you to the Poconos or Atlantic City. He can afford it."

"Actually, I've been wanting to go up to Foxwoods in Connecticut. I hear the winnings are a lot better there than in Atlantic City."

"Then make Walter take you. It's beautiful country up there on that reservation."

"You know, I think I will. I'm going right next door and drag his lazy behind out of bed. I'll let you know when we're leaving."

Thank God. "That's fine. I'll see you later."

"Okay. Oh . . ."

Oh, shoot!

". . . I'm making a banana pudding later. Want some?"

"Thanks, but I don't have much of an appetite these days."

"Of course. I understand, but don't worry, I'll make you a special one when you're ready."

"Thanks, Gert." Celeste closed the door before Gertrude cleared her stoop. As much as she liked Gertrude's old-fashioned custard banana pudding, banana pudding was the last thing on Celeste's mind. She was anxious to get back to Willie's Pandora's box. She took the stairs two at a time back up to her bedroom and went right to riffling through the pictures left in the box. Thank God for small favors. Willie had kept the negatives for all the pictures. She could easily replace the three pictures she had tried to destroy, but—

"Oh, God." Tears leapt to Celeste's startled eyes. The last three pictures that were facedown in the bottom of the box she had turned over. It was her own bed, in her own bedroom, on which Willie and Patrice had made love. Even now, the same lavender and white bedspread they lay atop in the picture covered the bed. Willie had not respected her, his child, or the home they had worked hard to make together. Oh, God. How could he?

Folding over, her head to her knee, Celeste wept silently because she didn't want to bring Gertrude running to her door again. That was the thing about row houses; the walls were never thick enough. Celeste cried until her head throbbed and her back pained her. She got slowly up off the floor, stepping on the pictures, her heart heavy, but her soul full of anger. Standing at the foot of the bed, she gathered up the corners of her once favorite summer bedspread and pulled it off the mattress. She balled it up and threw it out into the hallway. It was trash now, nothing pretty about it. Four years ago, she'd paid fifteen hundred dollars for the bed. It was supposed to last twenty-five years. It hadn't. She'd never see her money's worth.

Riiiing!

As if sleepwalking, Celeste checked the caller ID on the base of the telephone. It was Bryson. She answered, "I found the pictures."

"Oh, God," Erica said.

"Where's Bryson?"

"He's at work. I decided to stay home. Celeste, what are you gonna do with the pictures?"

"I'll talk to you about that later. Right now, I need for you to go over to my parents' house to pick up Justine."

"You want me to bring her to you?"

"No. Keep her at your house. Can she spend the night?"

"Of course . . . sure. Celeste, are you going to confront Patrice? Is she back in the city?"

"Erica, you know where my parents live, right?"

"Of course. We have their address. Celeste—"

"Erica, pick Justine up this morning—as soon as you can."

"Okay, but—"

"I'll call you tomorrow. Tell Bryson not to call me."

"But, Celeste—"

Celeste abruptly disconnected the call, but she immediately called her parents. "Mother, Erica, Bryson's wife, will be stopping by this morning to pick up Justine."

"Why?"

"Please get her ready. Send her clothes, too."

"Celeste, what's this about?"

"Mother, just have Justine ready, I'd appreciate it."

"Celeste, what's going on?"

"Is Katrina coming in from Washington today?"

"No. She has to stay over a few days to take care of Gordon's business with his job. Celeste, what's wrong? Why are you talking to me like this, and why is Erica taking Justine? She's fine right here."

"Mother, I want my daughter at her uncle's, and I don't feel like explaining why. Just do it."

"Just a minute, young lady. I don't like your attitude or your tone, and I will not pack Justine off without an explanation."

"What in the world is going on?" Richard asked in the background.

"Your daughter has lost her ever-loving mind, ordering me to pack Justine's things and hand her over to Bryson's wife. She ordered me! She—"

"Mother! If you don't hand Justine over to Erica, I will come out there and take Justine myself. Either way, she's leaving your house this very day. And if I have to come out there myself, you may never see my daughter again."

"My God, Celeste! What in God's name is wrong with you?"

"Let me talk to her," Richard said. "Celeste, what's going on? What's happened?"

Tears streamed down her face. "I want my daughter out of the line of fire—immediately."

"What in the world are you talking about? What line of fire?"

"You and Mother have never understood how much Katrina hated me."

"Is that what this is about? You and Katrina's petty arguments?"

"See. My point. As usual you're dismissing what I have to say about Katrina. You and Mother have always done that, which is why—"

"Okay, Celeste! I'm listening. What has Katrina done to you now? When we talked yesterday and you were still in Washington, you said nothing about any fights between you and Katrina."

"That's because the fight wasn't between me and Katrina. At least not directly. It was between me and Patrice."

"Celeste, for God's sake! Patrice is a child. You can't take anything she says seriously."

"Oh, I guess I shouldn't be taking these pictures I have of that *child*, Patrice, screwing my husband serious either, huh?"

The abrupt silence that followed the startled gasp on the other end of the telephone was broken by Stella asking, "What is she saying? Richard, what is she saying?"

"Dad, have my daughter ready." Celeste ended the call with a light touch of the talk button on her phone. She wanted Justine at Bryson's so she wouldn't have to hear her parents say, "You're upsetting your daughter," or "We'll keep Justine until you come to your senses." The funny thing was, while Celeste was taking a shower, she came to her senses. She was going to not only hand the pictures over to Detective Vaughan, but she was going to send pictures to the *New York Daily News* and the *New York Post*. They had run the original articles about Willie's murder; why not run pictures of him with his mistress? But first things first. She needed to either get more pictures developed or scan the pictures into her computer and print them herself.

Fresh out of the shower, Celeste sat in her bathrobe at the computer scanning the pictures onto the computer in the den. The reckoning for Patrice and Katrina was as close as the Internet.

Riiiing!

A quick glance at the caller ID on the telephone handset and Celeste saw her parents' number flash onto the small display. She didn't answer, and she didn't listen to the message they left. She had no intention of giving her parents the opportunity to browbeat her out of what she had her mind set on. Her scanning done, she went onto the Web sites of the *New York Daily News* and the *New York Post*. She had to take care of her business with them before handing the pictures over to Detective Vaughan. She wasn't about to let him stop her either. This game was going to be played by her rules.

CHAPTER
28

Finally finished with running around under the blistering Washington, D.C. sun, Katrina sat soaking in a cool tub of water, tired, but extremely grateful that she had settled much of Gordon's business on his job—the rest she'd take care of from New York. Other than the impending lawsuit for his illegitimate child's share of his estate, which was a matter of time and financial calculations, this whole nightmare would soon be a distant memory. For now, there was no need for her to waste a single brain cell worrying about how much Joan might actually get for her kid. Gordon hadn't been rich. There wasn't much to be had. Joan's lawyers were not going to be able to touch her house in Brooklyn, nor could they touch her and Gordon's insurance policies, which she'd mostly paid for and on which she and her children were listed as beneficiaries. Gordon's pension was in her name, and so was his very small stock portfolio. Joan's kid might get social security payouts and a few dollars from Gordon's savings, but there would be very little else Joan could get her hands on for that kid. Whatever Gordon had accrued in the little time he was living his double life, Katrina had no interest in, including that house he'd lived in with his mistress—she could have that little two-bedroom Cape Cod style house.

On her last afternoon in Washington, with Lorna and Patrice

at her side, Katrina had relaxed and played tourist. They had made it to the Lincoln and Washington Monuments, skirted the White House, and visited the Smithsonian. To top off their day, they were going out for a great meal at a great restaurant, and after a good night's sleep, they would be homeward bound—that was, except for Patrice. As strange as it seemed, Katrina felt as though she'd been given a new lease on life. No husband, a daughter going off to college, another daughter in her middle teens able to fix her own food, and her youngest, Gordy, potty trained and easily entertained by Rocket Power and Pokémon cartoons, or a popular Game Boy cartridge. What more could an attractive, young widow ask for?

A quick tap at the door—Lorna stuck her head into the bathroom. "Grandma's on the phone."

"As you can see, Lorna, I am sitting in a tub full of water."

"I told her that, but she said to tell you to come to the phone—it's very important."

"Did something happen to Gordy?"

"She didn't say, but she sounded hysterical."

"Damnit. I hope it's not more bad news." The bathwater washed from Katrina's body as she stood. "What's Patrice doing?"

"She's laying on the sofa watching TV."

"Tell her to get started changing her clothes since she takes forever and a day to get ready. You go change, too." Katrina quickly wrapped a towel around her wet body and padded out into the bedroom to answer the phone. "Yes, Ma. What's so *very* important? Did something happen to Gordy?"

"Didn't you check your messages?"

"Nope, not yet. What's up?"

"Your sister called."

Katrina clicked her teeth. *Damn. Now what?*

"Katrina, Celeste said something really disturbing about Patrice."

"Oh, that. Patrice was a bit nasty to her, but I straightened her out."

"That's not what Celeste is talking about. Celeste says she has pictures of Patrice having sex with Willie."

Katrina's mouth would have hit the floor if it hadn't been attached to her jaw.

"Did you hear me, Katrina? Celeste said Patrice was sleeping with her husband, Willie. His brother's wife came over to pick up Justine, and although she didn't wanna talk about it, she said it was true. Katrina, what in the world is going on? Do you know anything about this?"

"What else did Celeste say?"

"What do you mean, what else did she say? Are you telling me it's true?"

"Ma! Just tell me what Celeste said!"

"Don't yell at me!"

"I'm sorry! Ma, what else did Celeste say?"

"She told your father she wanted Justine to go to Bryson's house because she wanted her out of the line of fire."

"Oh, shit!"

"Katrina, it's really true?"

"I gotta talk to Patrice. I'll call you back."

"Katrina! Katrina!"

Katrina slammed down the telephone. "Patrice!"

Patrice lifted her head. "Whatcha callin' me like that for?"

"Get in here!"

"Sounds like you're in trouble." Lorna quickly claimed the remote control.

"Shut up, mind your business."

"I said get in here, Patrice!" Katrina could feel her heart pounding in her ears.

Patrice bolted off the sofa. "Whatcha yellin' for?"

"Close the door."

As soon as Patrice closed the door, Katrina rushed at her, slapping her hard across the face. With her fists she pounded her relentlessly over the head, while cursing her with each blow. Screaming, Patrice ran about the room trying to escape her mother's attack, but Katrina was always on her heels. She didn't care that her towel had fallen from her body and that her anger was blinding her in her pursuit of her daughter. Beating Patrice was the only thing on her mind.

Lorna burst into the room. "Ma! What you doing? Stop! Stop it!" Lorna grabbed Katrina, trying to hold her back while Patrice, crying hysterically, cowered in the far corner of the room.

"Let go of me, Lorna!"

"Ma, we're gonna get thrown out of here!"

Katrina pushed Lorna off of her. She snarled at Patrice, "How could you be so *stupid?*"

"What did she do, Ma? What happened?"

Katrina ordered Lorna, "Get my underwear and something for me to put on!"

Lorna hurriedly took from one of the dresser drawers a pair of black panties and a black bra. She handed them long-armed to Katrina. She then went back to the closet to get a pair of white pants and an orange blouse.

All the while glaring at a beaten Patrice still crying in the corner on the floor, Katrina was shaking hard as she yanked on her underwear and roughly stuffed her breasts into the cups of her bra.

Her chest was heaving; her lips were trembling. "I could kill you."

Totally confused, Lorna looked from Patrice to Katrina. "What did she do, Ma?"

"Lorna, go into the other room."

"I can't know what's goin' on?"

"I said *go* into the other room!"

"Dang! That's not fair!" Lorna dragged her feet as she left the room. She barely made it out of the bedroom before Katrina slammed the door at her back. "Man! People actin' all crazy up in here." Lorna immediately pressed her nosy ear to the bedroom door.

Patrice whimpered, "Ma, what did I do?"

"You stupid fool! How in God's name did you let that *asshole* take pictures of you fucking him?"

Patrice gawked stupidly at her mother.

On the other side of the bedroom door, Lorna covered her mouth to hold silent her scream of disbelief.

Although Katrina saw utter shock and terror in Patrice's eyes, it didn't matter. "That's right, Patrice, Celeste knows. Celeste has pictures of *you*, stupid, and Willie doing God knows what. You were stupid, Patrice. Don't you know if you lie, if you cheat, if you do anything in the dark, you don't take *pictures* that will expose you in the light of day? How stupid can you be? It's a wonder you never got pregnant."

"Oh, my God," Lorna mouthed to herself while staring at the door as if she could see right through it.

"Ma, I wasn't tryin' to get pregnant. I—"

"I could kill you!" Katrina again rushed at Patrice—balled up tight in the corner with her arms covering her head—kicking her on the thigh, hurting her own big toe. "Damnit!" She grimaced from the pain.

Patrice cried from the blows inflicted by her mother's foot, but she also cried from unadulterated fear.

"Your grandparents know, Patrice. Willie's brother knows. Tell me, Patrice, why in the world would you let that bastard take pictures of you having sex with him?"

"Those pictures were just for us, Ma. Nobody was ever supposed to see them."

"Stupid! Willie is dead! He's not here to keep those pictures hidden! Celeste found them. Do you know what that means, Patrice? Do you?"

"Ma, I . . . I didn't—"

"Shut up! You didn't what? You didn't know what you were doing? I guarantee you, Celeste knows what she'll be doing if she hasn't done it already. Celeste is going to the police. She's going to have you picked up, and once the police fingerprint you and match your prints to any one of the set of prints found in that motel room, you'll be arrested, Patrice. You'll be charged with murder!"

"Mommy, please. Please don't let them arrest me."

Katrina flopped down on the side of the bed. "Such stupidity! God, how can you be my child?" Her shoulders began to shake. She began to cry.

Outside the bedroom door, Lorna ran to answer the urgent knock at the hall door. It was the manager.

"Miss, you and your family will have to find other accommodations elsewhere."

"Maa!" Lorna called. "This guy says we gotta leave."

Dressed only in her underwear, Katrina opened the bedroom door. "We're leaving. We'll be out in an hour. Lorna, get in here and help me pack." She closed the door, yanked on her pants, and went about snatching clothes from the closet and the dresser. "Get up, Patrice. Pack your bag."

"Ma, I don't wanna go to jail. I didn't kill Willie."

"Shut up, stupid! Keep your mouth shut and get your ass offa that floor and pack your damn clothes so we can get the hell outta here."

Lorna timidly entered the room, but she didn't have to be told to be quiet. She said nothing as she, too, went about packing her suitcase. *Did Patrice say she didn't kill Uncle Willie? Why would she say that? Were they doing it when Uncle Willie got killed?* Totally stupefied, Lorna kept stealing glances at Patrice, wondering how could she have slept with Uncle Willie. No wonder she hated Aunt Celeste; she'd been screwing Aunt Celeste's husband.

As angry as she was, Katrina couldn't keep the tears from falling. She was just as much to blame as Patrice. She should have put a stop to the affair, but no, she'd let her hate for Celeste cloud her mind and dictate her decision to say nothing. She should have known that a pervert like Willie would take pictures, the egotistical bastard. Damn, how had she and Patrice both messed up this bad? Now Patrice was in deep shit, and Celeste was going to go after her full throttle. She had to stop Celeste, but how?

CHAPTER
29

"Pictures Link Murder Victim to Wife's Niece!"

The story of a dead man's infidelity and of a young girl's treachery didn't make the front page of the Friday edition of the *New York Post,* but it did garner a three-inch column on page sixteen. The paper declined the use of the pictures, although they did use a picture of Willie, smiling his bright toothy smile. They made sure to spell correctly his and Patrice's names. Celeste's name was spelled correctly, also. She was named as the widow and the aunt, who was "shocked and dismayed" by the discovery of sexually explicit photographs exposing the affair. *How true.* Celeste sat transfixed, staring at the article, not fully satisfied that she had exposed Patrice's trailer park lies and Willie's infidelity, but certainly justified in exposing them. All she had to do now was sit back and wait. She knew that Katrina had been back home since late last night with Lorna, minus Patrice. That didn't surprise Celeste. She figured Katrina would try to keep Patrice away from the police and from her, too, but that was all right. Patrice wouldn't be hard to find—the world wasn't that big.

"Damn!" Bryson tossed his copy of the *Post* onto the coffee table. He stepped, unapologetically, across Erica's legs on his way to barreling through the kitchen door with the force of a man who had no one to take his anger out on but the door itself.

Not bothered by Bryson's little tantrum, Celeste cooly shifted her eyes from the kitchen door to Erica. She folded her paper, set it on her lap, and folding her hands, interlocked her fingers like she had in elementary school—she was a good girl. From the kitchen came the sound of the refrigerator door being slammed.

"He'll get over it," Erica said.

Like I care. Celeste didn't bat an eye.

"Do you think Katrina's seen the paper?"

"My parents have. So I'm sure she has."

"Why don't you plug in your phone?"

"Nope. I want her to come over."

Erica started shaking her head. "I don't know, Celeste. This . . . this is bad."

"No, bad was when Willie and Patrice were sneaking around behind my back. This, this is good. Exposure is good for the soul. No telling who might see this article and relate. Perhaps they'll stop what they're doing before their affair sees the light of day."

"Tell me something, Celeste." Bryson came back into the room with a cold beer in his hand. "Did you have to put Willie's picture in the paper for everyone to know who he was? I told you about those pictures because the cops didn't have a lead. I didn't have to tell you. I could have kept the whole damn mess to myself."

"So you would've—"

"I got this!" Erica said, stopping Celeste. "Let me straighten out my man."

Bryson looked at his wife in disbelief. "So it's like that?"

"First off, babe, if you hadn't told Celeste, I would have told her myself."

"But she's wrong, Erica! We argued about this all the way here."

"Think about it, Bryson. Willie was her husband. Patrice her niece. If I were in Celeste's shoes, after seeing the pictures that were in that box, I would've called the *National Enquirer* and posted the raunchiest of those pictures on the world wide web—big-time. I think you should be grateful for that itty-bitty article."

"Y'all just don't understand. Willie was my brother."

"We understand. Don't we, Celeste?"

Celeste acknowledged with a single slow blink of her eyes. She could kick herself for not spreading the pictures all over the Internet, but, hey, it wasn't too late. Detective Vaughan had the originals, but she had copies printed from her computer. He'd appeared to be embarrassed for her, but he couldn't hide his elation that a lead had dropped into his lap. "We'll talk to her," he'd said, "see what she can tell us. What's her address?"

"For my sake," Bryson said, "and for Justine's, why couldn't you have just told the police about Patrice and kept the pictures out of it?"

"Bryson, leave Celeste alone."

Bryson ignored Erica. "I mean, did you have to make Willie look so bad? My brother was human, Celeste. He made a mistake. Did you have to let the world know what he did?"

Celeste met Bryson's angry glare with a cool, unfazed gaze. She didn't need to waste her energy fighting with Bryson—he was no threat to her. There was a bigger battle destined to be fought.

"You were wrong, Celeste. That wasn't right."

"I hope you told Willie how wrong he was."

"I did! I told you what I said to Willie."

"Then you should have stopped him. You should've—"

"Willie was a grown man! I couldn't stop him from doing a damn thing! He—"

"That's exactly right, Bryson!" Celeste was tired of Bryson's anger at her. "Willie was a grown man, and grown men should know better. They should know there are serious consequences for adultery, but even worse consequences when family's involved. It's too bad his cheating ass isn't alive to suffer the consequences of his stupidity. Hey, but Patrice is alive. I want her to receive her first lesson in retribution from her *auntie.*"

"So you get your revenge, Celeste. What if someone tells Justine about this article?"

"Willie should've thought about what effect his affair with my niece would have on his daughter if his daughter ever found out."

"She's right."

"Aw, come on."

"Bryson, none of this would be happening if Willie hadn't had the affair with Patrice in the first place. In fact, Willie wouldn't be dead if he hadn't snuck off to get with Patrice."

Celeste muttered, "Each path you take."

"Damnit, Erica, I know that. But my mother is gonna have another heart attack for sure if she hears about these pictures. I didn't tell her, remember?"

"Well, babe, it's not like your mother's gonna read the paper. She's almost blind from the glaucoma, and that double hip replacement confines her to the nursing home down in Tennessee. Besides, you haven't see her yourself in years, and she didn't even make it to Willie's funeral, so I don't think you have anything to worry about. Who's gonna tell her?"

"News travels."

Celeste hadn't thought once about Willie's mother. There was no reason to. She'd met Mildred Alexander only twice in all the years she and Willie had been together. The single mother who had raised two sons was never very maternal, according to Willie, and he could remember from the time he was six, Mildred telling him and Bryson that she couldn't wait for them to graduate high school. When that day came, his mother literally kissed them good-bye and relocated to her hometown of LaVerne, Tennessee, vowing to never return to New York City. The two times Celeste had seen her were when Willie yearned to see his mother, but after the second visit, when Willie saw that Mildred couldn't care less that he was there, he said he'd never visit her again, and he hadn't. That was seven years ago. He spoke to her on her birthday in March and on Christmas Day. That was it.

"They're your pictures, Celeste. Don't let me or Bryson tell you what to do with them."

"Well, damn," Bryson said. "Sometimes, Erica, I wonder if you're for me or against me."

"For you, babe. Don't ever doubt it. But like I keep telling you, right is right, wrong is wrong."

Shaking his head disgustedly, Bryson turned away from Erica.

"Look at you two," Celeste said. "I don't want y'all fighting over this. I don't want your marriage in jeopardy because of any decisions I make about these pictures. Bryson, let's be real. When you told me about the pictures, did you think I was supposed to keep them a secret, like Willie did?"

"Not from the police, Celeste, but damn! You didn't have to go to the tabloids."

"Yes, I did. I wanted what Willie did to be out in the open. It was a way to get even."

"Couldn't you have gotten even by putting Patrice in a head-lock and beating the hell outta her?"

"If I did that, her mother wouldn't feel the pain."

"Oh, shit. You did this because of Katrina?"

"Bryson, I'd be lying if I said Katrina had nothing to do with my decision. I believe she's just as guilty as Patrice."

"That's not right, Celeste."

"Babe, I can see where Celeste is coming from."

"Then explain it to me, because I'm not getting it."

"Okay, listen. Suppose Katrina knew all along about Willie and Patrice. That would mean that she condoned her daughter's affair with her sister's husband. Now, if that's true, that makes Katrina—"

"Just as guilty of the affair as Patrice," Celeste said, finishing Erica's sentence. "And in a court of law, Katrina's knowledge of the affair would be an accessory after the fact, if not before. So Katrina—"

"Needs to be punished, too," Erica concluded.

"Are you two supposed to be lawyers now?"

Buzzzz!

"If I ever find out that Katrina knew," Celeste said, ignoring the doorbell, "I'm gonna—"

Buzzzzzzz!

"Aren't you gonna get the damn bell?" Bryson asked impatiently.

"You get it." Celeste shifted her behind in her chair, recrossed her legs, and got more comfortable. "I don't feel like wearing my-self out." She knew how hard and long the day was going to be. Sore feet was the last thing she needed on top of the mental gym-nastics she was going to be putting her brain through. And if she guessed right—all hell was about to break loose.

"Where is she?"

The sound of her father's voice didn't surprise Celeste.

"In the living room," Bryson said.

What did surprise Celeste was that her mother had come, too. Well, she was ready for both of them, but neither seemed to know what to say. They stood across the room with grim, bitter looks on their faces, obviously blaming her for exacting revenge on their precious grandchild.

"Mother, it's so rare I get to see you here."

Abruptly standing, Erica cut her eyes at Celeste, but she said graciously, "Mr. and Mrs. Reese, would you like to sit down?"

Both Richard and Stella sat where Erica directed them, but they continued staring at Celeste. Bryson took a long swig of his beer. Erica went off into the kitchen.

"So," Celeste said, trying to sound as nonchalant as she could, "what brings you *both* here on this bright, beautiful day?"

"How could you, Celeste?" Stella asked. "How could you do such a spiteful thing?"

Richard took Stella's hand and squeezed it. "Let's not get off on the wrong foot."

"Mother, why am I not surprised that you asked that?"

"This is not a game, Celeste. Because of that article, the police are going after Patrice. They wanna question her. They think she may have something to do with Willie's murder."

"Good to hear they're doing their job."

Erica came into the room carrying a tray with two glasses filled with ice water. She set the tray on the coffee table and offered a glass to Stella.

Stella ignored the glass held out to her. "Aren't you the least bit concerned about Patrice?"

"Was she concerned about me?"

"Celeste," Richard said, "Patrice is only a child. She—"

"Dad, that child didn't have any problem spreading her thighs with my grown-ass husband."

"My God, Celeste," Stella said. "Are you gonna let your anger at Willie destroy your own niece?"

That screaming headache was back, but Celeste refused to rub her forehead. "Is that what I am, Mother? Angry?"

"Don't mince words with me, Celeste. You didn't have to go to the press . . ."

"That's what I told her," Bryson said.

"Well, I did."

". . . and you didn't have to turn those pictures in to the police."

"Patrice is not a murderer," Richard said.

"Oh, so I guess she's just a little slut who had a habit of meeting with my husband in motel rooms?"

"How dare you—"

"How dare I what, Mother?" Celeste shot up out of her chair and charged at her mother, forcing her and her father to rear back. "How dare you come into my house with your long face and accusatory eyes, blaming me, when I'm the one that's been wronged. *I'm* the one that was cheated on by *my* husband with *my* niece—my blood. Patrice is equally to blame. Both of them had a moral obligation to respect me—Willie, our marriage; Patrice, our blood. Instead of coming into my house ready to damn me to hell, Mother, for exposing a little slut, you should have walked in here and said how sorry you were that I'd been hurt. But no! You come in here to do what? To chastise me, to scold me for being a bad girl? No, I don't think so. I won't allow you to fault me, chastise me, or put guilt on my head. "

"Celeste, sweetheart," Richard said, speaking slowly and calmly, "we're not blaming you for what Patrice did. She was wrong. We all know that."

"Do you in fact know that, Dad, because I was beginning to wonder. I mean, if you need to see the pictures to truly accept what Patrice and Willie did, I have copies. They're right over there." Celeste pointed to printouts from her computer laying on top of the credenza between the two windows. She'd had Erica put them as far away from her as possible after she and Bryson had gotten their eyeful.

Richard and Stella both turned to look where Celeste was pointing, but neither made a move to get up. When they looked back at Celeste, she saw the pained expressions on both their faces, but that was not enough to make her back down.

"Let me tell you all something," Celeste said, looking at Bryson and including him in what she was about to say. "I won't let any of you make me the culprit. I am not the one who lied, who cheated and slithered around in the dark behind Willie's or Patrice's back. They screwed me. And if there is one person in this room who can't see that, or can't understand why I don't give a rat's ass about Patrice or what happens to her, then that person"—Celeste looked from Bryson to her parents—"or all of you, can get the hell outta my house."

Everyone stared at Celeste in stunned silence. That was, everyone except Erica. She exaggerated clearing her throat.

Celeste didn't think she'd made her point strong enough. "And I mean get the fuck out now."

Stella gasped. Bryson turned his beer up to his mouth and downed the last drop, while Erica reached out and touched Celeste's arm, but Celeste already knew that Erica was in her corner.

Richard slowly got to his feet. Celeste's nose began to sting. Of all people, she never thought her father would be the one to walk out on her. Going around the coffee table and standing in front of Celeste, Richard opened his arms, and before Celeste's beaded tears could run down her cheeks, she fell against his chest, grateful that he wasn't abandoning her.

"But what about Patrice, Richard?" Stella asked. "We have to help her."

"Yes, we do. But we have a daughter we have to take care of, too."

"Patrice needs us more than Celeste does. Celeste can take—"

"Be quiet, Stella! We have an obligation to Celeste first and foremost. She's right. Patrice was old enough to know what she was doing was wrong. If she didn't kill Willie, a good lawyer will prove her innocent. We can't turn our backs on any one of our children. If we do, this family will fall apart. Now, you let Celeste be. She—"

Buzzzzzzzzzzzzzz! Buzzzzzzzzzz! Buzzzzzzzzzzzzzz!

"Oh, Lord." Stella started fidgeting with her glasses. "That must be Katrina."

CHAPTER
30

There wasn't a soul who didn't know who it was that was laying on the bell. Celeste glimpsed fear on her mother's face, anticipation on Bryson's, a cocky glint in Erica's eyes, and a dark scowl creasing her father's brow.

Buzzzzzzzz! Buzzzzzzzzzzzzzzzzzzz!

Celeste started for the door.

Richard hurried past Celeste. "Stay here."

"I can answer my own door."

"That's not what you said earlier," Bryson reminded Celeste.

"Sue me, I changed my mind." Again she started for the door. Bryson stopped her this time.

"Would you please let go of me?"

"Celeste, don't you know anything about combat? You never rush headlong at your enemy. You don't know what they have waiting for you."

"You're talking nonsense," Stella said. "My girls are sisters, not enemies."

"Yeah, Bryson. Katrina and I are sisters. We're the best of friends."

"You can stop the sarcasm," Stella said.

Katrina shoved the door open the minute Richard unlocked it. "Where's that bitch?"

"Don't come in here talking like that."

"Dad, let her in. I'd love to see my sister."

"Bitch, I'll fu—"

Richard snatched Katrina hard, yanking her back. "What did I just tell you?"

Katrina tried to free her arm. "I'm gonna kill her!"

Richard squeezed Katrina's arm harder. "You're not doing any such thing! You are going to sit down and act like you got some sense."

Stella stood. "Katrina, we do have to sit down and talk about this."

"I'm not here to talk to her. I'm here to kick her ass."

"Bring it on, *sister.*"

"No!" Richard roared. "There will be no fighting in here. Katrina, you will behave yourself."

"Dad, you saw what she did! She libeled my daughter in the damn newspaper!"

"Granted, that may not have been the best way to handle this, but—"

"Get it right," Celeste said. "Libel is an untruth, a malicious lie. Did I lie about something?"

Katrina lunged at Celeste but was yanked back by Richard. "Bitch, you—"

"I said cut it out, Katrina, and I mean it!"

"She lied on my daughter!"

"What did I lie about? The affair or who the affair was with?"

"You're trying to put your husband's murder on Patrice. She had nothing to do with his murder."

"Says you. I figure if she can screw my husband, she can kill him, too."

"Bitch—"

"Katrina!" Stella shouted.

"If you weren't woman enough to please your man, somebody had to do it."

"Funny, you of all people should say something like that. What is it that your husband did again?"

"Fuck you!"

"Oh, yes. Gordon married another woman, a white woman, and made a baby with her all while he was still married to you. Hmm. Could it be, Katrina, that you weren't taking care of your man's needs?"

"Let go of me, Dad!" Katrina struggled to get closer to Celeste. "I'm gonna kill her. She's accusing my daughter of murder because that bastard of a husband of hers didn't want her."

"You can't change the facts, Katrina," Celeste said. "Patrice was sleeping with Willie."

"That's a lie!"

"It's the truth, Katrina," Bryson said. "The pictures don't lie. See for yourself."

"I don't wanna see any damn pictures. Y'all probably doctored them."

"If only that were the case," Bryson said. "Katrina, my brother was seduced by your daughter."

"Liar!"

"Don't call my husband a liar!" Erica exclaimed.

"Neither of you know my daughter and can't say a damn thing about her. So mind your damn business."

"Wait a . . ."

"Katrina!" Richard bellowed. "Get control of yourself. Stop this nonsense."

". . . minute," Erica said. "I don't know who you think you are. Instead of barging in here and calling us liars, you need to ask yourself why your daughter was sleeping with her uncle."

Bryson had his hands full with holding on to Celeste. "Katrina, don't be disrespecting my wife. Your daughter—"

"I got this, Bryson!" Celeste said, putting up her hand, stilling his tongue. "This is my battle. Katrina and I are on familiar ground."

"Celeste, don't—"

"Dad! Stay out of this. My sister and I need to talk about why her daughter was screwing my husband. Why her daughter, the tramp, killed Willie—"

"That's a damn lie! Patrice didn't kill Willie! But I'm glad he's dead. He deserved to die for raping my daughter."

"Oh, hell no!" Bryson said. "Willie didn't rape Patrice. She—"

"Those pictures don't show rape," Celeste said, "and cheap-ass motels is where most men take whores."

"Fuck you, bitch!"

Stella shook her fists. "Would y'all please stop cursing?"

"My daughter had your man, bitch, and if he were still alive, he'd be with her right now."

"Over my dead body," Richard said.

"And mine," Celeste said. "It's too bad that little tramp isn't six feet under with Willie right now."

"Oh, God. Y'all stop this!" Stella shouted. "I didn't raise y'all like this."

Katrina smirked. "Patrice is more woman than you'll ever be, and Willie knew that."

Celeste balled up her fists. "You knew about the affair, didn't you?"

"Richard, make them stop!"

Richard tightened his hold on Katrina. "I'm taking you out of here."

"Yeah, bitch, I knew. I should've taken pictures my damn self."

"Katrina!" Stella shrieked. "My God."

Celeste pounced on Katrina before Bryson could stop her. She punched her in the face, and before Katrina had a chance to recover, Celeste punched her upside her head. To Celeste's ears, Katrina's screams sounded like a wild animal. Katrina broke loose from Richard, rammed Celeste into Stella, and all three fell onto the sofa, pushing it back. A flurry of fists landed awkward punches, some hitting Stella, who screamed out of panic. Katrina grabbed a fistful of Celeste's hair, pulling it, hurting her, but Celeste clawed savagely at Katrina's hands, drawing blood, making her release her hold on her hair. Shouts of "Stop it!", "Do something!" filled the room. Richard and Bryson both took hold of Katrina and pulled her off of Celeste, but Katrina caught hold of Celeste's oversized T-shirt, refusing to let go, pulling Celeste, the sofa cushion, and Stella onto the floor. It wasn't until Bryson used brute force, twisting Katrina's wrist, that he was able to get her to let go of Celeste. He hefted Celeste up onto her feet and swung her halfway around, away from Katrina.

Erica rushed to help a gasping Stella up off the floor. That's when she kicked something. Looking down, she saw that she had kicked a videotape. She picked it up and looked at the label—Dialacom. Erica tried to get Bryson's attention, but he was totally occupied with trying to hold on to Celeste.

"Get offa me, Dad!" Katrina shouted.

Richard shook her. "Stop this!"

Stella was gasping still and clutching her chest.

"Let go of me!" Celeste was breathing so hard her throat was hurting. "Bryson, let go!"

"No! You gotta calm down."

"Look what you're doing to your mother," Richard said. "You girls are acting a fool."

Stella was crying. Celeste didn't know if her mother was crying because she was hurt or because her daughters were fighting like animals, but she had no time to see about her.

"Get her outta my house!"

"Bitch, I ain't going anywhere till I kill you!"

"Are y'all crazy?" Richard slammed Katrina up against the wall and held her there with his powerful forearm across her collarbone. Katrina fought wildly, kicking and clawing at her father. "Enough! Goddamnit, I said enough!" He pressed harder on her collarbone, but Katrina fought harder.

"I'm gonna kill that bitch!"

"You're wrong, Katrina!" Richard said. "If you knew Patrice was sleeping with Willie and did nothing to stop her, in God's name why didn't you?"

"Why, Katrina?" Stella asked incredulously. "How could you let that happen?"

"You wanna know why? I hate that bitch, that's why."

Celeste asked, "Isn't that what I've been telling y'all all my life? Katrina has always hated me?"

"That's right, bitch, I knew, and I laughed at it."

"You low-life, scandalous piece of trash!"

"Bitch, so are you."

Celeste tried to pull away from Bryson. "If I get my hands on you again, I'll show you my bitch."

"Y'all gotta stop this!" Richard pushed even harder against Katrina's collarbone. She grimaced from the pain. "You're sisters!"

"I'm no sister of hers," Celeste said. "I knew she knew. I bet she even put her tramp of a daughter up to it."

"And if I did? Whatcha gonna do about it? You wanna kick my ass? Come on."

Richard took hold of Katrina's face, pushing her head back against the wall, squeezing her cheeks hard until her mouth gaped from the pain. Squealing and squirming, Katrina tried to free herself, but Richard was unrelenting in his hold on her.

Nose to nose with Katrina, Richard snarled, "Stop it or I'll break your damn neck myself, so help me God."

With her mouth grotesquely twisted and gaping, Katrina froze in a bug-eyed stare.

"How could you let Patrice sleep with your sister's husband? Why would you let that happen?"

Katrina tried to speak, but her words were garbled. Saliva streamed down her chin, and tears slipped down her face onto Richard's hand. She dug her fingernails into his wrist. He didn't flinch.

"You answer me, Katrina!"

Katrina couldn't answer—her father was squeezing her cheeks so hard her teeth were embedded in them.

"Don't you get it, Dad?" Celeste asked. "Katrina was trying to hurt me, like she's always tried to hurt me. But she was so blinded by her hate for me, she didn't realize that it was her own child she was hurting. She's responsible for Patrice becoming a murderous whore."

"Oh, Lord," Stella cried, holding her head. "I can't take this."

Richard abruptly released Katrina's face. "Did you put Patrice up to sleeping with Willie?" He stepped back from her.

Katrina worked her mouth to ease the pain and realign her jaw.

"*Did you?*"

"I had nothing to do with them getting together!"

"Then when did you know?"

"You can't put this on me. Celeste—"

"*When,* Katrina? When did you find out?"

"Months ago, all right! I found out by mistake. I saw Patrice with Willie."

Richard groaned, "Oh, God."

Celeste felt light-headed. Hearing Katrina admit to seeing Patrice with Willie sickened her. "Your daughter slept in my bed, with my husband, in this house."

Stella groaned and lowered her head.

"For a whole year, damnit, they had an affair. And you knew, Katrina. No matter how much you hated me, you should have loved your daughter enough to protect her, to make her understand that she was doing wrong. Did you get some sort of perverse pleasure from seeing your child with my husband?"

Seething, the veins in Richard's neck popped as he clenched his jaw.

"Well, did you, Katrina? Answer me!"

"Damn right! Every time I thought about Patrice and Willie together, I knew that you were getting fucked just as hard."

Slap! Richard's right hand slap snapped Katrina's head into the wall.

Celeste started for her, too, but Bryson still had a firm hold on her.

Deep guttural sounds of sobbing were all that came from Stella.

Glaring bullets at her father, Katrina started to move away from him.

"You take one step, and as God is my witness, I will knock you down." The hard, unblinking glare in her father's eyes told Katrina that he was not threatening her. He meant every word.

"You've always loved *her* best. You've never been on my side."

"Katrina, there is no taking sides with wrong, and you were *dead* wrong."

"Amen," Erica said.

"You're gonna pay for this," Celeste vowed. "I swear to God, if it's the last thing I do, I will make you pay for—"

"There isn't a damn thing you can do to me!"

"Oh, no? I wouldn't bet on that. Even if your daughter is convicted of murder, the conviction will be on your shoulders."

"Patrice will never be convicted."

"I wouldn't bet on that," Erica said.

"Who the hell are you?"

"Just an interested bystander, but I was thinking. If Patrice's fingerprints are found in the room, and the bodily fluids that we all know were found on Willie match Patrice's DNA, all of that places her at the scene of the crime."

"Oh!" Bryson said. "And don't forget that 911 call from a female reporting that Willie was dead. They should be able to match Patrice's voice."

"Good one, babe," Erica said. "Now, if you put that evidence with all those nasty pictures and the fact that Patrice is Celeste's niece, geez, Katrina, do you think your daughter can handle twenty to life?"

"You don't know what you're talking about. Just because Patrice was with Willie don't mean that she killed him."

"Hey, people have been convicted on less circumstantial evidence. I know. Working in the system, I've seen it."

"My daughter won't be convicted. She didn't kill Willie."

Celeste gave Erica a wink. Erica's job as a paralegal served her well. "Well, Katrina, if Patrice is convicted, you can only blame yourself. You should have stopped her."

"Maybe you should've known where your husband was spending his free time."

"Damn, Katrina," Bryson said. "Even I can't believe you went there. It's like the pot calling the kettle black."

"Go to hell, Bryson. In fact, all of you can go to hell." Her cheek was still smarting. Katrina moved cautiously away from her father. "I don't owe any one of you a damn thing—not an explanation, not a single answer to any of your asinine questions."

"Oh, you will answer to someone," Richard said. "I will be telling the police where they can find Patrice."

"Dad, do you hate me so much that you'd turn your own grandchild in?"

"That's just it, Katrina. I love Patrice enough to do what's right by her. Which is what you should have done."

"I'm a good mother, and you can't say that I'm not."

"Celeste, call that detective you've been working with. Tell them that Patrice is down in Chapel Hill with Dorothy Grant. I have the address at home."

This time, Katrina grabbed on to Richard. "Dad, please don't. I don't want Patrice to see the inside of a cell. Don't bring her into this."

"She's been in it from the start," Celeste said.

"This is your fault!"

"No, Katrina," Richard said. "This fault belongs solely on your shoulders."

It was as if her father had slapped her a second time. "I hate all of you!" Katrina rushed from the house, slamming the door hard enough to make it sound like a clap of thunder. She had to get a lawyer for Patrice.

"You know she's going to call Patrice," Richard said, settling on the sofa next to Stella, who had finally stopped crying.

"She's too late," Stella said sadly. "Lorna told me this morning that she told one of those detectives where Patrice was down in Chapel Hill. Katrina is already too late."

Thank you, Lorna. Thirsty, Celeste gulped from one of the glasses Erica had brought into the room earlier for her parents.

"I can't wait for all of this to be over," Bryson said, sitting for the first time since Katrina stormed into the house.

"Look at what was under the sofa," Erica said, handing the tape to Celeste.

"Is this—"

"I believe so. I don't know how it got under the sofa."

"Is that the tape someone broke in here for?" Bryson asked.

"It might be," Erica replied.

"Well, folks," Celeste said, "I think this case is about to burst wide open. I wonder if Patrice is on this tape, too?"

CHAPTER
31

SPRING!

Last September when Patrice was brought back to New York and charged with Willie's murder, there was no joy in Celeste's heart. It was a sad time for the family and the final severing of the fragile vein that connected Katrina and her children to the family. She permitted no contact between her children and their grandparents, which hurt Mother and Dad to their hearts. In the months leading up to Patrice's trial, Justine grew an inch and a half taller, turned eight in early April, and was learning to play softball without her father's coaching. Nothing was the same, and as the second week of May got under way, so too did Patrice's trial.

On one side of the courtroom Celeste sat with her parents, alongside Bryson and Erica, while Katrina sat on the far side of the courtroom with Lorna and people that Richard said were Gordon's family. Poor Lorna, she didn't know where she belonged. At times she looked yearningly over at them, smiling a sad, weak little smile when Katrina wasn't looking, but she couldn't move away from her mother. It was where she belonged. Day to day, it was easy to see the strain in Katrina and Lorna's relationship pushing them farther apart. They never did sit shoulder to shoulder; they never did see eye to eye on very much. A divided courtroom wasn't all that divided their family. Katrina blamed all of them for turning Patrice in. For some reason, she lay no guilt at Patrice's feet, while everyone else felt Patrice was guilty as sin and not just of the murder.

Every day Celeste studied Patrice sitting at the defense table, seemingly younger than her twenty years, exuding youthful innocence in her white and pastel blouses, looking so much like a private school debutante.

Without a murder weapon or witnesses, the prosecutor, Robert Gladstone, argued his case against Patrice on circumstantial evidence. He portrayed Patrice as a scorned young woman hot for her aunt's husband, who turned to murder when Willie wouldn't leave his marriage for her. Willie's cell phone log posted more than two hundred calls over a six-month period from Patrice, and the house telephone log showed that Patrice had called the house the morning Willie slipped away to meet her. It showed that Willie's supervisor, Andrew Coleman, had called also.

When questioned about his call, initially, that was before he knew that Willie's videotape had been found, Coleman said, "I'd missed Willie at work the day before and wanted to wish him the best on his vacation." But once he was questioned about the videotape and the morning of Willie's death, Coleman came clean about the early morning telephone conversation. He was subpoenaed to give testimony for the prosecution in Patrice's murder trial—seems he had seen her with Willie the morning of the murder.

"On the telephone, I tried to make a deal with Willie to not show the tape to anyone, but he refused to deal. I drove to his house that morning, but he was pulling off as I was driving into the block. I recognized his SUV, so I followed him. I didn't know where he was going, but I was going to catch up with him at the first traffic light and try to talk to him. But Willie was speeding. Within minutes, he picks up this girl and heads out on Atlantic Avenue. I followed him to this motel in East New York, and when he and the girl got out, I knew I had something serious to bargain with."

"Did you speak to him?"

"No."

"What did you do at that point?"

"I left. I saw all I needed to see."

"Do you see the girl William Alexander was with on the morning of July sixth in this courtroom?"

Andrew Coleman looked directly at Patrice. "That's her in the blue blouse sitting at the defense table."

"Thank you. Mr. Coleman, did you kill William Alexander?"

"No."

There was no evidence of Coleman being in the motel room, but his fingerprints were evidence of his breaking into Celeste's house with the keys he'd copied that were left behind in Willie's desk. He was charged with breaking and entering. Just as Willie would have wanted, the bird's-eye view of Coleman stealing computers from Dialacom on his secret tape freed Tyrel Johnson and convicted Andrew Coleman of grand larceny.

While on one hand Willie's tape of Coleman saved a young man from being wrongly convicted, his pictures of himself and Patrice damned his own soul to hell and got Patrice accused of his murder; especially after it was determined that it was her DNA left behind on Willie's body and her panties left behind under the pillow in the motel room.

"What woman would leave her drawers in a sleazy motel room after she'd been laid?" Erica asked. "Didn't her mama teach her better than that?"

Celeste saw no humor in Erica's words, but she thought it mighty funny when Katrina, called as the first witness by the defense, brazenly testified, "Yes, I knew about the affair." Everyone's eyes widened in surprise when she added, "I saw nothing wrong with it. If my sister couldn't hold on to her man, that was her problem."

On cross, Mr. Gladstone asked, "Did you kill William Alexander, Mrs. Dawson?"

"I didn't, but maybe I should've. Then my daughter wouldn't be sitting in this courtroom charged with his murder."

"No, Mrs. Dawson, maybe if you had stopped your daughter

when you discovered the affair, then perhaps none of us would be here."

Katrina showed her annoyance by setting her face in a readable mask of contempt.

"Were you home, Mrs. Dawson, on the morning of July sixth at five-thirty A.M. when your daughter was talking on the telephone with the decedent?"

"Yes, I was sleeping."

"Were you aware of that telephone call at all that morning?"

"No."

"Were you aware that your daughter left the house that morning around five forty-five A.M.?"

"Not until she came back."

"What time did she get back?"

"Around eight-thirty that morning."

"Did she tell you where she'd been?"

"No."

"Did you question her about where she'd been?"

"No."

"Did the defendant look disheveled or distraught or disturbed in any way?"

"No, not that I noticed."

"I'm sure you'd tell the court if you noticed anything out of the ordinary with your daughter, wouldn't you, Mrs. Dawson?"

"Objection. Argumentative," the defense attorney said.

"Sustained," the judge ruled.

Mr. Gladstone continued, "Who else was in your home on the morning of July sixth at five-thirty A.M.?"

"My son, Gordon, Jr."

"How old was Gordon, Jr., at that time?"

"Ten."

"Was he asleep?"

"I assume so."

"You have another daughter, Lorna Dawson."

"Yes."

"How old was Lorna Dawson?"

"Fifteen."

"Was your daughter, Lorna Dawson, home on the sixth of July at five-thirty A.M.?"

"No. She had spent the night at a girlfriend's house."

"Was there anyone else at home on the morning of July sixth?"

"Yes, my late husband, Gordon Dawson."

"To your knowledge, Mrs. Dawson, was Mr. Dawson asleep or awake at five-thirty A.M. on the morning of July sixth?"

"I personally have no knowledge of my husband being awake."

"Do you know if Mr. Dawson left the house at any time before you awakened?"

"Not that I'm aware of. Look, I was sleeping. I have no idea what was going on while I was asleep."

In her four hours of interrogation, Katrina in no way tried to camouflage her anger for Gordon's betrayal, her strong dislike for Willie, and her raw hatred for her own sister, which to anyone's ears was more powerful than her moral and maternal obligation to her own daughter. There was little doubt that Katrina did more harm than good to Patrice's defense.

On the fourth day, Patrice's attorney, Valdermere Austin, announced, "The defense calls Albert Waterman to the stand."

"Who's he?" Richard asked.

Celeste had forgotten about meeting Albert Waterman in Washington. She quickly explained the professional and personal relationship between Albert and Gordon. Richard's and Stella's eyes widened. Bryson and Erica exchanged knowing looks. Still, they all wondered why Albert was there at all.

While all heads turned and looked at Albert as he passed down the center aisle toward the witness stand, Katrina never looked his way. She hated that Albert was called as a witness. He had nothing to do with Patrice or Willie, just Gordon, but Mr. Austin explained earlier, "Any link, any connection to a defendant by a witness, no matter how minute, is important. Your husband was home on the morning of July sixth and Patrice admits she spoke to him before she snuck out of the house."

"Look at that." Erica nodded toward Katrina. Although hushed, Katrina and Lorna were having words—more like Katrina was. Her lips were flapping.

"What do you suppose is going on?" Richard asked.

No one ventured a guess, but they couldn't pull their eyes away. Those onlookers close enough to hear were listening intently.

"Poor Lorna," Celeste said. "She—"

Katrina suddenly elbowed Lorna, pushing her away. At once, Celeste and Richard stood. Clearly about to cry, Lorna started out of the courtroom, but Richard quickly reached out and caught her by the hand, pulling her into his arms, embracing her briefly before sitting her down between himself and Stella. They both held her while she muffled her crying on Richard's shoulder. It was obvious by the angry scowl on Katrina's face that she didn't like it one bit that Lorna was sitting with them.

"The judge is watching us," Celeste whispered, keeping her eye on the judge's stern, reproachful glare.

"What happened?" Stella whispered to Lorna.

"She's upset because I called Albert—she hates him."

"I bet," Richard said. "How's she been treating you and Gordy?"

"She screams all the time."

"I guess she's upset about this trial," Stella said.

"Yeah, that, plus she curses Dad all the time. You know what Dad did?"

"We all know about that," Celeste said in a low voice.

"No, this is something else. Dad took all of his money out of his pension plan . . ."

Oh, man! Celeste thought.

". . . and he cashed out all the insurance policies in his name."

"Oh, man," Bryson said, "I know Katrina was fit to be tied finding that out."

"She was and still is."

"So how are you all making it?" Richard asked.

"Ma quit her job at the insurance company, and now she sells software and computers."

"That's good money," Celeste said.

"It is, but Ma works all the time. She's hardly ever home."

"Your mother should have called me," Richard said. "I would have helped her."

"She ain't gonna never call you, Granddad, none of y'all. She said y'all don't exist to her or us anymore. But I told her me and Gordy wanted to see y'all, and she wouldn't let us. And just now, because Albert's here, she told me to get away from her."

"That's all right, baby," Stella said. "She won't stay mad at you forever."

"I don't know," Erica said. "Look at the way she's looking over here."

"God, if looks could truly kill," Celeste said.

"She's real mad at you, Aunt Celeste. She—"

"Don't worry about it." Celeste leaned over her mother to touch Lorna. "Being angry at me is a state of being for your mother. I'm used to it, but what about you? Are you all right?"

Shaking her head, Lorna began to cry again. Celeste wasn't worried about Lorna. Once she got over the hurt, she'd be okay, too.

It took nearly ten minutes for Mr. Austin to establish who Albert was and what his relationship was to Gordon. "Mr. Waterman, it seems you acted as Mr. Dawson's confidant. Is that so?"

"Yes."

"So in addition to Mr. Dawson confiding in you that he was married to two women at the same time, he confided many other things of a highly personal nature to you. Is that so?"

"Yes."

"Mr. Waterman, did you have an occasion to have a conversation with Mr. Dawson upon his return to Washington, D.C., on Sunday evening, July seventh, after his visit with his family in New York City?"

"Yes."

"What did Mr. Dawson say about that visit? His exact words."

"He said he couldn't keep up the pretense."

"And what pretense was he referring to?"

"Objection," Mr. Gladstone said. "Witness cannot testify to what he thinks someone was referring to unless that fact was stated."

"Sustained."

"Mr. Waterman, did Mr. Dawson in fact say what pretense he couldn't keep up?"

"Yes. He said he couldn't keep up the pretense of the marriage he had with his wife, Katrina Dawson."

Katrina sat forward. "He's lying!"

The judge shot Katrina a warning glare, muting her tongue.

"And how did Mr. Dawson say he would end the pretense?"

"He said he intended to divorce his wife, Katrina Dawson . . ."

"That's a lie," Katrina said again.

". . . and legally remarry the wife he had in Maryland."

"That's a damn lie!" Katrina jumped to her feet.

The judge pounded his gavel twice. "Mrs. Dawson! Sit down."

"But he's lying! Gordon never planned on divorcing me."

"If you do not sit down and be quiet, Mrs. Dawson, you will be barred from these proceedings."

Sitting down hard, Katrina itched to get her hands on Albert. He was lying. It couldn't be true that Gordon had planned on divorcing her. That would mean that Joan would have won over her, and that could never be. She silently cursed Gordon for the umpteenth time. She closed her eyes to shut out the jurors, the spectators, those people that used to be her family, all of whom she sensed were staring at her.

Bowing her head, Stella prayed for Patrice, Katrina, and Lorna.

Celeste and Erica exchanged knowing glances. What passed between them was an understanding of how and why Gordon would make such a decision.

"Proceed," the judge ordered.

"Mr. Waterman, did Mr. Dawson tell you anything specific about the morning of Saturday, July sixth, in his home in Brooklyn?"

"Yes. Gordon said he was on the way to the bathroom when he overheard his daughter, Patrice, talking on the telephone to a man."

Looking at the prosecutor, the judge cooly raised his brow, but Mr. Gladstone had no intention of objecting.

"Did Mr. Dawson say how it is that he knew the defendant was speaking to a man?"

"Actually, Gordon said he asked his daughter to whom she was speaking, and she said she was talking to a girlfriend, Willamina."

"Then, how did Mr. Dawson come to conclude that the defendant was talking to a man, if the defendant said she was talking to a girlfriend named Willamina?"

"He said he knew she was lying because—"

"Objection. Witness is testifying to a conversation he had with someone who made a judgment on the verity of someone else's statement."

"Sustained."

Mr. Austin was in no way deterred. "Did Mr. Dawson say what it is he overheard the defendant say, specifically, on the telephone to give him the impression that the defendant was talking to a man?"

"Yes. Gordon said, after he'd spoken to his daughter, he didn't move away from her door. He said he heard her say, 'Willie, I'm juicing. Don't you want some of this?' "

Patrice lowered her head shamefully, while Katrina again closed her eyes. Celeste rolled her lips inward and held them that way as she thought about how Willie had betrayed her.

Again, the judge stared at the prosecutor's table, but again Mr. Gladstone opted to not object to the hearsay that Albert Waterman's testimony was sprinkled with.

"Mr. Waterman, what if anything did Mr. Dawson say he did about what he'd overheard?"

While Katrina was expecting to hear Albert say that Gordon did nothing but go back to bed, Celeste began to sense that there was a reason beyond proving that someone else had known about Patrice and Willie's affair.

"Gordon told me he followed Patrice out of the house that morning."

Patrice gasped and turned to look at her mother sitting behind her. Katrina pulled herself to the edge of her seat. She'd had no idea that Gordon had even left the house. He'd been there when she awakened, sitting in the kitchen in an undershirt and a pair of jeans, drinking a tall glass of orange juice. He'd never said a word about leaving the house.

Katrina glanced over at her parents and Celeste, at their startled expressions. She gave them a smug look.

Mr. Gladstone rapidly took notes.

"Mr. Waterman, you contacted my office just two days ago. Why is that?"

"I live in Washington, D.C. I had no idea what was going on here. I found out about the trial because I received a call from Lorna Dawson, who called to say hello and to let me know how she was doing."

Katrina cut her eyes angrily at Lorna. Lorna was already looking at her mother but quickly dropped her gaze.

To her grandparents, Lorna explained, "I couldn't talk to Ma, and she said she'd disown me if I called any of y'all, and she said she'd know if I called y'all. So I called Albert."

"It's okay. We understand."

"Mr. Waterman, did you talk to Lorna Dawson often?"

"No. We'd spoken maybe two or three times before this last time a few days ago, which is when she mentioned what was going on with her sister."

"What did Lorna Dawson say about the trial?"

"Lorna was very upset about her sister and her family. About the trial, she said that her sister was charged with killing her aunt's husband, William Alexander."

Gritting her teeth, Katrina kept shaking her head. Because of Lorna, Patrice was going to be convicted. Albert had to know something or why else was he on the stand?

"So why did you contact me, Mr. Waterman?"

"Because I had a letter in my possession, dated July tenth, that Gordon gave to me with the instruction that I wasn't to open it unless something happened to him."

"Objection. The State had no knowledge of the existence of a letter, and we have, therefore, had no opportunity to examine this document."

"Your Honor, the defense also had no knowledge of this letter, but its existence is vitally important to my client's case."

"Your Honor, introducing this letter at this late date is prejudicial against the State's case. Defense—"

The judge brought the gavel down hard, silencing the prosecutor. "Sidebar," the judge said, ordering both Mr. Austin, with the letter in hand, and Mr. Gladstone to the bench. The judge proceeded to read the letter to himself, making everyone, including the attorneys, wait for a determination on whether they'd ever learn what Gordon was about to tell them all from the hereafter.

Bryson whispered to Erica, "Man, I hope they don't suppress that letter. We'll never know what's in it."

"You think Gordon knew something about who killed Willie?" Erica asked.

"Albert said he could straighten everything out," Lorna said.

"Oh, God." As incredulous as it seemed, Celeste wondered if it was possible that Gordon knew the truth.

Mr. Gladstone didn't look too happy when he turned away from the judge. Both he and Mr. Austin returned to their respective tables, but Mr. Austin continued to stand.

"Counselors, considering the timeliness of the witness's appearance, the court will allow the letter."

From a folder, Mr. Austin took a copy of the letter and passed it to Mr. Gladstone. In his own hand, he held the original handwritten letter. "I submit said letter, received from Mr. Albert Waterman, marked Exhibit fifteen, into evidence."

"Marked and entered," the judge confirmed.

Mr. Austin approached Albert and handed the letter to him. "Mr. Waterman, is this the letter you originally received from Mr. Dawson?"

"Yes."

"Mr. Waterman, something did happen to Mr. Gordon Dawson on Sunday, July twenty-eighth, three weeks after the murder of William Alexander. Is that so?"

"Yes. He died."

"Did you open the letter upon the death of Mr. Dawson?"

"No, I did not."

"Why not? You were instructed by Mr. Dawson to open the envelope if something happened to him."

"I know, but so much was going on, initially I forgot about the letter."

"When did you remember about the letter?"

"Two days after Gordon died."

"Did you tell Mrs. Katrina Dawson about the letter at that time?"

"No."

"Why not?"

"Well, I tried. At least twice, I tried to tell Katrina Dawson that we had to talk, but she wasn't much interested in speaking with me."

"Why didn't you insist on speaking to her?"

"Mrs. Dawson isn't the type of person one insists on doing anything to or with. She's not exactly the easiest person to approach."

Katrina huffed and folded her arms high and tight atop her chest, while Erica whispered to Celeste, "Is that not the truth?"

"Then again, to be fair," Albert said, "when I was attempting to speak with Mrs. Dawson, she was dealing with the death of her husband, the issue of his bigamy, and the special relationship Gordon and I shared."

"I see. Mr. Waterman, before you read this letter to the court, why is it that you didn't speak to the authorities here in New York or in Washington, D.C., about the contents of this letter?"

Albert took a pensive pause. "Mr. Austin, Gordon had just died. His two wives had just learned that he was a bigamist. I know it sounds bad, but Gordon was really a good person. His life was spinning out of control because of bad decisions, but he was a good man and a good friend. I loved Gordon. After I realized that Mrs. Dawson wasn't going to ever hear me out, as time went by, I decided to not tell anyone about the letter—that is, until I found out about Gordon's daughter, Patrice, being on trial for murder."

Albert looked over at Patrice. "I'm sorry I took so long to come forward. I hope you understand. I didn't want people to know that your father was a murderer."

The bomb of silence that dropped following the pandemonium of gasps that exploded in that courtroom, Celeste could still hear and feel two weeks after the letter had been authenticated as being written by Gordon.

"I followed my daughter out of the house." Albert began reading Gordon's words. "Patrice's head was so high up in the clouds, she didn't see me come out of the house a minute behind her. While she waited on the corner across the street, I sat in my car waiting to see who it was that was picking her up. I prayed that I was wrong, that I hadn't heard what I thought I heard. When I saw that it was Willie, my wife's brother-in-law, I knew then that I would kill him. Killing him was the first and only thought in my mind.

I followed that rapist bastard out to that motel in East New York and watched him, with his arm around my daughter, take her into that sleazy motel room with the intention of using her like a street whore. I sat in my car, cursing and banging on my dashboard with my fists, wanting to get into that room to kill him with my bare hands.

That prick-ass son of a bitch was fucking my baby. Patrice was my firstborn. I changed her diapers, I helped her with her homework, and that bastard was ruining her, robbing her of her innocence. The longer they stayed in that motel room, the more pissed off I got. When I couldn't take waiting one minute longer, I got my tire iron from my trunk. I jimmied that cheap-ass lock and opened that door. What I saw, when I entered that damn room, filled me with a rage that shook me to my very core.

With all my might, I tried to knock that raping-ass bastard's head off his body. I knew when that iron cracked his skull that he was dead. I left that room regretting nothing. I had saved my daughter from a predator, and that's all that mattered."

EPILOGUE

CELESTE

No one apologized to Patrice, and no one tried to call Katrina. As far as the family was concerned, if Katrina had exposed the affair the minute she found out, Willie might be divorced, but he'd be alive, and Gordon might still be a dead bigamist, but he wouldn't be on the books as a murderous one. Whoever said, ". . . time heals all wounds," had never met Katrina. The case against Patrice was dismissed that day in court, and together she and Katrina, arm in arm, walked out, leaving Lorna behind without a concerned glance. By nightfall when Stella and Richard hadn't heard from Katrina, they took Lorna home to her.

Katrina blocked the door and wouldn't let Lorna in. "She doesn't live here anymore."

"That's nonsense," Richard said. "This is your child, Katrina. You need to grow up and be a better mother to your children."

Katrina slammed the door in their faces. That was two years ago, and as far as Celeste knew, Katrina hadn't set eyes on Lorna since. Lorna was living with her now. She was in her senior year of high school, a mainstay on the honors roll, and had applied to Columbia and Princeton, both offering her scholarships. If only Katrina knew, she would be proud. But that was all right, Lorna had her Aunt Celeste to stroke her ego, give her a pat on the back, and smother her with love. Justine no longer called Lorna her cousin; she told everyone that Lorna was her sister, and Lorna liked that, although it was clear that she missed Gordy and Patrice. She never talked about going back home or about the mother who had disowned her. Thank God she was close to Justine, just as Justine was close to her cousins Kevin and Kevon. Bryson meant what he'd said after Willie died; he didn't allow Celeste to shut him and Erica out of her or Justine's life. For Celeste, Bryson was indeed the brother she never had, while Erica was the sister she was supposed to have.

Holidays came and holidays went. Stella, the ever prayerful mother since before Patrice's trial, kept Katrina's name in God's ears, while continuing to send birthday and Christmas cards to her wayward daughter. Lorna sent birthday and Mother's Day cards in hopes of getting Katrina to speak to her, but although the cards were never returned and they surmised that Katrina hadn't moved away, the cards were never acknowledged either. Stella hoped and prayed that in time Katrina would come around, but Celeste was more realistic. When a person carried hate that deep inside, it became a part of her, like a cancer that fed greedily on its host. Katrina would never speak to any of them again, that Celeste was sure of, and like her mother, she kept Katrina in her prayers.

Celeste saw no reason to hold on to her anger at Katrina, Patrice, or Willie. She didn't want the hate to fester in her soul. Besides, it wasn't like she had to break bread with Katrina or Patrice ever again in life or like Willie was there to remind her of his infidelity. Of course, it helped that she followed her mother's advice and thought of Willie as the man whose sole purpose had been to leave her the precious gift of her daughter. Once Celeste took that to heart, she was able to get over the hurt. Justine was indeed a precious gift. Celeste was moving on with her life with no intention of looking back.

She started dating Isaiah Vaughan when Patrice's trial ended. Isaiah really was a great guy, but Celeste was taking it slow. She was in no hurry to replace the band of gold she no longer wore. She had two daughters to raise, and that was enough for now.

KATRINA

Katrina straightened her back a tad more, sucked in her already flat stomach a quarter of an inch more, and smiled broadly as she made her way past the many well-wishers congratulating her on winning the coveted Brain Trust Award. As she accepted the twelve-inch crystal vase from Harold Warrick, the president of Brain Trust Educational Software, outwardly Katrina smiled modestly, but she was heady with the knowledge that she definitely deserved the honor. She had worked her ass off over the past two years selling the grade school software to as many parents throughout the city of New York as she could. When she'd first decided she could no longer sit behind her desk performing the mundane task of processing auto insurance claims as a claims adjuster, with her coworkers looking cross-eyed at her since that article about Patrice ran in the newspaper, she started looking for another job. Being a software salesperson would have never crossed her mind, except for the notice she received from Gordy's school about Brain Trust Educational Software. She'd made the appointment with the salesperson just to see what they had to offer Gordy and spent more time talking to the salesperson about the job of selling software and computers and how much it paid. In no time, she was sold on the job, and Gordy had enough academic software to get him through to college.

Since joining Brain Trust, Katrina discovered she truly enjoyed talking parents into buying software to enhance their children's learning experience. In the first year, she outsold everyone in the New York City area. By the end of her second year, she had outsold every salesperson in the northeast sector. She could talk parents into buying air if she had a mind to, and almost did once when she told a woman in Starett City, who complained about the odors that came from the dump site near the Brooklyn housing complex in Spring Creek, she could breathe easier if she supplied her own oxygen. The next time she saw the woman, the woman had been trying to purchase her own oxygen tank. To her, Katrina ended up selling a bundle of educational software for her own daughter and one each for her three nephews! The nephews didn't have a computer, so Katrina sold her a computer as well. That commission paid for a great pair of diamond earrings she had her eye on. Yes, she deserved the Brain Trust Award.

"We all know Katrina," Mr. Warrick said. "She never takes no for an answer. A no just makes her push harder. If a parent gets away from her, then that parent can't be had."

The audience laughter pleased Katrina. They all knew she was tough and was no laughing matter.

"What's remarkable about you, Katrina, is that you pitch our products to the parents in Brownsville the same as you do to the parents in Chelsea. Great skill. Which reminds me, I'm thinking about creating another award just for you."

Katrina smiled.

"The Most Miles Traveled by an Employee in a Given Year Award. Katrina, you logged in more than four thousand miles in the past year . . ."

The wows and applause filled the room.

". . . I didn't know a person could travel around the five boroughs that many miles. Katrina, how do you find the time to be on the road so much?"

"I gave up my addiction to bingo." Katrina had never played bingo in her life. That little fabrication got a good laugh from Mr. Warrick and the audience.

"I guess we all should," Mr. Warrick said. "Thank God you didn't have to give up your family. We at Brain Trust value our families. Katrina, take a bow, you're heads above us all. You'll be missed on the road, but as north east sales director, you'll have another challenge ahead of you to get your salespeople to hold up the incredible standards you've set. Congratulations."

With the final applause Katrina left the stage with a fake smile and a heavy heart. She hadn't told anyone at Brain Trust about Gordon or Patrice, and spoke not at all about any part of her family life. Mr. Warrick had no idea how close to home he'd hit when he said, "Thank God you didn't have to give up your family." In a way she did, in order to earn a living. Gordy was no longer a baby—he was thirteen—but he needed to have her around more. He had his own key and was good at fixing microwaveable macaroni and cheese and burgers. Sure he had complained about her not being home enough, but she had no choice. She needed the money to keep living the way she was accustomed to.

Without Gordon's paycheck, it was hard. And, of course, what the bastard did when he'd borrowed seventy-five percent of his pension and cashed out the life insurance policies in his name messed her up financially. But the hell with Gordon; he had not destroyed her. What he'd done disrupted her life; it didn't break her. She was doing quite well for herself.

Since turning her back on Lorna two years ago, she hadn't spent a dime on her. From her mother's letters, she heard that Lorna was living with Celeste. Good riddance to both of them. Patrice was out on her own, living with some guy up in Harlem she met at City College. She didn't have to give her money any longer either. When the trial ended and Patrice was cleared, Patrice had still wanted to go south for college, but the money wasn't there and she'd ended up having to get a job at Dunkin Donuts to help pay for her tuition at City College. Moody and rebellious, she'd started staying out for days at a time, and within six months, she had moved out with this Rashaad guy she'd brought home only twice.

"I'm a grown woman, Ma. You can't tell me what to do anymore." That was Patrice's pat response whenever Katrina tried to tell her that she couldn't live with Rashaad. On the day Patrice was moving out, Katrina had said nothing, done nothing. Patrice had cut the apron string for herself.

Katrina left the awards banquet just as she had arrived—alone. There were no men in her life; she hadn't had time to play the dating game. She needed to make money, and unless there was a man out there ready to pay her bills, she otherwise had no interest. She was tired anyway.

As soon as Katrina walked into her house, she smelled cigarette smoke. She yelled up the stairs, "Boy, have you been smoking?"

Gordy didn't answer, but Katrina could hear his television, so she knew he was still up. She'd deal with him when she went upstairs. She went to check the answering machine. There was one message.

"Ma, stop blowing up my voice mail," Patrice's annoyed voice said. "I have a life, you know. I can't call you every three minutes or every day. I'll call you Sunday afternoon if I get a chance, but stop bugging me."

Katrina stared at the answering machine. She'd be lying to herself if she said it didn't hurt that Patrice had no time for her or even wanted to talk to her. Whatever Patrice's life was, Patrice wasn't willing to include her. How ungrateful was that, when she had been the only one to stand by Patrice when the rest of the family wouldn't? She was the only one who had believed in her innocence. She needed a drink.

Taking her fill of the vodka and orange juice she kept plenty of, Katrina went straight up to Gordy's room. He was on his back reading a magazine with the television blasting.

"You've been smoking again, haven't you?"

Gordy kept his head in his magazine. "Nope." He raised the magazine higher, completely covering his face.

Katrina snatched the magazine out of Gordy's hands. "Boy, I'm talking to you."

"Dang, Ma! You buggin'."

"I'm not stupid, Gordy. I smell smoke. I don't smoke, so there shouldn't be a smoke smell in this house. Where're the cigarettes?"

"I ain't got no cigarettes." Gordy picked up his television remote and pushed the volume higher.

"Don't you lie to me, boy!"

Katrina went to the wall socket and yanked the television cord out, killing the picture and sound instantly.

"Ma!"

Rushing back at Gordy, she grabbed his face, forcing his mouth open. She smelled his breath. It was foul with the smell of cigarettes. She slapped his face hard.

"Don't you lie to me."

Gordy jumped off the bed. "You ain't gotta hit on me!" He rubbed his cheek.

"I will knock your head off if you lie to me again." Katrina began ransacking the room, tossing discarded clothes, books, and papers in her search to find Gordy's hiding place. Under a conspicuous basketball cut in half on the floor in the corner, she found what she was looking for—an ashtray full of cigarette butts and—

"What is this?" She inspected the stubbed-out butts that lay next to smaller butts that were definitely not cigarettes.

"It ain't mine."

"Don't lie to me, Gordy."

"My friends were over! They—"

Katrina threw the ashtray at Gordy, and although he saw it coming, he didn't duck out of the way in time. The heavy plastic ashtray and all of it ashes and butts hit him in the chest, leaving a gray and black powdery stain.

"That hurt, man!"

"Didn't I tell you you were not to have any company when I'm not home! And what thirteen-year-old boys are you hanging out with that are smoking cigarettes and marijuana?"

"They don't smoke. They was just tryin'—"

"Stop lying!" Katrina started at Gordy. He started backing away the closer she got.

"Boy, I will not have you smoking or running around here acting like a wild animal." She caught Gordy by the tail of his oversized T-shirt just as he turned to make a run from the room. She was about to yank him back to her when he turned suddenly and caught her hard across the nose with his arm.

Katrina let go of Gordy's shirt as she stumbled backward. She grabbed her nose. "You hit me!"

"You was holdin' on to my shirt. I wasn't tryin' to hit you, but you was tryin' to beat up on me."

"You hit me!" Katrina again started toward Gordy, but she was stopped by the sudden wetness in her hand. "I'm bleeding. Son of a bitch! You gave me a bloody nose."

"I didn't do it on purpose. You was pullin' on my shirt."

The blood began flowing quickly, forcing Katrina to hold her head back. "I'm gonna kick your ass as soon as I stop bleeding."

Katrina pushed past Gordy, out of his room, and hurried to the bathroom. It was a while before she could get the bleeding to stop. In her bathroom mirror she saw that her expensive russet Georgette gown was spotted with her own blood. She went looking for Gordy. He wasn't in his room. In the past year he had been acting out, talking back, and hanging with some of the roughest kids in school and in the neighborhood. He had been expelled twice in the last month and showed no signs that the counseling sessions she was paying good money for were helping.

"Gordy!"

He was nowhere to be found in the house. She went to the front door and discovered that it was unlocked. She had definitely locked it when she came home. Out on her front stoop in the late fall chill, Katrina looked up and down the block. At midnight when Gordy still had not returned, she knew it was time to call the police, but before she could make the call, the telephone rang.

"Gordy?"

"Gordy's with me, Ma," Patrice said.

Thank God. "You tell that boy to get his ass back here before I—"

"He's not coming back tonight. I'll bring him home in the morning, after you've calmed down."

"Did he tell you what he did? He hit me, Patrice. He gave me a bloody nose."

"Were you hitting on him?"

"No. I was trying to talk to him. Gordy was smoking in his room. I am not going to allow him to smoke in this house."

"I'll talk to him about smoking, Ma, but you can't be beatin' up on him."

"Patrice, I want Gordy back here tonight. I'll call the police and have them pick him up, take him to a juvenile facility if—"

"Ma, if you do that, you'll lose me and Gordy, just like you lost Dad and Lorna."

Those words cut Katrina deep and silenced her tongue. That Patrice would hurt her like that was daunting.

"Go to bed, Ma. Gordy will—"

Katrina slammed the phone down. She couldn't listen to another word out of Patrice's mouth, although Patrice was right. She'd lost them all—Lorna, Patrice, and Gordy. No one cared about her, and she wasn't going to care about them anymore either. She had herself to worry about and take care of. The hell with them all.

Katrina went about her ritual of making herself another vodka and orange juice in a tumbler-sized glass so she wouldn't have to keep getting up. In her dimly lit living room, she folded her legs under her body on the sofa, and with nothing but the sounds of her own breathing filling the room and the occasional street noises of a loud motor passing by her front door, she drank her vodka and orange juice, hoping that when sleep finally came, it would bring her no dreams and no thoughts of her children, of Gordon, or of Celeste. Ironically, that was what she feared most—Celeste. Too often Celeste had come in Katrina's dreams, telling her, "No good ever comes of a lie or a liar." In reality, Celeste had never said anything like that to her, but in her dreams, Celeste was always there with her arms out, as if she wanted to embrace her. If she dreamed that dream tonight, it would make her mad as hell. Maybe tomorrow she'd think about getting Gordy back, but for tonight, she needed to sleep the sleep of the weary.

WHAT'S DONE IN THE DARK

GLORIA MALLETTE

ABOUT THIS GUIDE

The suggested questions are intended to
enhance your group's reading of this book.

DISCUSSION QUESTIONS

1. The sisterly bond between Celeste and Katrina was broken early in life by Katrina's betrayal. Is it ever okay for a sister to go out with a guy another sister likes?

2. Katrina's betrayal was only a symptom. Were there deeper issues like jealousy and sibling rivalry at play long before Katrina slept with Celeste's boyfriend?

3. If one sibling (Katrina) dislikes the other, is there anything the other sibling (Celeste) can do to keep the peace, or is their relationship inevitably doomed?

4. Do you think Celeste and Katrina's parents, Stella and Richard Reese, contributed in any way to the hostile relationship between Celeste and Katrina? Should they have done more to stem the animosity between them when they were children? What could they have done?

5. Katrina's dislike for her sister, Celeste, was perceived differently by each of her own daughters. Why did Lorna like Celeste, and why did Patrice hate her? Do family members who do not get along always pass their feelings on to their children and thereby cause an irreparable rift in a family for generations?

6. Katrina was wrong to allow her daughter, Patrice, to continue seeing Celeste's husband. In the long run, did Katrina do more harm to her sister, Celeste, or to her daughter, Patrice?

7. Ironically, both Celeste's husband, Willie, and Katrina's husband, Gordon, were having affairs behind their backs. Once these affairs were brought to light, should Celeste and Katrina have forged stronger bonds to support each other? Do you think Katrina would have been more sup-

portive of Celeste if her own daughter had not been involved?

8. If you had been Celeste, would you have allowed your par-
    ents to pressure you into going to help your sister if your
    sister had never been nice to you? Is blood truly thicker
    than water?

9. Should Celeste have taken her niece, Lorna, in knowing
    that her sister, Katrina, would hate her for it? Did Celeste
    take Lorna in out of spite for Katrina, or is she really sin-
    cere in her love for her niece?

10. Will Katrina take her anger at her parents and her hatred
    for her sister to her grave, or do you think time and cir-
    cumstance can soften her feelings?